THE UNLIKELY ALLIES

BOOKS BY GILBERT MORRIS

THE HOUSE OF WINSLOW SERIES

The Honorable Imposter	The Iron Lady
The Captive Bride	The Silver Star
The Indentured Heart	The Shadow Portrait
The Gentle Rebel	The White Hunter
The Saintly Buccaneer	The Flying Cavalier
The Holy Warrior	The Glorious Prodigal
The Reluctant Bridegroom	The Amazon Quest
The Last Confederate	The Golden Angel
The Dixie Widow	The Heavenly Fugitive
The Wounded Yankee	The Fiery Ring
The Union Belle	The Pilgrim Song
The Final Adversary	The Beloved Enemy
The Crossed Sabres	The Shining Badge
The Valiant Gunman	The Royal Handmaid
The Gallant Outlaw	The Silent Harp
The Jeweled Spur	The Virtuous Woman
The Yukon Queen	The Gypsy Moon
The Rough Rider	The Unlikely Allies

CHENEY DUVALL, M.D.[1]

1. The Stars for a Light
2. Shadow of the Mountains
3. A City Not Forsaken
4. Toward the Sunrising
5. Secret Place of Thunder
6. In the Twilight, in the Evening
7. Island of the Innocent
8. Driven With the Wind

CHENEY AND SHILOH: THE INHERITANCE[1]

1. Where Two Seas Met
2. The Moon by Night
3. There Is a Season

THE SPIRIT OF APPALACHIA[2]

1. Over the Misty Mountains
2. Beyond the Quiet Hills
3. Among the King's Soldiers
4. Beneath the Mockingbird's Wings
5. Around the River's Bend

LIONS OF JUDAH

1. Heart of a Lion
2. No Woman So Fair
3. The Gate of Heaven
4. Till Shiloh Comes
5. By Way of the Wilderness

[1]with Lynn Morris   [2]with Aaron McCarver

GILBERT MORRIS

the UNLIKELY ALLIES

Minneapolis, Minnesota

Published by Bethany House Publishers
11400 Hampshire Avenue South
Bloomington, Minnesota 55438

Bethany House Publishers is a division of
Baker Publishing Group, Grand Rapids, Michigan.

Printed in the United States of America

Library of Congress Cataloging-in-Publication Data

Morris, Gilbert.
     The unlikely allies / Gilbert Morris.
         p.   cm. — (The House of Winslow ; 1939)
     Summary: "Mallory Anne Winslow, daughter of missionaries in Africa,
follows God's call to carry the Gospel to the Lapps in the Arctic. But her
work is interrupted when Norway is invaded by the Germans"—Provided
by publisher.
     ISBN 0-7642-2779-3 (pbk.)
     1. Winslow family (Fictitious characters)—Fiction. 2. Sami (European
people)—Norway—Fiction. 3. World War, 1939-1945—Norway—Fiction.
4. Americans—Norway—Fiction. 5. Women missionaries—Fiction.
6. Arctic Regions—Fiction. 7. Norway—Fiction. I. Title II. Series:
Morris, Gilbert. House of Winslow.
     PS3563.08742U54   2005
     813'.54—dc22

                                                                  2005018575

To Gale Towne—

Many years have gone since we were all a clan in Forrest City, and there are many empty places. But the memory lingers on, and one day we'll all sit down at the Master's table together.

Here's to all the Gilberts, Gale, and especially you!

GILBERT MORRIS spent ten years as a pastor before becoming Professor of English at Ouachita Baptist University in Arkansas and earning a Ph.D. at the University of Arkansas. A prolific writer, he has had over 25 scholarly articles and 200 poems published in various periodicals and over the past years has had more than 200 novels published. His family includes three grown children. He and his wife live in Gulf Shores, Alabama.

CONTENTS

PART FOUR
November–December 1940

THE HOUSE OF WINSLOW

★ ★ ★ ★

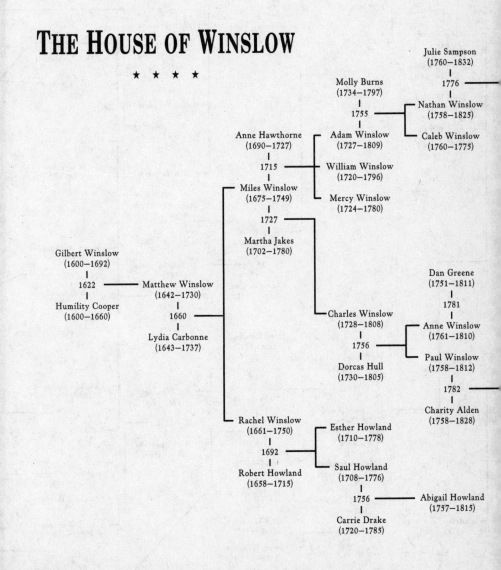

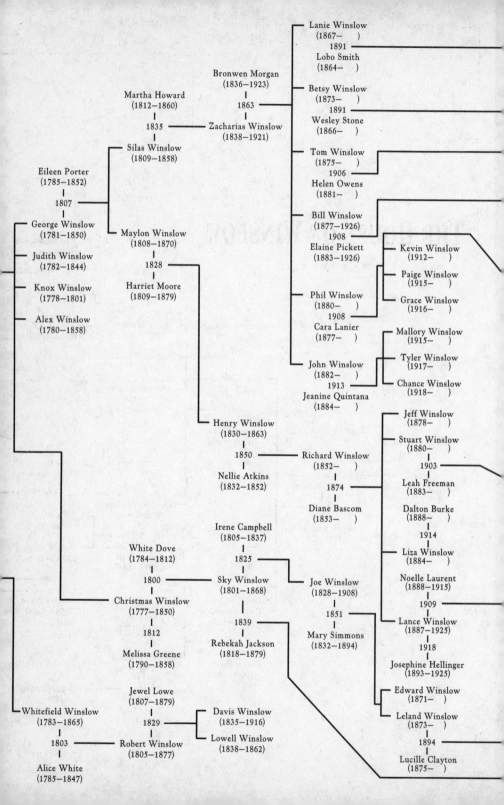

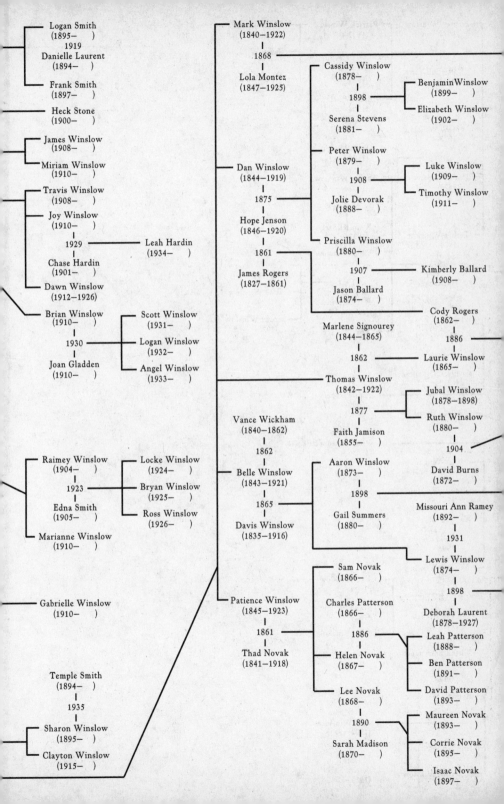

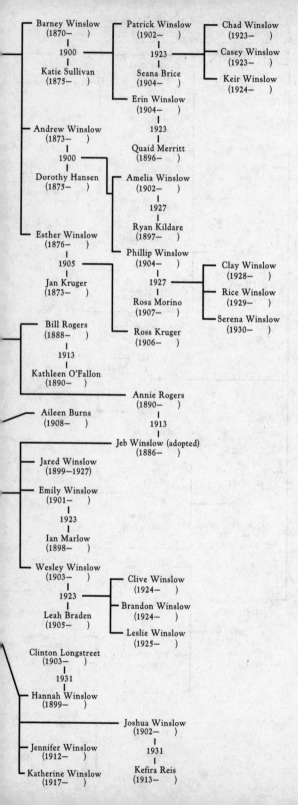

PART ONE

March 1938–May 1940

★ ★ ★

CHAPTER ONE

THE CALLING

★ ★ ★

Lifting its head suddenly and making a quick half-turn, the black-maned lion's nostrils swelled as it sniffed the air. It froze, jowls dripping blood from the wildebeest it had been feeding on, golden eyes glittering in the bright African sun. Its body was one long coil of hard muscle, a killing machine. As the wind stirred the long grasses of the veldt, the beast crouched and began advancing toward a stand of tall grasses fifty yards away.

Mallory Winslow tried to stay absolutely still as she crouched low in the grass, unarmed and defenseless against one of the largest lions she had ever seen. The lion padded by noiselessly, like a tawny ghost, so close she could see the powerful muscles rippling under the hide. She had been close to lions many times before and had even killed one once, but then she'd had a powerful rifle in her hands and had been accompanied by her father and two other hunters.

Even so, she was not alone. She glanced at Ubo, the Masai warrior crouched at her left hand, his ever-present spear in his hand. Just the sight of him gave her confidence, for he was the pride of the Masai warriors. His spear was his most precious possession, which he had carefully anointed with animal fat and polished until it gleamed. Two black ostrich feathers were attached to its tip with a string of beads.

Mallory felt a touch from Ubo, and she knew he was saying silently, *I am here. Do not be afraid. You are a daughter of the Masai!*

The lion froze and stared at them for what seemed a long time. Then suddenly the lion coughed deep in its chest, turned, and ambled back toward the carcass of the wildebeest.

Again Mallory felt the touch of Ubo's hand, and she glanced at him. With his head he signaled a silent retreat. Mallory followed him for nearly half a mile. Finally Ubo stopped, planted the butt of his broad-headed spear in the ground, and turned to the young woman.

"That lion is beautiful," he said in the Masai tongue.

"Yes, Ubo."

Mallory studied Ubo's tall, lithe figure. Masai warriors had been known throughout their history as absolutely fearless. Visitors to the Masai country were always impressed by their intelligence and beauty. Ubo stood several inches over six feet and was as lean as a panther. He wore a single garment, a red tunic with one strap over his right shoulder. His inky black hair had been dyed with ocher and lay in tiny rows arranged neatly on his head. Around his forehead was a string of beads, red and white and blue, meticulously made by his sweetheart. His earlobes had been elongated and decorated with tiny beads, and a chain of the same material hung around his neck. He had coated his legs with ocher mixed with fat and, while it was still wet, had drawn intricate patterns.

"I thought he was going to charge, Ubo."

"So did I, but you were not afraid."

Mallory smiled, looking up into his deep brown eyes. "I am never afraid. Not with my friend Ubo to protect me."

Ubo took in the young woman who stood before him.

As always, he marveled at her, for she was not like other women. He had known her since she was a child. Mallory Anne Winslow had jet-black hair and dark violet eyes, a color Ubo had never seen in anyone else. She had an olive complexion, oval face, and a wide mouth. She was very tall for a woman, a trait she had inherited from her father, John Winslow. Her violet eyes and black hair came from her mother, Jeanine. She was now twenty-two years old, and Ubo remembered the time she had talked him into letting her accompany the warriors of his tribe on a lion hunt. No woman was ever permitted, and even now Ubo could not understand how she had finally gotten him to agree to it. He smiled a gentle, thoughtful smile and shook his head. "How is it, daughter, that you can get me to do anything you like?"

Humor gleamed in Mallory's eyes, and she turned her head to one side, a manner she had when she was amused. "You have to let me have my own way because I'm such a good child."

Ubo laughed deep in his chest. "I remember when you were a little girl, all skinny and thin, but you thought you were too tall."

Mallory smiled at the memory. "I was ashamed to be so tall. I thought a woman should be small."

"A woman should be as God has made her. He made you tall, and I remember once I threatened to cane you if you didn't stand straight."

"I remember. I think you would have done it too."

Ubo's eyes clouded with sadness, and he said, "Come. It is time to go."

As the two made their way back toward the compound, Mallory surveyed the African landscape. This was all she had ever known, except for one visit to the United States when she was fourteen. This was her world—the twisted trees, the vistas of space, the herds of animals that shook the hard-packed earth like thunder as they raced across it. She had learned all the names of the beasts, the birds, and the vegetation from the tall Masai who walked beside her, adjusting his steps to hers.

"What is it like, this place to which you go?" Ubo asked.

"Norway? Why, it's altogether different from Kenya."

"Different how, daughter?"

"It's very cold there much of the year. It snows, and the waters are all covered with ice."

"Tell me again about the snow and the ice."

Mallory had tried before to explain snow and ice to Ubo, yet she herself had only seen pictures. Her one visit to the States had taken place in the summer. There were no adequate words in the Masai language to convey *cold*. There were many words for heat, but cold was a foreign concept—at least the kind of cold that freezes water. She was good at languages and had picked up Masai simply by spending time with the Masai people. She had learned French and German in school, as well as Latin at her father's insistence, and during the last two years she had learned to speak Norwegian with Anna Jorgensen, a missionary from Norway.

"I do not understand this cold land you speak of," Ubo said. "Are there any lions there?"

"No. Not a one."

"Then how do warriors prove their courage?"

"I don't think they do. Not the way the Masai think of it."

"And what is the name of the people you will go to tell about Jesus God?"

"They are called Lapps."

"Tell me about them."

"Well, let's see. . . . They live in the very coldest part of the country, and they keep cattle for their livelihood."

"Oh!" Ubo said, delighted. "That is just what we do. Ubo own many cattle—wealthy man!"

"Yes, but their cattle are different, Ubo. I've seen pictures. They're smaller than your cattle, with big antlers, and they're called *reindeer*. The Lapps keep herds of them, and they eat them and use their hides to make their clothing and tents."

"Do they mix their blood with milk for their drink?"

"I doubt it." Mallory laughed at her friend. "I think only the Masai do that."

As the compound came into view, a wave of sadness washed over Mallory at the realization that she would be unlikely to see this dear friend of hers for many years. "Don't forget me, Ubo."

He laid his hand on the young woman's head—a very unusual gesture for him. "Not while the rivers flow! You go to tell people about Jesus. I will pray for you—and you must pray for Ubo and for your Masai family."

"I will every day, Ubo." When he removed his hand, she simply whispered, "Good-bye," then turned and walked away.

Ubo watched her go, knowing that he was losing something precious out of his life. He had learned to love this young woman, and it had been Mallory Winslow who had led him to worship Jesus—something that the other missionaries had failed to do. As she disappeared inside the walls of the mission compound, he walked away, his shoulders bowed with grief.

★　★　★

"Mallory—here you are!"

Mallory had seen Paul Joubert's vehicle parked in front of the main building of the compound. She knew he would be there—and she knew she had to talk with him—but now as he came toward her, she wished he hadn't come.

Paul approached her with a sober look on his square face. He was not a tall man and was stocky and muscular. He was an Afrikaner, a man of twenty-five whose fair skin was sunburned, as usual. He put out his hand to greet her, and when she took it, he enclosed both of hers. "I've been waiting for you for two hours. Where have you been?"

"Oh, I just wanted to take one more look around before I left." Mallory shook her head and added wistfully, "I'm going to miss this place."

Joubert released her hand and stood quietly watching her. "I need to talk to you. Where can we go?"

"Let's walk down by the river."

"Good."

As the two made their way toward the serpentine river that watered the compound's fields and vegetable garden, Paul said, "I see most of your family is here."

"Yes. It's my going-away party."

They reached the bend of the river and stood on the bank, neither of them speaking.

Paul broke the silence. "You know why I've come."

Mallory faced him and noted, not for the first time, that he was about an inch shorter than she was. When it came to young men, it had always been that way. Those she had liked had been short and stocky, but this was not what troubled her most at the moment. She was about to hurt Paul, and she dreaded it, for she had become very fond of him.

"I can't marry you, Paul."

Paul came from a wealthy family of mine owners, and he had met Mallory in college. Those had been good days of close friendship, but after they had come back home, he'd begun to pressure her to marry him. He was a good Christian man, but Mallory sensed that he was far more attached to worldly things than she was. This would be natural, since his family had great possessions; nonetheless, it disturbed her.

"We must marry," he insisted. "You know how much I love you, Mallory . . . and I think you love me too."

With that he swept Mallory into his arms and kissed her. She did not resist, yet he sensed that her heart did not return his ardor. Releasing her, he stepped back and his lips grew thin. "What's wrong? I thought we had an understanding."

"I made a mistake, Paul. You know we can't marry. I'm

going to do missionary work in Norway. Your life is here."

"I've never accepted that."

"I know you haven't, but you must."

"Look, there's another way. I've mentioned it before. I've been thinking about it a lot and have talked to my family." Paul's face grew animated. "The mines are doing very well. Why, Mallory, we could send and support five missionaries to Norway, if you like. Then you wouldn't have to go."

Mallory suddenly felt tempted. It would indeed be easy to marry Paul. Life would present no difficulties, and she would not have to leave her beloved Africa. But even as this thought came to her, she pushed it aside.

"God has called *me* to go—not to send others in my place."

Paul continued to plead with her, but he finally saw that he was not going to change her mind. "So this is your final decision, Mallory?"

"Yes, it is. I'm sorry, Paul."

Paul Joubert was a stubborn man, but also practical. When he saw that a cause was lost, which happened rarely in his life, he never wasted his strength on a useless battle. "Will you write to me? You'll come back before too long and then we'll see."

"I'll call you on the shortwave radio."

Joubert shook his head glumly. "Well, I won't stay for your party. I'll say my good-bye here."

Mallory put her arms around him and gave him a sisterly hug. She felt a sense of loss, but she had known this moment must come. "Good-bye, Paul. I wish you well."

The two made their way back to the compound in silence, and Paul returned to his car. He started the engine and drove away, never looking back.

★ ★ ★

"I have a letter here for you to give to my sister Eva."

Anna Jorgensen, a tall woman with fair hair and blue eyes, was sitting next to Mallory at one of the tables in the communal dining room of the compound. The room was crowded with well-wishers who had gathered to send one of their own to far-off Norway. Anna smiled at Mallory. "I think God must have a sense of humor."

Mallory lifted an eyebrow. "What do you mean by that?"

"Well, He called a woman from the land of ice to come here to Africa under a blazing sun, and now He's calling a woman from this place to go and freeze in order to present the Gospel to the Lapps. It would have been much more economical if He had called me to preach to the Lapps and you to preach to the Masai."

Mallory laughed. "It is rather ironic. You know, Anna, I've often thought of the verse in John that says, 'He that believeth on me . . . out of his belly shall flow rivers of living water.'"

"What about it?"

"I think most of us would rather dig a channel. If we wanted to get water from point A to point B, we would make that channel as straight as we could. But a river doesn't go like that, does it?"

"No. It meanders and twists and turns. I see what you mean. God does things we can't understand." Anna reached over and put her hand on that of the younger woman. "I'm glad you're going to the Lapps. They need Jesus desperately."

"Doesn't anyone witness to them—the native Norwegians?"

"Very little, I'm afraid. The church has grown cold in Norway. And from what Eva writes me, it hasn't changed much. But God will allow you to witness to them."

The two women had grown close over the past two years, ever since Mallory had announced that God was calling her to be a missionary to the Lapps in Norway. She knew this desire had been birthed, at least in the beginning, by Anna's wistful comments that the Lapps were without God and no one seemed to care. This had created a desire in Mallory that she felt was of God, yet she had waited for months before telling anyone. The Winslows had a strong missionary heritage, and her decision had been respected by her parents and the other missionaries.

As Anna spoke quietly about life with the Lapps, Mallory's eyes fell on her parents, and a warmth washed over her, for she loved them dearly.

Her mother, who had been Jeanine Quintana before she had married John, was a striking woman, still very attractive with her black hair and violet eyes. John was her second husband, her first husband having died, leaving her with a considerable inheritance.

Mallory spotted her two brothers toward the other end of the table, engaged in a lively argument. It seemed they were always at odds with each other. Tyler was two years younger than Mallory and Chance three years younger. They both looked very much like their father, and people often mistook her brothers for twins.

At the end of the table sat Barney and Katie Winslow with their daughter, Erin, and their son-in-law, Quaid. Mallory's father had once tried to explain how she was related to this arm of the Winslow family, but it was complicated, and she hadn't tried to remember the details. She did know, however, that Erin, who was eleven years older than she was, had met Quaid Merritt in America. He was a pilot, and now the two of them used their planes for missionary work.

Barney's brother and sister were both there also, along with their spouses. Andrew and his wife, Dorothy, sat across from Esther and her husband, Jan Kruger, the Krugers' only son, Ross, was engrossed in an animated conversation with Quaid Merritt.

Mallory felt a glow of pride at being a part of the Winslow family, and when Barney stood up suddenly, she felt a rush of emotion. He had been the first of the Winslows to come to Africa, and now at age sixty-eight, with his hair gray and his figure somewhat stooped, he still seemed a strong man.

"All right. Let's have a little quiet here. I'm going to make a speech."

"Oh no!" Ross said. "Get your wallets out, everybody. He's going to take up a collection!"

The laughter went around the table, and Barney could not help grinning. "I'll skip the collection this time, but I do want us to join together in wishing well our latest missionary addition to the family." Barney's eyes turned to Mallory as he said, "*Sending* missionaries is new for us. We're the ones who have always gone, and now a Winslow will be preaching the Gospel in Europe. I want you to know how very proud I am of you, Mallory."

Mallory's face grew warm as she listened to Barney's words of love and affection. Then, to her surprise, he finished with, "Now, let's have a sermon from the newest missionary in the Winslow family."

Not expecting to be put on the spot like that, Mallory rose slowly to her feet and looked around at all the family and friends she knew would be praying for her. "I feel so incapable of doing this job," she began. "But if you'll all pray for me, as I'll pray for you every day, I know I'll have the victory." The crowd broke into smiles and clapped, some voicing their agreement and praise to God at her declaration of faith. Then as they quieted, she spoke, more confidently now, about how God had blessed her with such a wonderful family.

"What are the Lapps like?" her brother Chance asked when she paused for a moment. "Tell us about them."

"What I know about them I've mostly learned from Anna," Mallory replied. "They are a small group, no more than twenty thousand, and they live in Lapland, which is the northern part of Norway, Sweden, Finland, and Russia. I plan to work primarily with the Lapps who live in Norway, because I don't know a word of the other languages. Nobody knows where these people came from, but it was probably Russia. They are short people with high cheekbones, dark hair, and olive skin. Their way of life is very simple. They've tamed huge herds of wild reindeer, and they follow these herds to use for their food and clothing."

She ended by saying, "I don't mind telling you I'm a little afraid of what life will be like for me there in such a cold, primitive place, but my heart is very joyful that I'll be telling the Lapps about Jesus."

"How will you approach them?" Chance questioned. "I know you've learned Norwegian, but I thought they spoke another language called Lapp."

"That's true, but most of them speak some Norwegian. And I'll pick up some of their language after I get there. As for how I'll approach them . . . why, it'll be the same as it is here. I'll try to hold up Jesus to them."

John Winslow smiled. "That's the only way, daughter. Your mother and I are very proud of you."

"We're all proud of Mallory," Barney said. "And we'll be expecting glorious victories for the kingdom of God."

Mallory felt a lump in her throat. She was leaving all she'd ever known, and life in northern Norway would be very difficult. Here she had always been surrounded by loving, supportive family and friends. There she would be alone in a strange, alien world. But looking around in that dining hall at all the loving faces of these people she knew would be praying for her, she was filled with a new confidence that told her she could not fail.

CHAPTER TWO

A NEW WORLD

★ ★ ★

Mallory's stomach fluttered uneasily at her first sight of Norway. Standing on the deck of the ship that had brought her from Africa and gazing at the dark, forbidding wall of rock that rose out of the churning waters, her apprehension grew. The snow-covered peaks above were beautiful, but cold and remote. She could not say why, but they seemed very different from the warm majesty of Kilimanjaro and other African mountains.

The skies were blue and the clouds were white and fluffy on this beautiful April day, which somewhat mitigated her fear of the dangerous-looking fjords. As they approached Oslo, Mallory peered eagerly ahead at the crowded harbor, filled with shipping vessels of all kinds. The winters in Norway were so dismally long and the northern days so short that as soon as the spring sunshine arrived, people made the most of their daylight hours. Anna had told her that from November on, the country was dark and wet; then the frost and snow would come, transforming the Nordic gloom into brilliant white under a cloudless blue sky. While she was in Africa, Mallory had looked forward to the snow and learning how to ski, but now the thought of winter was far from her mind.

The ship pulled into the dock, and Mallory made her way down the gangplank with the other passengers, her eyes searching the crowd. She spotted a young woman about her own age with a young man standing beside her. The woman waved and called her name, and as Mallory stepped onto Norwegian soil for the first time, a strange feeling enveloped her. *I'm here at last. I'm really here!*

"Hello, Mallory. I'm Eva."

The young blond woman with blue eyes came forward with a broad welcoming smile. She wore a simple blue dress that picked up the color of her eyes, and an energy flowed from her that Mallory sensed at once.

"This is my fiancé, Lars Klovstad," she said in Norwegian.

"Welcome to Norway," Lars said in his deep voice. He was a tall, powerfully built man with sandy hair and light blue eyes.

"I'm glad to meet you, Mr. Klovstad."

"Just call me Lars. We're not very formal here. Your Norwegian is good."

"Anna and I have worked hard on it. I'm afraid my pronunciation may not be the best."

"Much better than my English," Eva said with a laugh, her lively eyes sparkling. "We're going to take you to the house where you'll be staying for a while. Then we'll go out and eat."

"The car is right over here," Lars said. "Are you ready?"

★ ★ ★

Mallory was delighted with the trip through Oslo. It was not a large city, she observed, but seemed expansive with its buildings spaced far apart. The center of Oslo was as busy as any other capital, and Eva pointed out the streets with pride. "This is Karl Johans Gate. Gate means street, of course. Most of the city's important buildings are here."

They reached the end of the street where stood an impressive square white building, the Royal Palace. Masses of lilacs blossomed all around it, and their heady scent floated over the city.

They passed the Parliament Building, where, as Eva explained, Norway's national assembly met. Across from there stood the University of Oslo and the National Theatre.

"I'll be taking some classes there at the university this summer, if possible," Mallory said.

"Oh yes. That's all been arranged."

"That's the Oslo Cathedral over there," Eva said, pointing, "and there's the square with the fruit and flower market."

"That church was built in 1699," Lars said, "and has been restored several times since then. You'll have to visit it."

"Oh, what's that?" Mallory asked as Lars expertly maneuvered the car down the busy street.

"That's Frogner Park, one of Oslo's showplaces," Eva said. "It has an open-air swimming pool and a magnificent rose garden."

"Do you like sculpture?" Lars asked.

"I've only seen Masai sculpture."

"Well, Gustav Vigeland is the foremost Norwegian sculptor. There are nearly two hundred of his statues here in the park—many made of granite or iron, and some in bronze. He worked on them all of his life."

"I'd like to spend some time there and see them," Mallory said.

"Oh, we'll have plenty of time to see the sights."

They drove into the residential area, where Mallory took in the late-nineteenth-century stone houses. As they made their way into the suburbs, Mallory looked first one way and then the other at the brightly painted wooden houses. It was all so different from Africa. Many of the streets were narrow and winding, and blue-and-white trams clattered around the sharp corners of the thorough-fares.

As they reached the edge of town, Lars pulled up in front of a small farmhouse painted a brilliant yellow with light blue trim. When they went inside, Mallory exclaimed, "What a lovely house!"

"Yes, it is nice, isn't it?" Eva said. "My grandfather built it. He's gone now, of course, so Lars and I will live here after we're married."

"It doesn't have as many windows as houses have in England or America, but here we like our homes to be cozy in the cold winter. If we want the out-of-doors," Lars said with a grin, "we've got plenty of that. But indoors in the winter, we like to close out the cold and ice and enjoy a nice roaring fire."

"You can give her your lectures on Norwegian architecture later, Lars," Eva said with a laugh. "Come along. Let's take Mallory's bags to her room and then go get something to eat."

The three went to a restaurant, and Mallory got her first taste of a Norwegian meal. There was a hot fruit soup, which in Norwegian was *fruktsuppe*, followed by brown river trout, and roasted reindeer steaks with cranberry sauce. For dessert they had a wonderful concoction of golden-colored cloudberries with thick whipped cream.

"This is delicious!" Mallory exclaimed.

"Did you really mean what you said in your letter about how the Masai mix blood and milk and then drink it?" Eva asked, leaning forward, her eyes intent.

"Oh yes. They milk the cow, and then they puncture its neck and drain the blood into the milk. And then they plug the wound with cow dung, stir the milk up, and drink it down."

"Oh my! You never tried it, I hope," Lars said.

"Certainly! It's very good."

They talked for a while about the new customs she would encounter in Norway and among the Lapps before Eva changed the subject with a touch of sadness. "You've come at a hard time. Europe is very unsettled right now."

In 1938 Europe was indeed unsettled. Adolf Hitler had risen over the continent like a dark specter. He had organized the National Socialist Party and had unified Germany, which had been practically demolished by the Great War. In 1935 Hitler had defied the Treaty of Versailles, announcing that he would create an army of a million men, which he did. That same year Hitler had marched into the Rhineland, and no one had opposed him. The Nazis had grown in power until finally, in 1938, Hitler took over Austria, annexing it to Germany. Since then he had announced that the Czechs should surrender to the Third Reich, and Neville Chamberlain, the British prime minister, had caved in, declaring to his nation, "I believe it is peace in our time."

Winston Churchill, a member of parliament, however, had warned, "Be ready for war. We must stop Hitler now."

"This man Hitler," Mallory said, "I don't understand why England or France doesn't stop him. Nobody in Africa understands."

"We don't understand either, but we're safe here," Lars said. "Norway is neutral."

"Lars, no one is safe with a maniac like Adolf Hitler," Eva said grimly. Then she forced herself to smile. "But let's not think about such things now. You're going to love this country, Mallory."

"I think I will."

"You'll freeze to death, though," Lars said with a grin. "I understand you've never even seen snow."

"No, I never have."

"Well, just wait. You'll see plenty of it!"

"Yes, and you must learn to ski," Eva said. "I've got an instructor lined up for you. But first you need to settle in here and rest up from your trip."

★ ★ ★

A week later Eva brought home a tall young man with tawny hair and dark blue eyes. "This is Rolf Bjelland," she announced. "He will be your skiing teacher. Rolf, this is your pupil, Mallory Anne Winslow."

"I am so happy to make your acquaintance," Rolf said in precise English.

"Why thank you. Your English is very good."

"I like to study, but I like better to ski."

"Rolf was born in Narvik," Eva said. "He knows the Lapps very well."

"Not too well," Rolf objected, shaking his head. "They're a strange people, but I have spent some time with them."

"I'd be very interested in whatever you can tell me about them," Mallory said. "Perhaps you can tell me about your experiences with the Lapps while we're on our way to the mountains."

"I would be very glad to do that." Rolf spread his arms, palms up. "Well, is everybody packed?"

"We're all ready," Lars said, picking up his suitcase that he had placed by the door. Eva turned off the lights as the group made their way out the door.

"I brought some skis that I think would do for you," Rolf told Mallory. They stuffed all of their belongings into Lars's car. "You have never skied?"

"No. I've never even walked on snow."

"You have a fine teacher," Rolf said, slapping himself on the chest.

"And modest too." Eva laughed. "Watch out for this one, Mallory. He considers himself a ladies' man."

"Pay her no attention, Miss Winslow," Rolf retorted. "For you, I'm just what the doctor ordered, as they say in English."

★ ★ ★

The trip to the mountains was a delight to Mallory, both because of the gorgeous scenery and because she found Rolf, Eva, and Lars to be the best of company. They made their way there with scores of happy Norwegians who had begun their summer holidays. Dressed in gaily colored sweaters and anoraks, they all headed toward Nordfjord, some five hundred kilometers northwest of Oslo, where the snow still coated the upper slopes. Mallory found the air cool, sharp, and refreshing after the stifling heat of Africa.

The mountains were beautiful to Mallory. The ground was covered with mosses and lichens, and the lakes were fringed with bog cotton grass. Dense turfs of low-lying plants included rose-tinted heaths, saxifrages, and many species of white- and blue-blossomed Arctic plants. Mallory delighted in the clear mountain lakes, the foaming waterfalls, and the fast-flowing rivers. As they drove higher into the mountains, the road sometimes passed through dark forests and other times clung to rocky mountainsides with breathtaking views of glaciers and fjords.

It took the better part of the day to get there, but they weren't in any hurry. They stopped along the way to eat, and Mallory found the food quite delicious. For snacks they nibbled on hearty crackers and sweet goat's milk cheese.

When they arrived at the ski area, they hauled their packs into a *hytte,* a furnished cabin that offered a bed for the night very cheaply. Eva and Mallory stayed in a room with two other women, and the men shared another room.

That evening the foursome gathered outside around a huge fire, joining with the other travelers in their singing and folk dancing. Mallory learned that the oldest surviving type of Norwegian folk music was called *kveding,* which was unaccompanied singing. She even learned the words to some of the songs and was able to join in the singing.

Rolf insisted on teaching her some of the folk dances, and it was during one of these sessions she found out that his reputation as a ladies' man was well deserved. They had been dancing around among the crowd, and he had drawn her off to one side into the shadows of the tall fir trees, out of sight of their chaperones, Eva and Lars. She had tried to pull away, but he had caught her and kissed her before she could move.

"Rolf, don't do that!"

"Don't do what?"

"Don't kiss me. I'm not used to it."

"But I think it's my duty to get you used to it." Rolf's eyes danced with merriment, and when he reached for her again, she pushed him away. "No! Eva warned me about you. Anyway, I'm too old for you."

"You're only four years older than I am. When I'm sixty-five you'll only be sixty-nine. Besides, I think women should marry younger men so they can wait on their wives when they get old."

Mallory could not help but laugh. "You're going to have to find yourself a young Norwegian girl."

"No, I think I like older African women. Yes, that's what I like." Rolf reached for her again, but she laughed and turned away, going back to the fire to look for Eva and Lars. When he followed her, she said, "You're just my skiing instructor, Rolf. Stick to your job!"

★ ★ ★

Mallory found that skiing came easily to her, for her balance was good and was fearless. Rolf was a good instructor, although he never missed an opportunity to touch her, and she had to be constantly on her guard. She quickly learned to take the slopes at a fair rate of speed. She knew she would never be as good as Rolf or others who were practically born on skis, but she was satisfied with her progress.

They skied for the better part of a week, and on the last night before they all went back to Oslo, she was sitting on the couch with Rolf in front of the fire inside the hytte. The others had all gone to bed, and the fire crackled and hissed and snapped, making a comforting noise in the silence.

"You know what?" Rolf asked, staring into the yellow flames.

"What?"

"I think I'm falling in love with you."

"Don't be foolish. Eva says you're going through all the girls in Oslo alphabetically."

"That's not true! She's always telling those stories on me."

"Well, even so, you can't be interested in me. I've come to Norway to do a job."

"You can be a preacher. That's all right with me. It would be nice to be married to a preacher." He turned, and she could see a smile playing about his lips. "What about it? You think we should get married this summer or wait until winter? Maybe we'd better wait until winter. You'll need a man to keep you warm then."

Mallory burst out laughing. She could no more be angry with Rolf than she could be angry at a puppy.

"Good night, Rolf."

"Don't forget. When winter comes, we'll be married."

Mallory went to her room, where three other young women were already sleeping on cots, and she simply lay down fully dressed. She liked Rolf and had had a wonderful time with him in the mountains, but she knew her real work would be beginning soon.

★   ★   ★

September brought cold winds to Oslo, and snow began to fall. Mallory stood looking out the window, thinking of how much she had enjoyed the summer and the courses she had taken at the university. She had taken a Norwegian language class with other people from all parts of the world, as well as a class in Norwegian history and a third in Lapp culture. She had become close friends with an older woman named Sigrid Undset. Sigrid was a famous writer, having won a Nobel Prize for her work. She was interested in Africa and had invited Mallory to her house one afternoon for tea. Since then the two had met many times.

"And so you are leaving tomorrow for your work with the Lapps?"

Sigrid poured the tea, added some sugar to her own cup, and sat back. "You'll find it very uncomfortable. I don't know much about the Lapps, but they live roughly, I understand."

"Yes, they live in small tents. They are nomads, moving around to follow the reindeer."

"They seem to be almost another species," Sigrid said. She was a short woman, strongly built, with brown hair and brown eyes. "I don't know how you'll ever get through to them."

"They need Jesus just as we all do."

Sigrid smiled. She had discovered that this young woman had a single-track mind, and now she listened as Mallory spoke of the work she planned to do. Sigrid blew gently across her hot tea and then took a cautious sip. "I'm worried about this war," she confessed after Mallory mentioned her own concerns.

"It's getting worse, isn't it?"

Indeed, Adolf Hitler had rallied his storm troopers at Nuremberg and announced that the Czechs must surrender to the Third Reich.

"Do you think Hitler will invade Czechoslovakia?"

"It's inevitable, Mallory. They've already started. They've been attacking Jews." She hesitated, then said, "I will have to leave this place soon."

"Leave! But this is your home!"

"My life will be in danger if they invade Norway."

"No, that's not possible!"

Sigrid nodded. "They've already taken the lives of educated Jews in Czechoslovakia and many other places. I will have to leave when they attack Norway."

Mallory shook her head. "Norway is neutral. Hitler will never invade a neutral country."

Sigrid looked at the younger woman, and there was a profound wisdom in her eyes when she said, "You don't know this man Hitler. Nothing will satisfy him but ruling over Europe, perhaps even the world."

"That could never happen."

Sigrid did not answer but looked down at her hands.

"It will be all right, Sigrid," Mallory said quickly. "God is in His heaven."

"But man is on earth," Sigrid said quietly. "And while this madman is loose, no one on earth is safe."

CHAPTER THREE

THE STRANGE GUIDE

★ ★ ★

"Well, there it is, Mallory—Narvik, Norway. Not exactly London or Paris, is it?"

Mallory stared at the small village that lay spread out before her, flanking the dark gray ocean. They had seen some spectacular scenery as they had driven a thousand kilometers north from Oslo. It was certainly a far cry from New York or Paris—or even Oslo. She glanced quickly at Rolf and smiled. "I think it's nice. It's much larger than most of the villages in Africa."

Rolf Bjelland took his right hand off the steering wheel and put it around Mallory, drawing her close. "I wish I didn't have to leave you here," he complained. "But I've got to get back to the university. My fall classes will start soon."

"Rolf, you're hugging me again!"

"Of course I am. That's what pretty girls are for—to be hugged." He laughed at her struggles to escape and then released her. "You'll love my parents. I told them all the good things about you and left out all the bad."

"What bad things are there that you left out?"

"That you won't let me love you. I think it's terrible," he said, turning to give her an engaging grin. "It's the least you could do for a poor scholar who's taught you to be the best skier in Africa."

Rolf had certainly been an enjoyable companion for Mallory as she had begun adjusting to life in a new culture. During her stay at Oslo, he had been constantly at her side, and they, along with Eva and Lars, had taken two other trips to the ski slopes in the mountains, where he had indeed made a proficient skier out of her. He had also tried to prepare her for the bitter Norwegian winters, which sounded even more difficult than Mallory had imagined after being used to the sultry climate of Africa. During all that time he had romanced her incessantly, but always with a light spirit. Mallory had developed a great affection for the young man, and now she smiled at him. "I may have a few bad things to tell your parents about their son."

"Go ahead. They'll never believe it. I've been spoiled beyond belief."

"I can believe that!"

Rolf continued teasing her in a jocular fashion as he turned down toward the sea. "There's my home right there."

"Why, what a charming house, Rolf. It's wonderful."

"I was born in that house. You think we ought to put a sign out in front saying, 'Rolf Bjelland Born Here'?" Without waiting for an answer, he stopped the car, leaped out, and dashed around to open the door. "I can't wait for you to meet my parents."

Mallory smiled at the young man's exuberance. "I'm going to miss you, Rolf."

"Good. Absence makes the heart grow fonder."

At that moment the door opened and a couple came out. "Hello, Mother, Father. Here she is—the woman who refuses to marry your son. I think you ought to take a stick to her."

"It's you who needs the stick!" Rolf's father was a tall, broad-shouldered man with iron-gray hair and a weathered complexion. He put out his hand. "I'm Norman, and this is my wife, Hulda."

"Come in by the fire," Hulda said. "I would guess that son of mine hasn't fed you."

"I'm so glad to meet you," Mallory said. "And, no, he hasn't fed me today."

"Well, come in," Norman said. "Dinner has been ready since early this morning. Momma has been cooking a feast."

Mallory entered the house, where a cheerful fire crackled in a hearth that warmed an open area including a sitting room, dining area, and kitchen. The fragrance of fresh bread baking filled the room. She looked around, noting the low ceilings with exposed beams and the wooden walls weathered to a silvery gray. The walls were liberally covered with drawings and paintings. The sturdy wooden furniture, polished smooth with age, was simple but appeared comfortable.

"You come this way," Hulda said to Mallory, "and I will show you where you will be staying."

"I feel like this is such an imposition."

"Nonsense. It'll be good to have company. I'm afraid you'll find life here very boring. There's really nothing to do."

Hulda led Mallory down a short hallway and showed her through a door into a pleasant bedroom with white furniture. White curtains at the window with a blue-flower border matched a handmade blue-and-white quilt on the bed, and a dark blue rag rug warmed up the hardwood floor. "Why, this is a beautiful room!" Mallory exclaimed.

"It was our daughter's, but she's married now. Make yourself at home while I go put supper on the table."

Rolf entered the bedroom as his mother left, carrying Mallory's suitcases. "I'd better help you unpack."

"No thanks. I can take care of that myself."

He set one suitcase on a chair and the other on the floor. "Your parents are very nice."

"I'm glad you'll be staying here with them. They get

lonely. I don't get up here much except during vacations." He opened the closet door. "Hurry up and unpack. I'm starved."

"You're always starved. If you'd be so kind as to wait in the sitting room, I'll be done before you know it."

Twenty minutes later the four of them sat down to a meal that would have fed an army.

"This is delicious soup," Mallory said. "What is it?"

"Hulda's secret formula," Norman said with a grin. "She's only going to give it to Rolf's bride. She guards her recipes jealously."

"You might as well give it to her now, then," Rolf said. He had stuffed his mouth full of a buttery roll and spoke around it in a muffled tone. "She's going to marry me sooner or later—when she stops being so stubborn about it."

"I'm not stubborn!" Mallory objected. "I'm just too old for you."

"You'll have to be careful of him," Hulda said. "He's been chasing older women since he was fifteen years old."

"And caught a few of them, I daresay."

Mallory flashed a smile at Norman.

The fire crackled and popped in the fireplace, and the pleasant smell of burning wood mingled with the odor of the fresh bread.

"I understand you're going to be working with the Lapps," Norman commented. He sipped dark tea from a huge cup. "They're a strange people. Do you speak Lapp?"

"No, I don't. But Rolf tells me that most of the young people learn Norwegian in school."

"That they do these days. Back when I was a boy before the schools were here, you couldn't communicate with them. Things are different now."

"However are you going to get to them?" Hulda asked. "They wander all over the north country, all the way to Sweden and Finland . . . even the Soviet Union."

"God will provide a way," Mallory said, smiling.

"I understand your whole family are missionaries," Norman commented.

"Yes, we all came from America originally, but I was born in Kenya and have never been anywhere else—until now."

At the end of the meal, Rolf stood up. "Well, if you'll excuse me, I've got to go." He embraced his parents and then said to Mallory, "Walk me out to the car. You wouldn't want my folks to see you kissing me good-bye."

Mallory could not restrain a smile. "I'll walk to the car with you, and we'll shake hands."

"All right. Have it your way."

As soon as they got out to the car, Mallory said, "Rolf, you've been such a help to me, and it was so nice of you to work out the arrangements with your parents. They're lovely people."

"Oh yes. We Bjellands are all lovely people. Did you mean that about a handshake?"

"Yes!" Mallory put out her hand, but Rolf quickly leaned forward and kissed her full on the lips.

"I'll be back before you know it. Watch out for these young fellas around here. They're a bad lot."

"I'll write to you," Mallory said. She watched as he got into the car and waved as he drove away.

When she got back into the house, Norman grinned at her. "Was it a nice handshake?"

"I expect you know Rolf better than that. He stole a kiss before I could even move."

"He's a rash young fellow. Now, why don't you finish getting unpacked and relax a bit, and tomorrow we'll give you a tour of the village."

"I'd like to see the village, but I'm sure I can find my own way."

"No, we'll go with you," Hulda said. "I've told everyone you're coming, so I'm afraid you may find that they'll be staring at you. Visitors are quite a novelty up here. We don't get many."

After cleaning up the next morning after breakfast, the

three put on light jackets and left the house for a two-hour stroll around the village of Narvik. The Bjellands knew everyone, of course, which was not saying much in the small village. Many of the people were fishermen, Mallory discovered, and she could not keep their names straight. They were so very different from African names. When she mentioned this to the Bjellands, Norman simply shrugged his shoulders and said, "You'll learn their names in time. How long will you be here?"

"Not very long, I hope. I just need to figure out where the Lapps might be at this time of the year, and then I can get started."

Norman shook his head, a doleful expression on his weathered face. "I can't think how you're going to make it. People born in this country would have a hard time living way up north with the Lapps, and here you were brought up in sweltering Africa. Are you sure God's called you to do this?"

"Yes, I'm sure."

"Now, you leave her alone, Norman," Hulda said quickly. "If God has called her, He'll make a way."

★   ★   ★

In the days that followed, Mallory thought often of Hulda's words—*"If God has called her, He'll make a way."* She was anxious to get on with her work with the Lapps, but there was one obstacle that was preventing her from doing so: no one knew where they were. She took long walks in the village and got to know some of the shopkeepers by name, but as the weeks went by, the weather continued to get chillier. Mallory noticed that many of the local residents still were not wearing jackets, but she needed to pull hers tight around her to stay warm. Some days, the wind off the sea hit her like an icy fist, and the sky joined with the horizon, making one seamless unit.

For most of September, Mallory felt cut off from the

outside world. Narvik almost seemed like another planet, but rumors from the outside still made their way to the little village, and newspapers—sometimes weeks or even months old—arrived on the fishing boats when the weather permitted. With time on her hands, Mallory pored over the papers, reading in detail how Hitler had promoted himself to military chief earlier in the year and how in March he'd had a day of unparalleled glory. The dictator who had left Austria in his youth as a penniless artist was cheered by thousands as he returned to Vienna to pronounce the *Anschluss*—the union of Austria and Germany. It had been a bloodless victory, but everyone in Europe knew it was not the last aggression they could expect from Adolf Hitler.

Mallory wrote to her parents and brothers, to Eva and to Sigrid, and there were times when she was tempted to give up on her plan. She could not simply walk out of Narvik and into the wild north country and find the Lapps. She had to have a guide.

While staying with the Bjellands, Mallory attended the Lutheran church with them. The pastor, Peter Knudsen, was a fine preacher and welcomed Mallory warmly. He was intensely interested in her plans to evangelize the Lapps, but he was not too encouraging.

"The Lapps," he had told her, "are very resistant to the Gospel."

Mallory asked him what their religion was, and he shook his head. "I don't really know," he admitted. "It's almost as if they don't have any, although I'm sure they do. Every people has a god of some kind."

October brought more of the same routine for Mallory, and before she knew it, it was well into November. She could hardly believe she was still in Narvik. Rolf's parents didn't seem to object to Mallory's extended stay, but Mallory was growing almost desperate with anxiety. She decided to seek God more earnestly and made up her mind to fast and pray for two days, and knowing that it would be impossible to conceal this from the Bjellands, she announced her intentions.

"Why, that's a fine idea," Hulda said. "We'll join you. No meals for two days, Norman."

The three set themselves to the task of seeking God, and Mallory stayed mostly in her room. She found she could not pray constantly, and much of the time she simply meditated on the Word, turning over the pages of her Bible, hoping that God would speak to her through one of the verses.

The second day she thought little about food, and late in the afternoon she heard a knock on the front door. Norman and Hulda were both out of the house, having gone to the village to visit some friends, so she went to answer it. When she opened the door, she found Pastor Knudsen on the step.

"Good morning, Miss Winslow."

"Why, good morning, Pastor. Won't you come in?"

When he entered, she said, "The Bjellands aren't here, but they'll be back soon."

Knudsen pulled off his hat, which was covered with fine flakes of snow, and held it in his hands. "I need to speak with you."

"Well then, let me take your coat."

"No, I'll not stay. I have a sick family to visit, but something came to my attention I thought might be of interest to you."

"What is it, Pastor?"

"A young Lapp woman has been arrested. She's in the local jail."

"What has she done?"

"She's been charged with drunkenness and disorderly conduct. I'm afraid she's going to be sentenced to three months if someone doesn't pay her fine. She doesn't have any money, of course."

"Does she live here?"

"No, and she is a rather disreputable young woman, I'm sorry to tell you. I went in to talk with her, and she's a rough one. Curses every breath! I thought I'd heard profanity among the timbermen and the fishermen, but this one—well, I won't go into that. She has no morals where men are concerned. Took up with a blacksmith and was just living with him out of wedlock."

"How old is she?"

"Oh, probably only in her early twenties." He hesitated. "If you are still intent on finding the Lapps, she can take you to them. But you'd have to pay her fine . . . and . . . well . . . perhaps I've come in error. This is actually not something I would advise you to do."

"But, Pastor, this is clearly from God!"

"From God? What do you mean?"

"The Bjellands and I have been fasting and praying for two days now that God would open a door to get me to the Lapp people, and this is it!"

His face twisted with a wry expression. "Well, if you can put up with her ways, she can get you to the Lapps, all right. Maybe this is from God, but if you were my daughter, I wouldn't permit it."

"Thank you for coming by, Pastor. I believe God has used you in this way."

"You're actually thinking of going out into the wilderness with that woman?"

"If she'll take me, I'll go," Mallory said simply.

★ ★ ★

Stepping into a cell at the tiny local jail, Mallory found herself the object of a pair of cold eyes. The woman's name, she had been informed by the sheriff, was Orva, and like Pastor Knudsen, the sheriff had also warned Mallory about her temperament. "She's a bad 'un, miss. I'd have nothin' to do with her. Jail might take a little of the starch out of her."

As the sheriff closed the cell door behind Mallory, she greeted the woman warmly in Norwegian and introduced herself. "I understand your name is Orva."

The woman did not speak or make a move but sat sullenly on the bunk. Her black hair was tied back with a leather thong, and Mallory noticed that her eyes were golden brown and somewhat oriental looking. Her face was broad, and she had dark skin with wrinkles around the corners of her eyes. She was wearing well worn men's clothing. For a moment, Mallory thought she didn't understand the language.

"Well, what do you want?" she finally grunted.

"I'm sorry about your trouble, Orva. Pastor Knudsen told me about you and thought you might be able to help me."

The woman raised a dubious eyebrow and smiled cynically. "You want *me* to help *you*?"

"Yes. I know that comes as a surprise, but I've come to Norway to live with your people, the Lapps."

"What do you want with us?" She asked the question with a disdainful sneer and punctuated with some of the language Pastor Knudsen had warned her about.

"I'm a missionary, Orva. Do you know what that is?"

"No."

"It means I want to tell your people about the God I serve."

"We have our own gods!" The words were cold and hard, and there was something savage about the woman's expression. She looked very strong, and as Mallory explained what she wanted to do, Orva simply shrugged. "You will die. No white woman could live like we do. Besides, we don't need any white woman's god!"

"I know you feel that way, and I hope to change your mind. What I would suggest is this—I understand you're going to have to stay in jail for three months if someone doesn't pay your fines. Do you think anyone will?"

"I don't know anyone who would pay for me."

"I will."

A flicker of light touched the woman's dark eyes. "Why?"

"Because I want you to take me to your people, to be my guide. I can't do it by myself, but if you would go with me and help me, I think I can."

"You'll give me money?"

"I'll pay your fine, and I'll pay you for guiding me."

Orva got up and stood squarely facing Mallory. "I don't want to be in jail," she admitted sullenly.

"Then you'll guide me?"

"You'll probably die."

"That's not your problem. You can introduce me to your people."

Suddenly the woman smiled, revealing a missing front tooth. "My own family tries to avoid me when they can."

Mallory was taken aback, but she quickly recovered and said, "If you can find them and keep me from getting lost and starving, I'll pay you."

"All right, I'll do it. Anything to get me out of this place." She stood up and went over to the bars, which she shook violently, cursing the jailer and everyone else who came to mind.

★   ★   ★

Thirty minutes later the two women entered the Bjellands' house to find the couple sitting at the table. They looked up, alarm showing clearly on their faces. "I know you'll think this is foolish," Mallory told them, "but I believe God has sent this woman to help me find the Lapps." She went on to tell them of the pastor's visit and her own trip to the jail.

"When will you be leaving?" Hulda asked, her eyes not leaving the dark, strong face of the stranger, who revealed not a flicker of emotion.

"We'll go to buy the equipment we'll need first thing tomorrow morning, that is, if you don't mind. Is it okay if Orva stays in my room with me tonight?"

Norman and Hulda exchanged a look, and Mallory saw

Norman give Hulda the slightest nod.

"Yes, of course that's fine," Hulda answered.

Mallory took Orva into her room, where she quickly packed her bags. Orva watched silently and finally asked, "How are you going to carry those?"

The thought had not even occurred to Mallory. "Why, I don't know."

"You can't carry them on your back, can you?"

"No, I can't, but—"

"You'll need a tent. Do you have one?"

"No, but I'll buy one tomorrow."

Orva snorted with disgust. "You'll never make it out there."

★　★　★

The next morning Hulda fixed them a hearty meal to break their two-day fast, and then Orva and Mallory set out to buy supplies for the trip. Orva took Mallory to a shack on the outskirts of Narvik where an old Lapp man lived who was some distant relation to Orva. Apparently, he had given up the wandering life, preferring the warmth of four strong walls around him. After a suitable amount of haggling in their native tongue, they agreed on a price for a sled and one reindeer.

Orva turned to Mallory and told her the amount they had agreed on. After a moment's hesitation, Mallory pulled some bills out of her purse. Orva grabbed them and separated out several for the old man, who grinned at them toothlessly and nodded. She put the rest in her pocket.

"I'm going into town to buy something to drink," she said, smirking at Mallory's uncomfortable expression. "Just as soon as I hitch up this reindeer."

When the sled was ready, Orva motioned to Mallory. "Come on, let's go."

Mallory smiled her thanks to the old man, and they began walking back toward town, with the reindeer plodding along behind them, pulling the small sled that would serve to carry their provisions.

The wind made a shrill, keening whistle, and the cold bit at Mallory's face as the two women leaned directly into it. Every now and then, Mallory turned to make sure the reindeer was still following, even though Orva held the reins. It was a strange-looking animal and much smaller than Mallory had imagined a reindeer to be, but it seemed strong enough, and the wooden sled trundled after as the animal obediently followed the woman.

At the general store in town, Orva made most of the decisions. They left with a tent, cooking supplies, some canned and dried food, and warmer clothes and thicker boots for Mallory. Orva also bought two gallons of whiskey. Mallory started to protest at this waste of money, but Orva immediately snapped, "I get the whiskey or I don't go."

Mallory bit her tongue, knowing this was one problem she wasn't going to solve right away.

The two women loaded the sled down and then went back to the Bjellands' to pick up Mallory's things.

The older couple accompanied the two young women outside and watched as Orva made sure the reindeer was secured firmly in its harness. Mallory thanked the couple repeatedly for taking her in, and they assured her it had been no trouble and they would be praying for her. When Orva indicated that she was ready, Mallory waved to the Bjellands as she trudged along after the sled. She turned around and gave one last wave before turning a corner.

Norman shook his head. "We shouldn't have let her go, Hulda."

"We couldn't have stopped her. That young woman's got a mighty stubborn streak in her. My, how I'm going to miss her!"

CHAPTER FOUR

LIVING WITH THE LAPPS

★　★　★

"I'm afraid I can't go any farther, Orva."

A moaning wind almost drowned out Mallory's voice as she called out to the woman who had forged ahead tirelessly, leading the reindeer.

Orva turned to face Mallory, a look of satisfaction on her dark face. "This is as far as you can go, huh?"

"I'm afraid so. My legs hurt and I'm freezing."

Orva laughed a brittle laugh, one of the very few sounds she had made all day as the two had trudged across the land. "All right. I said you wouldn't make it, didn't I?"

"I'm sorry. I'll do better when I get toughened up."

Ignoring this, Orva pulled the tent off the sled and tossed it onto the cold ground, ignoring the tiny white particles of sleet that stung Mallory's face like beestings. Orva seemed impervious to the cold, even though she was dressed in much lighter clothing than Mallory was. She wore her heaviest clothing, including her new reindeer-skin boots and leggings, thick fur coat, and warm cap.

Mallory attempted to help, but even inside her thick

gloves, her fingers were numb. "I know how to put the tent up, but my fingers won't work."

Orva just kept working, and the tent went up mostly under her efforts. She turned and said, "Get inside, but don't go to sleep."

"No, I want to help."

"You're no help."

The curt sentence summed up Mallory's condition. Her legs ached fiercely from the difficulty of the icy walk. She had thought she was in good shape, but she was not accustomed to the cold, which seemed to increase her fatigue. Stubbornly, she stayed outside, unpacking the sled, and at Orva's direction began to gather whatever dried-up shrubs she could find. By the time Orva had fed the reindeer, Mallory had managed to get a fire started.

Orva glanced at Mallory, reached under the sled, and pulled out one of the jugs. Uncapping it, she took a long swig before offering it to Mallory. "You?" she said.

"No."

"I'll drink one for you, then." Orva took another swig, sighed gustily, and then capped it and put it back on the sled.

Mallory found it difficult to stay awake. She walked back and forth, beating her arms and stomping her feet as Orva dug through the supplies, found a can of beans, and opened it. She dumped it into a saucepan along with some dried meat and soon had a makeshift stew bubbling.

"Eat," Orva commanded.

Mallory squatted down and, holding the spoon awkwardly in her numb fingers, ate hungrily. As the stew went down, the warmth of the food and the small fire hit her hard. "I've got to go to sleep," she said.

"Get in the tent, then. I'll be in soon."

Creeping into the small tent, Mallory managed to get into the sleeping bag she had bought. She fastened it and almost immediately fell asleep.

She was startled awake when Orva entered the tent. Mallory could say nothing before the woman lay down right beside her and pulled a rough blanket over them both. She felt Orva's arms go around her and pull her close. "What are you doing?" she asked in alarm.

"Two are good," Orva explained. "Each one of us is a little stove. This is the way my people survive. Go to sleep now."

Even in the bitterly cold air, Mallory could smell the rank unwashed odor of the woman. She was to learn later that the Lapps did not change clothes all winter long. Added to this was the smell of alcohol on her breath. Nonetheless, it was warmer beside Orva, so ignoring the stench, Mallory tried to pray. But she was so weary she went to sleep before she could frame a single sentence.

★ ★ ★

"Come out!"

Mallory tried to dig deeper into her sleeping bag, but the grating voice persisted.

"Get out! Time to leave!"

Almost desperately Mallory shook herself awake and crawled out of the bag. The cold hit her like a physical blow. It was a fierce, biting, penetrating force that froze her flesh and seemed to sink deep into her lungs and all through her body. She struggled out of the tent and into the dark morning to find that Orva had cooked a breakfast of fried meat. A pan of water also bubbled over the fire.

"Eat."

Mallory quickly followed Orva's instructions, and as soon as she was finished with the sparse meal, Orva looked squarely at her. "You want to go on?"

"Of course."

"We can go back. You're not going to make it. This is only November. It will get colder yet in December and January."

The challenge angered Mallory. "If I don't make it, just put me on the sled and let the reindeer pull me."

"Hah!" Orva laughed, her eyes crinkling up till they were almost invisible. "I'll steal everything you have and leave you for the wolves."

Her threat silenced Mallory. She wasn't sure if Orva had said it in jest or was serious. Struggling with her numb hands and feet, Mallory helped as best she could to take down the tent. When the reindeer did not promptly obey Orva's order to come be harnessed, she struck it so hard with one of the tent poles that it staggered.

"Don't do that, Orva," Mallory said, shocked at her mistreatment of the animal.

"It's just a beast."

"He has feelings too. Don't hit him again."

Orva stared at her employer, silent for a moment. "You're too soft," she grumbled and shrugged. "You'll toughen up, though—if you live that long."

Before they set out again, Orva took a lengthy swallow from her jug. She lowered it and stared at Mallory, daring her to say something. "Aren't you going to preach at me?"

"I don't think you should drink."

Orva cursed and capped the jug, glaring at Mallory. "Don't tell me what to do. You'd die without me."

So the day began and continued with Orva leading the way and drinking. They traveled until almost midmorning before Mallory asked a question that had been puzzling her. "How come the sun sets so early in the afternoon?"

Orva looked around and grunted. "Better get used to the dark. Come December, you won't be seeing the sun for weeks."

Mallory shivered uncontrollably now, not only from the cold but from the realization that they were far enough north that the sun would soon be staying below the horizon. She tried to concentrate on putting one foot ahead of the other, but she felt as if she were in an alien atmosphere. The ground was hilly, uneven, and rocky, as well as being covered with snowy moss and lichens, which provided cushioning for their feet but was awkward and slippery to walk across. The farther north and inland they went, the colder it became.

At one of their resting places, Orva pointed toward some movement in the distance. "Look, reindeer herd."

"Is it your people?" Mallory asked hopefully.

"No." There was no further explanation. Orva did not believe in wasting words. "We go now," she said as she got up.

Mallory stuck it out until midafternoon, and finally she had to tell Orva she could go no farther. The sun had already set, and she was too tired to even help put up the tent, but Orva put it up quickly and efficiently. Once again it took all of Mallory's strength to resist the numbing effects of the cold. She walked back and forth stamping the earth, trying to get feeling into her feet, and beating her arms against her sides to restore circulation.

Orva cooked a simple meal, and after they had eaten, she fed the fire with a few more twigs. They both sat staring into the tiny flame. It gave off a pitiful amount of heat, and Mallory, hungry for warmth, crowded close. "Couldn't we build it up bigger?"

"It won't help. When it goes down again, it'll just seem colder."

The two women sat there quietly, Orva simply staring into the fire. There was a stolid hardness about her, and Mallory thought, *She's just like this land.* Mallory offered up a prayer before asking her companion, "Orva, will you let me tell you about my God?"

"You can if you want, but it won't do any good."

Mallory smiled at the invitation and began. "There is one God, Orva. He made all of this. He made the whole world and the stars and the sun and the moon. And He made us, you and me."

"He made everyone, you say?"

"Yes, of course."

"He's not a very good maker, then. I've seen some pretty pitiful specimens." Orva grinned and downed a swallow of her whiskey. "Go on. Tell me some more about this maker of yours."

Mallory struggled to get her message across, and finally she spoke about Jesus. "We were all so bad that there was no hope for any of us," Mallory said. The wind had died down, and an immense silence rested on the barren landscape. It was as if everything in the world had died and all was totally silent. Mallory's voice sounded thin and weak as she said, "God was holy and righteous. And He sent his Son to save us."

"To save us from what?"

"From hell."

"Hell? What's that?"

"It's a place where people go forever who are lost and die in their sins."

"And what is this hell like?"

"It's a place of burning fire."

Orva laughed and hugged the jug to her chest. Her eyes gleamed, and her teeth glowed white against her dark skin. "That's where I want to go, then. I've never been warm in my whole life. Yes, I want to go to hell."

Mallory was speechless. She struggled to find a way to explain what she meant, but no words would come. Finally she said, "For you and your people, I guess hell would be a place of eternal ice, with no fire and no warmth."

Orva blinked. "I wouldn't want to go to a place like that. I've had enough of that kind of misery."

Mallory did not know how to say what was on her heart. "Jesus is the Son of God, and He came to give us peace. To make everything right."

"He's got a big job on His hands," Orva said sardonically. "How does He propose to fix the mess we're in?"

"He came to earth and He died for us."

Orva grew still and fixed her dark eyes on Mallory. "He did?"

"Yes," Mallory said, encouraged at the woman's interest. She went on to speak of how Jesus was born without an earthly father, and this also interested her.

"He had no father? Just a mother? That can't be."

"It was the only time it's ever happened. God was His father, and Mary was His mother. So He was God and man."

"It makes a nice story," Orva said with a shrug. "This is what you're going to tell my people?"

"Yes, all about Jesus."

Orva slowly uncapped the jug, took a swallow, and expelled her breath with a gust. "Well, it'll make a good story to tell when there's nothing else to do."

★ ★ ★

For four long days Mallory Winslow struggled with the hardest journey of her life. She had thought it was hard to live in Africa under the blazing sun, fighting the heat and mosquitoes and other bugs and dangers of wild animals. But every day now she longed for an hour under that hot African sun. She had not bathed or changed her clothes, and the travel seemed endless. The landscape changed very little. Sometimes new snow would fall. Once she woke up to find the tent buried two feet deep, and it had taken all of the fortitude she could muster to come out and face the world. True, it was beautiful in its pristine stillness, but it was white and unbroken and treacherous.

It was almost noon by her watch on the fourth day of travel when Orva stopped short. "There."

Mallory was stumbling forward, concentrating on not falling down, when she looked toward the horizon. Her heart gave a queer lurch at the sight of movement.

"My people."

"How can you tell?"

"I have eyes, don't I? Come."

Mallory struggled forward, excited by the opportunity of meeting Orva's family. As they approached, she saw that a large herd of reindeer was digging at the snow to get at the vegetation underneath. She had never understood how they could survive in this inhospitable land, but obviously they had done so for hundreds of years.

When they drew closer, she could make out human figures, and she also saw a group of tents scattered in a random fashion. The reindeer grazed about them, and their arrival had attracted the attention of a number of people, who were walking toward them. She could see they were all wearing reindeer-skin boots and heavy coats.

"They won't be too glad to see me," Orva said. She halted the reindeer in front of the small group and spoke in the Lapp language.

The man who replied was short and broad.

"This is my father, Jagg—and my mother, Remu," she said in Norwegian. "This woman's name is Mallory."

Jagg's face was lined and seamed and had the texture of old leather. He had no beard, and his eyes looked Asian. When he spoke, his Norwegian was broken, but he ignored Mallory and said, "You come back. I told you, you'd have to obey me."

Orva laughed. "That would be different. I'll see if I can follow your rules for a few days, and then we'll see what happens." She grabbed Mallory's coat sleeve. "You'll be interested in this woman. She's come to tell us about a new god."

"We have gods enough already."

"Not like this one, you haven't." Orva turned and went over to two young people standing nearby who were dressed exactly like their parents. "How are you, Lorge?"

"I'm glad you're back, Orva."

"This is my brother, Lorge," Orva told Mallory. "He's fifteen. And this is Mayda. She's twelve."

"I'm glad to meet you all. It was good of Orva to bring me. I couldn't have made it without her."

"Here, I brought you a present." Orva rummaged around in the sled until she found one of the jugs she had brought. She handed it to her father, and Jagg's eyes brightened.

He uncapped it and smelled it, then grinned and took a

drink. "That's good," he said, expelling his breath lustily. He turned to Mallory. "What's this about a new god?"

Mallory wished for a more graceful introduction, but she saw she had to do the best she could. "I would like to stay with you awhile, and when you think it's right, I'd like to tell you about my God."

"You have better manners than some," Jagg said, staring at Orva, who was grinning at him. "You can stay for a while."

Relieved, Mallory nodded. "Thank you very much, Jagg. I'll try to be no trouble."

"You got anything to eat?" Orva demanded.

"Yes," Remu said. "It'll be ready in a few minutes."

"Good. I'm starved," Orva said.

The family's reindeer-skin tent was not large. The family ducked into the doorway one at a time, and Orva's mother went to work, taking the lid off a pan that was on the fire in the center of the tent. An opening at the top of the tent permitted some of the smoke to escape. The stench was awful—a mixture of unwashed bodies, cooking meat, smoke, and some other odors Mallory could not identify.

"You sit there," Jagg said as he sat down not far away.

"Thank you." Mallory sat down, and Orva's brother came and sat beside her. She turned and saw he was examining her as if she were a strange creature.

"What's your name again?" he asked.

"My name is Mallory. You speak very good Norwegian."

"I go to school, my sister and I. We learn there. Do you speak Lapp?"

"I'm afraid not." Mallory smiled apologetically. "Maybe you could teach me."

"It's not hard."

Mallory laughed. "Not for someone born here, but it might be very hard for me."

Mayda sat silently on the other side of Mallory as Lorge talked incessantly.

"How old are you?" he asked.

"I'm twenty-two. And you're fifteen, your sister said?"

"Yes. Do you have a mate?"

"No, I don't."

"Why not?" Mayda demanded. "Is something wrong with you?"

"No, I hope not. I just haven't found a husband yet."

The young people were intensely curious, and Jagg watched the exchange as his wife took the pan off the fire and apportioned the meat into several wooden bowls. She handed one to Mallory.

Mallory said a blessing silently and then watched the others to see what they would do. They were picking up their meat with their fingers and biting into it, so she did the same. It was tough and had a wild taste to it. "Very good," she said. "What is it?"

"Why, it's reindeer meat!" Remu said.

"You'll get lots of that around here." Orva said with a grin. "Fried or boiled or raw. That's what you'll eat."

"You live off the reindeer, then."

"Yes," Jagg said. "We make our clothes and tents from their hide. We eat their meat and drink their milk."

"How many reindeer do you have, Jagg?"

Apparently this question was too difficult, for Jagg thought hard, then said, "Many."

"I know," Lorge said. "We've got six hundred and twenty-three. My father's a very rich man."

"I'm glad to hear that. It must be nice to have so many reindeer."

After the meal was over, Orva disappeared and Lorge offered to show Mallory around. She took advantage of the boy's hospitality and spent the afternoon wandering through the camp with him. "How do you know which reindeer are yours?" she asked as they approached a massive herd.

"We cut their ears with a special mark." He showed her his family's mark on the nearest animal.

"I see."

Lorge peppered Mallory with questions too, and she

enjoyed their conversation, finding him a bright and curious young man.

"Do you think you'll ever leave here?" Mallory asked.

"And go where?"

"Maybe go to work in a city."

"No, I like it here," Lorge said. "This is my country, and these are my people."

Late in the afternoon, the family had another meal of reindeer meat. Mallory brought out some cans of vegetables from the sled and opened them up to share with the family, and they were delighted to eat them. *They must get awfully hungry for green things,* she thought. *I know I would.*

After supper, the rest of the family relaxed around the fire while Remu worked on a pair of reindeer mittens she was sewing.

"Too much trouble to put up the tent," Orva told Mallory as Mayda opened her mouth in a huge yawn. "You sleep here."

The fire was now very small, and the cold was closing in. She'd had no intention of sleeping with the family, but Orva took it for granted.

Mallory went to the sled to get her sleeping bag, then lay down where Remu indicated she should sleep. She was so exhausted the sound of voices quickly began to fade as she felt a body pressed against her on one side and then on the other. The smell was awful, but she had to admit that in the bitter cold, two were definitely better than one, and a whole family was better than two. She knew she would have a hard time adjusting to this life, but it was where God had put her, so she ignored the unaccustomed smells and drifted off to sleep.

★ ★ ★

A week had passed since Mallory and Orva had arrived, and Mallory was concerned at how quickly her food supplies were dwindling. She realized that she would soon be reduced to the same diet as the Lapps, and she dreaded it.

She was sitting quietly by the fire with Remu, toasting a bit of reindeer meat, when Orva appeared with a man. He was short and squat, as were all the Lapps, but somewhat older than Jagg, Mallory thought.

"This is Tarjin," Orva said.

"I am glad to know you, Tarjin."

"Tarjin is worried about you."

"Worried! Why would he be worried about me?"

Orva's face was expressionless except for a light of humor glinting in her dark eyes. "I told him you had no man, so he says you can be his number two wife."

"What!"

"Don't worry. His first wife is old. When she dies, you'll be number one. He has more than four hundred reindeer." Orva grinned at her mother. "You'd better take him up on his offer. It's a good one."

Mallory could see that Orva was making fun of her, and she resolved not to let it get to her. Hoping she was not offending the man, she said to him politely, "Tarjin, I thank you for your kind offer, but I do not want a man at this time."

Tarjin shook his head and walked away without another word.

"I didn't mean to hurt his feelings," Mallory said.

"Don't worry. You wouldn't be any good for him anyway. I doubt if you could skin a reindeer if your life depended on it."

Mallory laughed. "Well, I had my chance, and I turned it down. Thank you, Orva."

Orva studied the slight form of the tall woman. "You're not going to do any good here with your Jesus. You might as well go home."

"I feel confident that this is where God wants me to be, so I'd like to stay awhile longer."

★ ★ ★

A month had passed since Mallory had rejected Tarjin as her husband. She had run completely out of supplies and was reduced to living on charity, which meant eating nothing but reindeer milk and meat. She tried to help with the work as much as she could, but her contributions were rather pitiful.

Life there was monotonous and she became bored. She wrote letters, which she could not mail. She read her Bible. She wandered around in the darkness meeting the people and had learned many names. She could now distinguish between them and had found out that the Lapps had a subtle sense of humor. She had also found out that they had the same problems as other people.

One day she asked Jagg if he thought people would come to a service if she planned one, and he shrugged his shoulders. "They're free to come if they want."

The service took place in the open, since there was no tent large enough for them all to meet inside. A group of some twenty people, mostly women and children, stood around her to listen. It felt strange to have a service in the dark, but with the light of a fire reflecting the snow, she could see everyone's face.

"I'd like to tell you about a man named Jesus, who is my Savior," she began. She had asked Lorge to interpret for her since some of the older people spoke no Norwegian, and he did so happily. She spoke for twenty minutes, and she saw no response at all.

Finally she felt a sense of despair. She had difficulty choosing her words, and she could not tell whether she was making any impression. She ended by saying, "Jesus is the Savior of the world, and He loves every one of you." She focused on each individual face. "He loves everyone in the whole world." She said a silent prayer as they looked blankly at her. "Do you have any questions?"

No one spoke for a time; then one woman turned and walked away, and the others quickly followed.

That night after supper, Lorge said, "That was good. I like to hear about Jesus."

This was the only encouraging word Mallory had heard. She put her hand on the young boy's shoulder and mustered a smile. "Thank you, Lorge. That's kind of you."

"They listened, and they will come back if you have another service, and maybe others will come with them. And you can tell us more about Jesus."

"Do you think you might like to have Him as your friend?"

"Tell me some more about Him. Read to me again how He fed five thousand people with just a little bread and a couple of fish."

"All right, Lorge. Come along." She got her Norwegian Bible and read to him.

He followed her finger as she moved it along the printed page. "I wish I had a Bible," he said when she came to the end of the story.

"You can have this one. I have another one."

Lorge looked at her, startled. "Really?"

"Yes."

He took the Bible and thumbed through it. He looked up with a thoughtful expression in his eyes. "Thank you. I call you the Jesus woman. That's what the others call you too."

Mallory smiled warmly. "I can't think of anything I'd rather be called than the Jesus woman."

★　★　★

More than once in the weeks that followed, Orva told Mallory she was doing no good there. And, indeed, it seemed that Orva was right. She held service after service, and although the crowd grew slightly larger, even Jagg coming from time to time, there seemed to be little response. Occasionally someone would ask her a question, which pleased her greatly.

But it was discouraging work, and late one day she walked alone over the frozen ground in what seemed to be a lifeless world. The reindeer milled around, and, from time to time, one would come up and nuzzle her. They were strange creatures, half tame and half wild, and ordinarily she liked their attention, but now she paid them no heed.

Maybe I am wasting my time, she thought. *I haven't seen one person saved.*

Feeling discouraged, she headed back to the camp. When she got halfway there, she found Lorge standing in her path. "Hello, Lorge," she said.

"I want to know this Jesus you talk about. How do I do that?"

Mallory's heart leaped. "He's waiting for you to ask Him into your heart," she said, her eyes brimming with tears. "Will you do that?"

"If you will help me."

There under the thin light of the northernmost part of the world, Mallory Winslow led Lorge to the Savior. He was ready and willing, and when she told him to simply pray and ask Jesus to forgive his sins and come into his heart, she saw the tears in his eyes.

When he was finished, he looked up at her with joy lighting his face. "Am I a Jesus boy now?"

"Yes, Lorge. That's exactly what you are." Mallory reached out and put her arms around him, and in her heart she was saying, *Oh, dear God, if no more Lapps are saved while I am here, you have this one!*

CHAPTER FIVE

THE CHURCH

★ ★ ★

Mallory wrote the date firmly at the top left-hand corner of the paper—*March 20, 1939*. She stopped for a moment, then looked around, noting the busy activities of the Lapps. The beginnings of spring had come, and although there were still patches of snow, the reindeer were nibbling at the emerald blades that were pushing up through the soil that had been as hard as brick all winter. Dogs were barking, children were playing, and now a breeze that had a taste of warmth and the summer to come touched Mallory's face. She was sitting outside her tent writing on a board and felt a sense of contentment.

The winter had been hard for her, but she had endured. The bitterly cold weather had been hard enough, but the constant darkness had been a challenge also. Now that they had plenty of daylight each day, she was feeling better. She hummed under her breath as she wrote firmly on the paper:

> Spring is here at last—at least *almost* here. It's getting warmer, and somehow I am happier than I have been in a long time. The weather was the hardest thing for me,

of course. After living in the heat of Africa, moving into the ice and snow and bitter cold was terribly hard. But no harder than for the new missionaries who come to Africa unused to the heat.

Seventeen people have found Jesus! Isn't that wonderful? It's like a huge revival to me. Orva's whole family has been saved—except for her. But I will pray for her as long as I live. God has given me such a love for her. She has a hardness about her, but one day God will break through that.

In a few moments I'll be going to my last service here, at least for a while. The Lapps have drifted their herds back south, so now we're only a few miles away from Narvik. Orva's going to take me there, and Rolf will take me back to Oslo, where I'll stay with Eva and prepare for the next winter session. I'll come much better equipped next time.

The noise of children laughing caught Mallory's attention, and she stopped writing and looked up to see Lorge roughhousing with three small children. They were rolling on the ground, and all of them were full of giggles. A warm feeling came to Mallory as she watched the teenager. He was such a fine young man! He had developed into an outstanding Christian. It was only because he would be able to keep the young church going that Mallory dared to leave even for a time.

I wish I could tell you about the church here. It's composed mostly of women, but there are four men. One of them, Macoo, is very old, the oldest man in the tribe. But he loves God with all of his heart. I know that I've done the right thing in coming here. If something happens and I can't continue the work, there will be seventeen people in the kingdom of God that I will meet in heaven someday. Lorge will take my place leading the church until I can get back. He is on fire for God!

Even as she wrote these words, she heard her name being called and saw Lorge coming toward her. He was wearing a *kofte*, a blue woolen tunic that the Lapps wore in warmer weather. He also wore the unusual four-pointed cap stuffed with eiderdown that she had grown accustomed to seeing. Like all of the others, he was wearing colored ribbons and rosettes, and today, for the occasion of her last service, he was wearing a red silk scarf.

"It's time for the service," he said with a broad smile.

"I'm ready." Mallory hastily rose, stuffed her writing material into the canvas bag she kept some of her possessions in, and tossed it into the tent. As they advanced toward the group that had gathered, she asked, "Are you nervous about keeping the flock together while I'm gone?"

"Yes, I am."

She put her hand on the young man's shoulder. "You are a man now, Lorge. A man of God. I have never been so proud of anyone in my whole life! God speaks to you, and all you have to do is listen and then share what you hear with the little flock."

"I will do my best, sister, but come back as soon as you can."

"I will return next fall. And I'll have a special surprise for you then."

"What is that?"

"I'm going to bring a shortwave radio, and during the winter months, when we're cut off from towns, we'll be able to pick up stations from all over the world. We should even be able to get sermons, I hope, from everywhere."

"Oh, I can't wait for that!" Lorge beamed. "What else will you bring?"

"Some books for you to study, and perhaps some goodies for you to eat. You and the others."

As the two reached the group, Mallory received a chorus of greetings. "Good morning. Let's all sing, shall we? Mayda, I'll let you choose the first song."

"'Jesus Loves Me,'" Lorge's sister replied shyly.

"Good. You all know that one. Now let's sing to the Lord."

Mallory lifted her voice in song and encouraged everyone to join in. She saw that Orva had joined the group, but she was not singing. She was staring at Mallory defiantly, yet Mallory knew it was a victory for her even to be there. She had often begged Orva to come, but this was the first service she had ever attended.

The strains of the old song that had been a favorite in China for many years broke the silence, and it was a miracle to Mallory to hear the same song that had been sung around the world now being lifted to God here in the Arctic.

Everyone had a favorite song, and as always, Mallory let them choose them. Finally, when the singing was over, she opened her Bible. "This morning I'm going to ask you a question," she started. "And the question is, 'How much are you worth?'"

She saw a look of surprise wash across everyone's faces, including Orva's. "By the time I finish my sermon, I hope you'll be able to answer that." She opened her Bible and said, "This is in John 3:16. It says, 'For God so loved the world, that he gave his only begotten Son, that whosoever believeth in him should not perish, but have everlasting life.'" She looked up and felt the spirit of the Lord rising within her, as she often did. There were times when preaching was hard, but sometimes God simply gave her words, and all she had to do was speak them. It was like that now as she said, "You all know how much some things are worth. You know how much a reindeer is worth. You know how much your tent is worth or your boots. But what are *you* worth? How many reindeer are you worth?" She turned to a young woman and smiled. "Ormu, what would you take for your baby?"

"Nothing! She's mine."

"Yes, that baby is the most precious thing you have. What's the most valued thing you have, Gar?"

A young man whipped out a gleaming steel knife and waved it in the air. The sunlight caught the blade and caused it to flash brightly. "My knife!"

"Right. And what about you, Damar?"

An old woman whose face was seamed with many

creases from long years thought for a moment and then said, "My black fur coat."

"You know how much that is worth, don't you?"

As Mallory continued to talk about the value of their most precious belongings, she noticed that Orva was listening carefully.

"What would you think, then, is the most precious thing that God has?"

A silence fell across the congregation, but finally Lorge spoke up. "Why, He owns everything."

"That's right, Lorge. He owns all the reindeer in the world. All of the animals. All of the trees. The gold and the silver—everything. But He values one thing more than anything else. I read it to you a moment ago. 'God so loved the world, that he gave his only Son.' God's Son was the most precious thing to Him, and He gave that Son so that we might live."

Mallory helped the people to compare their own love for their children to God's love for His Son and tried to help them understand the magnitude of His sacrifice. She had their full attention. "Now I want to read you a story that I've read to you before. It's the story of the death of the Lord Jesus." She began to read the story of the Crucifixion, and when she had finished, she looked up and said, "That's how much you're worth. God says you're worth so much that He gave His Son that you might live.

"When I was thirteen years old, I was all alone out in the bush in Africa. It's so very hot there—hotter than you can imagine—and the sun was blazing down, and I was drenched with sweat. I had been listening to my father preach for weeks about Jesus, and that day as I walked along, I suddenly knew that I had to have Him in my heart. There was nobody else there—no singing, no sermon—but I just knelt down on the path and said something like, 'Jesus, I've been bad, but I want you to come into my heart. God, forgive me for my sins.'"

Tears came to Mallory's eyes as she said huskily, "Something happened when I prayed that prayer. I was just a young girl, but I knew something was different. The difference was that I wasn't alone anymore. I had Jesus living within me. Most of us live alone. We have people outside of us, but oh, how different it is to have Jesus on the inside!"

She told them with great fervor and warmth how wonderful it was not to be alone and to know that God was not separated from her anymore. She paused and looked over the gathering of eager faces waiting for her to continue. She thought of Jesus' words to His disciples, *"Follow me, and I will make you fishers of men."* She sensed it was time to draw in the net.

"Most of you have already asked Jesus into your heart, and I am so thankful to God for that. But there are some here who are lonely and some who are afraid. I'm going to pray in a moment, and when I do, will you pray with me? Just imagine you are in a tent and you hear a voice saying, 'May I come in?' All you would have to do is say, 'Yes, come in,' and that friend would come into the tent. It's that way with our hearts. The Bible says that Jesus stands outside and says to us, 'May I come in?' And He's waiting for you to say yes. You don't have to be wise or clever or super intelligent. Even a child can do it, as I did. So as I pray, I wish you would call upon Jesus and ask Him into the tent of your heart. Let's pray now."

Mallory prayed fervently and much longer than usual, but when she finally looked up, she saw that Lorge had gone to his sister Orva, who was weeping. At once Mallory went to them. She saw that Orva was standing stiffly, a tortured expression on her face.

"Orva, will you open your heart to God and ask Jesus to come in?"

"I'm . . . I'm too bad," she choked.

"We're all bad, Orva. But Jesus can make us so pure it's as if we had never done anything wrong."

As Mallory pleaded with Orva, she saw a desperate longing in the woman's dark eyes. But then suddenly Orva pulled away from Lorge and gasped, "I can't do it! I'm too bad!" She whirled and hurried away, her head down.

Tears were running down Lorge's cheeks as his sister left. Mallory put her arms around him and whispered, "Don't worry, Lorge. God is after her. Jesus will find her, and she will find Him. In the meantime, you will have to be faithful to keep the flock together."

Lorge nodded. "Pray for me, sister," he whispered.

"I will, and you pray for me. I'll be back as soon as I can."

★   ★   ★

Orva said almost nothing on their return trek to Narvik. The sled was much lighter now, so the reindeer was able to pull it easily over the patchy snow that was left on the tundra. When they arrived at the Bjellands' house, it didn't take long to unload Mallory's things.

As they finished unloading, Mallory said cheerfully, "Thank you so much for bringing me, Orva."

"You will come back, as you have said?"

"Oh yes, I'll be back next fall. Before you go, I have a gift for you."

"For me? What gift?"

Mallory straightened her fingers and removed the opal ring that her parents had given her when she was fifteen. "I want you to have this. When you look at it, think of me." She had seen Orva looking longingly at the ring many times, and when she handed it to the woman, Orva made no move to take it.

"I can't take your ring."

"Of course you can. Here. Let's see if it will go on your finger." She took Orva's hand and found that the ring fit on her little finger. Orva's hands were thicker than her own, but the little finger was just right. "There. That ring will remind you of me until I get back."

Orva dropped her head and could not speak. She

looked at the ring and said huskily, "I thank you. I must go now."

Mallory reached out and hugged the woman, but it was like hugging a post. Mallory kissed her on the cheek and said, "Good-bye, my sister. I'll see you soon."

Orva turned away without a word, but not before Mallory saw tears in her eyes. She watched the young Lapp woman walk away, leading the reindeer as she had done throughout their travels together.

With a prayer to God to watch over her and bring Orva safely to Him, Mallory noticed Rolf coming out of the house, followed by his parents.

★　★　★

"I'm worried about the Germans," Rolf said as he and Mallory were taking a walk along the water's edge at Narvik, watching the fishing boats coming and going. "You've been away from civilization and probably don't have any idea of what's been going on, do you?"

"No, I don't. Tell me, Rolf."

"Hitler's a crazy man, and nobody seems to be able to stop him. He's taken Czechoslovakia now, and who knows what's next."

Rolf filled her in on the details of all that had happened over the winter, both politically and back at the university. They stood and watched two men unload supplies from their boat.

"Before we go back, I've got to talk to you, Mallory."

"About what?"

"About us." Reaching out, Rolf took her hand and held it so firmly she could not pull it away. "I know you think I'm just a foolish fellow, but I haven't been able to think about anything but you."

"You're just infatuated, Rolf," she said quickly. She had a great affection for Rolf, but that was all it was. Now she saw that he was deadly serious about her and wondered almost frantically how she could tell him exactly how she felt without hurting his feelings.

"I want you to marry me," he said quietly. "I mean it, Mallory. I love you more than I ever thought I'd love a woman."

Mallory was aware that this was a critical moment, that if she wasn't careful she could destroy this good friend. She prayed quickly for guidance and then said softly, "Rolf, I've never met anyone I've felt more comfortable with, but I'm not thinking of marriage. God's called me to do a work. I'll be going back to the Lapps next fall, and you wouldn't be able to go there. You have your work at the university."

Rolf suddenly pulled her forward and kissed her on the lips. He did it so quickly she could not resist. "I know all about that, but we can make it work."

Mallory tried to gently extricate herself from his embrace. "But, Rolf, we've been talking about how uncertain the world is. With Hitler on the march, who knows what will happen? Why, he could even invade this country."

"He'd never do that." Rolf shook his head. "Norway's neutral like Sweden."

"I hope you're right. But the biggest priority in my life is serving Jesus. Is that the biggest thing in your life?"

He blinked with surprise. "Well . . . no. *You're* the biggest thing in my life."

"But God should be. Not any individual."

"I know I'm not a saint like you—"

"I'm not all that saintly," she interrupted. "I have problems just like you do, and I do care for you. But it's like a sister feels for her brother."

"I'm not your brother!" he exclaimed loudly.

They continued to argue the point, and finally Rolf said, "I'll accept what you are telling me for now, but I'm not giving up."

They walked back to the Bjellands' in silence, and Mallory went right to her room and flopped on the bed.

Their conversation had exhausted her emotionally. She thought back to the time she had said good-bye to Paul Joubert at the mission compound in Africa. That had been difficult, but not like this.

I've got to find some way to make him see that we're not meant for each other, she thought. *He needs to find someone his own age and with similar goals in life.*

★ ★ ★

Rolf and Mallory made the long drive back to Oslo together, where Eva welcomed her joyously as her roommate for the summer. Rolf was busy with some summer classes at the university but came to see Mallory nearly every day. Once when Mallory and Eva were alone, Mallory had told Eva about her problem with Rolf, and Eva had said, "He's never been serious about any girl before. Do you think you could ever care for him in that way?"

"I don't think so."

"Well, people can change. No one ever really knows about things like that." Changing the subject, Eva asked, "What will you do now?"

"I'll get ready to go back to be with the Lapps in the fall. I've got big plans. I'm taking some of my shortwave radio equipment back and lots of books for Lorge. I can see God is going to make him a missionary to his own people. He'll be their first pastor. Then I'll come back next April in time for your wedding."

"That seems like such a long time away," Eva said, giving Mallory a warm embrace. "I can hardly wait for that day."

★ ★ ★

Mallory discovered that she had lost weight and had worn herself out during her months with the Lapps. As the more temperate summer weeks passed, she spent a lot of time with her radio. She had brought all of her radio equipment with her from Africa, and she enjoyed tinkering with it and seeing what she could find on the airwaves. She talked with her parents and brothers in Kenya, and she began to collect news from all over the world. The more she listened, the more she learned it was, indeed, a dark hour for most of the world. Hitler's men were swarming over Europe, and nobody knew where he would stop.

She also spent much time with Sigrid, who was fearful of an invasion. "I've got to get away, Mallory. They will execute me for my writings if they invade."

"If it comes to that, I'll help you," Mallory promised. But in her heart she was convinced that Hitler would not invade a neutral country.

Each night she knelt down beside her bed and prayed for the Lapps. She knew that God had sent her there, and she ended every prayer by saying, "God, be with Lorge and with the little church there. They are your people, Lord. Don't let the wolves come in and destroy them!"

CHAPTER SIX

INVASION

★ ★ ★

The radio in front of Mallory crackled with a fierce intensity before a voice with a British accent cut through clearly. "The skies over Finland cleared in the past week, and Russian bombers punished civilian populations in Helsinki and elsewhere. Hundreds of Russians were killed in fierce fighting, and Soviet tanks were trapped in the snow and captured. Large numbers of prisoners were taken, and it is reported that Swedish, Norwegian, and Danish volunteers have been fighting with the Finns. The Russians, it is reported, are angry and frustrated, but there is no sign of a letup on the war of Russia against tiny Finland."

Mallory slowly turned the dial in front of her until she found a dance band playing in Cincinnati, Ohio. She stopped to listen to "You Are My Sunshine," which, the announcer informed the audience, was sung by Jimmie Davis. Mallory turned the dial again but could get nothing but war news, and all of it was bad. Since the German invasion of Poland in September 1939, which had plunged Europe into war, Russia had thrown its might against

Finland, and now the whole world was anxious over the newest atrocities of both Russia and Germany.

Snapping the radio off, Mallory sat back in her chair and absentmindedly took hold of her right hand to turn her ring, a nervous habit she had. She realized the finger was bare and suddenly remembered that the ring was now on Orva's finger. The thought of the hard young woman grieved her. As she had promised, Mallory had returned for another winter with the Lapps, where Lorge was doing a fine job as pastor of the fledgling congregation. With Orva's help, Mallory had taken all of the books she could gather, plus gifts for all of the members of the new congregation. She had tried to convince Orva that Jesus could help her, but Orva had brusquely rejected her, saying, "I don't need Jesus. I can't live like your Bible says."

Mallory had returned to Oslo in time to help Eva with her April ninth wedding. Now the day had come, and as Mallory clipped on her earrings, she could hear the church bells ringing in the distance. She was putting on her lipstick when Eva rushed in, crying frantically, "I can't find my shoes! Where are they? What could have happened to them?"

"I polished them," Mallory said quietly. She took Eva by the arm. "You've got to calm down. You'll never make it through your own wedding if you're this nervous now."

Eva Jorgensen laughed nervously. "You're right. I didn't think it would be like this. I'm scared to death!"

"Now, put all that out of your mind," Mallory said soothingly. "You're getting a great husband, and you're going to have a wonderful honeymoon and raise a sweet family."

"That's right," Eva said, giggling. "I'm acting like a teenager."

"It'll be all right. You'll see."

"Just you wait. I hope I'm there when you get married. You'll fall to pieces just like I am."

"I probably will. I think that's normal. Come on. I'll

show you where your shoes are, and then we need to leave for the church."

"Oh, Mallory, I'm so happy!"

"And I'm happy for you, but we've got to hurry."

The two women drove to the church, and it took all of the skill Mallory could muster to keep Eva calm. They entered the church and found the rest of the bridal party waiting for them. She accompanied Eva to a room set apart for the bride and helped her into her wedding dress.

Mallory stood back while Eva looked at her stunning reflection in the mirror.

"You're absolutely beautiful!" Mallory said with a sigh. "It's the most gorgeous wedding dress I've ever seen." The formal white gown had a fitted bodice that was decorated with tiny white pearls and buttoned down the back with two dozen satin-covered buttons. It had a high neckline, and the close-fitting long sleeves ended in a V on top of her hands in a delicately embroidered lace. The full skirt was also decorated with white pearls and flowed into a long train, which was also edged with the embroidered lace. A wreath of fresh flowers held her small veil in place, and it hung down to the middle of her back.

The bridesmaids came in, and there was much giggling and teasing until finally a knock on the door interrupted them, and a voice said, "All right. We're ready to start."

Eva looked like a deer caught in the headlights. The bridesmaids filed out, each offering a reassuring comment or a quick kiss on the cheek. Mallory kissed Eva and said, "It's going to be just beautiful. You'll see."

Mallory went through the door, and when her turn came, she walked slowly down the aisle of the old church, which was packed. She took her place in the front, and then when Eva appeared, Mallory breathed a sigh of relief. *She's going to be all right. She just had the usual bride's jitters.*

She watched as the bride came down the aisle, a smile on her face, and then when Lars Klovstad moved to stand beside her, they made a perfect picture. As the couple exchanged vows, Mallory had to blink the tears away, she was so happy for her friend. Looking out over the congregation, she saw that she was not alone in the happiness she felt for the young couple. Lars and Eva were favorites with everyone, and now as they began their married life, Mallory thought, *May they live happily ever after*.

★ ★ ★

The noise of the happy crowd resounded off the wood-paneled walls of the fellowship hall of the church, and the refreshments were disappearing at an alarming rate. The bride and groom stood surrounded by well-wishers, and Mallory turned from a conversation with the bride's mother to find Rolf at her side.

"Does this give you any ideas, Mallory?"

"What sort of ideas?"

"Well, look how happy they are." He nodded toward the laughing couple, who were flushed with pleasure. "You and I would be much happier than that."

Mallory had given up trying to discourage Rolf. She had told him in every way she could think of she was not interested in marriage, but he was persistent. She started to make a joke of it when suddenly a tall man burst into the room, yelling, "Invasion—it's come!"

The warning brought a stunned silence to the room, and then he cried out, pointing upward, "Parachutists are coming down out of the sky right now!"

Mallory joined the rush to get outside, noting that even Eva in her wedding dress was running toward the door. As soon as she got outside, she looked up, and her heart froze. The roar of planes high overhead sounded like angry bees, and against the blue of the sky, white parachutes were floating down by the thousands.

"German planes," Rolf said tensely. "They're coming down at the airport."

"But Norway's neutral."

Rolf shook his head, anger tightening his lips. "Yes, and

that's why they're able to do this."

She glanced over to see Lars speaking rapidly to Eva, and then the couple turned and ran toward her and Rolf.

"Come on, Rolf," Lars shouted, "we've got to stop them!"

As the two men raced away, Eva tried frantically to follow them, but Mallory caught her. "You can't go with them."

"Yes I can! Let me go, Mallory!"

But she held on tightly, and finally Eva grew still.

"Come help me get this wedding dress off, Mallory. I've got to be with Lars."

"Where is he going?"

"We've been expecting this invasion and have plans all laid out. We've organized a resistance, and Lars and Rolf have gone to set things in motion. But you must stay out of it, Mallory. This isn't your fight."

With her heart heavy, Mallory followed Eva to the church's bridal dressing room to help her. She knew that the world had suddenly changed—her world and the world of the Norwegian people. Adolf Hitler had stretched his evil arm out once again to bring terror to an innocent and helpless nation.

★   ★   ★

Six weeks later, Eva came into Mallory's room without knocking. Eva and Lars had been generous enough to offer Mallory a room in their house for as long as she cared to stay.

Strain marked Eva's face as she said abruptly, "You've got to get out of Norway, Mallory."

Mallory stared at her friend. The last few weeks since the wedding had gone by like a whirlwind. The paratroopers had quickly secured the airport, and transport Junkers had flown in with German storm troopers, who had taken Oslo. The Germans had struck all along the coast at

Bergen, Trondheim, and at Narvik with their blitzkrieg tactics. The invasion was ruthless, and although the Norwegian army had tried to defend their land, the coordination of air, land, and sea forces that Hitler had mobilized had struck the country like a sledgehammer.

"What are *you* going to do, Eva?" Mallory asked.

"We're going to keep working with the resistance, but you need to get out of Norway—if you can."

"But what will happen to the little church among the Lapps? I can't leave now."

"The Germans won't bother the Lapps. Nobody ever bothers them. They wander where they please. They don't have anything that the Germans want. Someday when this is over, you can return to them."

The two women talked briefly, and then Eva said, "Sigrid is going to have to leave Norway too, and you'd better leave with her."

As soon as Eva left the room, Mallory stood for one moment thinking, then went to her radio and switched it on, her jaw set. After it was warmed up, she began trying to reach Africa. She gave her call letters, and almost at once she heard her father's voice greeting her.

Without preamble, she summarized the latest news in Europe. Her father urged her to return home. He was worried for her safety.

"Dad, I can't come home now. I can't leave my friends."

With those words, Mallory knew she had made her decision. She would stay in Norway. She would help Eva and those engaged in the underground war as best she could. And she would return to her church among the Lapps. The world was at war now, and so was Mallory Anne Winslow.

PART TWO

September 1935–March 1939

★ ★ ★

CHAPTER SEVEN

A MEETING IN PARIS

★ ★ ★

As Rachel Mindel stepped outside of the Sorbonne library, she paused and glanced upward. A thin moon lay askew low in the south, and the Milky Way made a dull silver river against the sable blackness of the sky. During that instant a strange feeling touched her—a stray current of something out of her past, a half-warm regret and a pale sentimentality. She hesitated for a moment, conscious that she was longing for her homeland, but Czechoslovakia was a long way from Paris. With a quick shrug of her shoulders, she moved down the front steps.

The cool September air that filled Paris was laced with the city's odors, and as Rachel moved down the murky streets, lit only partially by feeble lamps, she could not shake off her yearning for her homeland. Paris was too big and busy, and after several months here, she was weary of the bustle of the thousands of people that swarmed its streets. She longed to walk in the woods next to her home, to watch the sunlight run fresh and fine against the towering trees, and to smell woodsmoke as it tinged the fall air.

Some of the streetlights were out, she noticed, and the ebony night spread itself over the street. She quickened her pace, for this dark street of Paris was no place for a young woman. *They say the human body is more muscle than anything,* she thought, *but that's wrong. We're made of memories, and most of those are snarled and tangled like a line on a fishing reel that has to be cut away because no one can straighten it out.* It was typical of Rachel Mindel to have such thoughts, for a poetic strain ran through her. There was also a strain of humor, and she smiled at her own thoughts as she hurried toward the next streetlight.

She never saw the man who stepped out of the alley and grabbed her arm with a powerful hand. She was whirled around before she knew what was happening. She smelled the rank odors of the man's body, and terror ran through her like a jolt of electricity. She opened her mouth to scream, but before she could make a sound, another hand closed on her slender throat. "Don't scream," he said in rough French. "Gimme your money."

Rachel struggled, dropping her purse and striking at the man's face, but he only laughed, pinioning both of her hands in his. He threw his other arm around her and laughed coarsely. "I'll have your money, and I'll have you too!" he growled in a hoarse whisper. Still holding her, he stooped over and grabbed her purse before dragging her back toward the open maw of the alleyway.

"Help me! Please, somebody help me!" Rachel managed to cry out, but her voice sounded pitifully thin.

"That's right. Go on and holler. It'll do you no good."

Her assailant's grip was frightening. He was as strong as a gorilla, and Rachel felt herself dragged along helplessly. She kicked at him and screamed, but her voice was cut off when the man grabbed her throat again and cut off her air so that her voice trickled off into a faint protesting murmur.

Suddenly from behind her, a man's strong voice broke through the darkness. "Turn the woman loose!"

Rachel was whirled around, her assailant still gripping

her tightly. She could see only the outline of the other man, enough to know that he was tall. "Please help me!" she begged.

"Let her go, you brute!"

Rachel was released so suddenly that she staggered and nearly fell. She saw a gleaming flash, and narrowing her eyes, she saw that her assailant had drawn a knife. He held it out in front of him and laughed deep in his throat. "Come on, hero. I'll gut you like a fish!"

Rachel could neither speak nor think clearly, but she saw her attacker move forward with surprising speed for such a large man. The tall man kicked at the other man's shins, knocking his feet out from under him. There was a dull snapping sound as his left arm hit the curb, and the man cried out in agony.

He managed to pull himself up into a crouch, the knife still in his hand. As he shoved himself upward, the tall rescuer also moved quickly. His leg shot out again, this time much higher, and the impact of his shoe striking the big man's jaw made a distinct crunching sound. Rachel blinked with astonishment as her attacker was driven backward. He fell over and lay still, the knife falling beside him on the pavement.

"Are you all right?" The tall rescuer asked Rachel, his face shrouded by the murky darkness.

"Oh yes. Thank you so much."

"Do you want to call the police?"

"No, I just want to get away!"

"Well, I suppose that's enough. It looks like he's got a broken arm and a broken jaw. When he comes to, he's not going to get far. Come on. I'll walk you home."

Rachel felt weak and helpless as she realized what had just happened. She stumbled forward and felt the man take her arm. The strength of his grip gave her a reassuring feeling, and when they reached the streetlight, she looked at him. She started to speak and then saw that the sleeve of his coat was sliced. "You've been hurt!"

"Yes, he did scratch me a bit."

"We'll have to get you to a hospital."

"It's not that bad."

In the pale gleam of the streetlight, Rachel was able to see his face now. He was over six feet, so she had to bend her head back to see him. He was young, in his early twenties, she guessed, and had strong features—high cheekbones, a broad mouth, and blue eyes that seemed to be studying her.

"We must get you to a doctor," Rachel said.

"No need of that—"

"Yes, you must have help," she insisted. Then she had an idea. "My landlady is a nurse. She can see to you if you won't go to a hospital. Come, I live very close to here."

The tall man hesitated.

She was a resolute young woman, and when he hesitated, she shook her head. "Don't be stubborn, now. That needs to be seen to."

"Well, if you insist. By the way, my name is Derek Grüber."

"I'm Rachel Mindel. Come along, Mr. Grüber."

★ ★ ★

Margot Billaud was in bed when Rachel arrived back at her apartment building with the man who rescued her. After banging on her door repeatedly, Rachel managed to rouse her landlady, who threw on an old blue robe and sleepily made her way to the door. Margot was a woman of little imagination, but she was an excellent nurse. She had married late in life, and her husband owned this apartment building, which brought in a good income, so Margot worked at her profession only when she chose to.

When she heard what Rachel wanted, she gathered her medical supplies and brought them up to Rachel's apartment. She directed the man into the kitchen and asked him to remove his shirt, then to sit on the table under the light. She inspected the four-inch cut on his right shoulder, wasting no time admiring the strength of his upper body. "That's not a very bad wound." She glanced at Rachel. "You should have better sense than to walk the streets alone at night."

She had Rachel fetch a pan of warm water and a clean cloth and began gently cleaning the wound. "What's your name?" Madame Billaud asked.

"Derek Grüber."

"You're not French."

"No." Grüber smiled. "My French isn't very good."

"Where are you from?"

"Germany."

As Derek Grüber spoke, his eyes were on Rachel, who was now standing slightly behind Madame Billaud. When he said the word *Germany*, he saw her visibly flinch, with a flicker in her eyes that told him he had hurt her with just a word. He was accustomed to this by now. Being a German in Europe was not easy these days. Adolf Hitler was a man who put fear into the hearts of most Europeans. He reminded them too much of the kaiser and of those terrible days of the Great War. Derek made no sign that he had noticed her reaction.

"What are you doing in Paris?" Madame Billaud demanded.

"I'm a student at the Sorbonne."

The woman was a quick, efficient nurse, and she had cleaned his wound and was now applying antiseptic. "Does that burn?"

"Yes."

"It hurts, but you need something to keep it from infection."

Madame Billaud taped on a bandage, and then she looked straight into his eyes. "I don't like your *führer*," she said abruptly, a keen edge to her tone.

"Many do not." Grüber began to put his shirt back on. As he buttoned it, he said, "I'll be glad to pay you for your treatment."

Madame Billaud snorted. Turning to Rachel, she said,

"Well, Mademoiselle Mindel, I hope you'll have better sense than to roam the streets of Paris after dark." She gathered up her medical supplies, gave the German one strong look of disapproval, then left the room, shutting the door with more force than was necessary.

"She's a little rough," Rachel said, "but she has a good heart."

"I'm sure she does."

"I attend the university too."

"Oh really. What are you studying?"

"I'm studying French, as well as music history. I would like to teach when I return to Czechoslovakia. What are you studying?"

"Ah, that explains the accent. I'm supposed to be studying engineering, but I'm taking courses in French literature as well." He saw her look of surprise. "My father will be unhappy. He thinks literature is for women and small children, not for grown men." He picked up his coat and put it on. "I best be leaving you now, Mademoiselle Mindel."

She accompanied him to the door and said, "I don't know how to thank you. You saved my life, and I'm grateful for that."

Derek studied her face. Not everyone would find her beautiful, but her face was pleasing to him. Her brown eyes were warm but mysterious, holding back some of what lay behind them. She had wide and clean-edged lips, and her complexion was fair and smooth. He admired the rich auburn gleam of her hair and the gentle slope of her neck and shoulders.

At his obvious admiration, she smiled demurely and a small dimple appeared in her right cheek. "I'll never forget you," she said simply. "I wish I could do something to make it up."

"Do you know anything about French literature?"

"Why, yes. As a matter of fact, I've studied it quite a bit."

"I'm struggling with one of my courses in that area. I don't suppose you'd care to help me along?"

Rachel did not answer, and Derek saw an inner struggle in her. "What is it?"

"I'm . . . I'm Jewish."

"That doesn't matter to me."

"It does to some Germans. It does to Hitler."

His face flushed in embarrassment. "I wish he didn't feel like that, and I certainly don't."

Rachel was not impulsive. She had learned to be careful, especially in Paris, but there was something clean and strong about this man, and she made a quick decision. "I'll meet you at the campus library tomorrow, if you'd like. We can talk about literature."

"Fine. What time?"

"Would one or two o'clock be all right?"

"One o'clock would be just right. I'll see you then." He turned to go, but she reached out and touched his arm.

"I meant what I said. I'll never forget what you did for me. You saved me from a terrible fate."

"I'm glad I was there. If I were you, I'd pay heed to Madame Billaud. It's not good to roam the streets of Paris after dark." He opened the door. "I'll see you tomorrow."

Rachel went to the stairwell and watched him exit the building, then saw Madame Billaud standing at her apartment door on the first floor looking up at her.

"Have nothing to do with him," she warned, pointing her finger up at Rachel. "He's a German."

"But he came to my rescue. That counts for something, doesn't it?"

Madame Billaud shook her head, a grimness on her face. "He may seem nice enough, but they're all the same. Stay away from him."

Rachel did not argue. "Good night," she said, then turned and went back into her apartment. When she closed the door, she walked over to the window and looked out at the street below, but he was already gone. "Thank God he came!" she said aloud before turning to prepare for bed.

★　★　★

"Sometimes I think a sidewalk café in Paris is the most interesting place in the whole world."

Rachel shook her head decidedly. "I don't agree. I think almost any woods in the world with trees and grass and a running stream is better than any café on any street in Paris." She took a bite of her cake.

"You're just a romantic," he said.

"I suppose I am, but then you are too." Rachel watched as surprise washed across Derek's face. The two had spent an hour and a half together at the library, talking incessantly. At Derek's suggestion, they had left and made their way to a small café with five tables outside, all of which were now filled. She watched his face as he talked, impressed with his strength. His wide mouth was expressive when he smiled, and she noticed a small faint scar shaped like a fish hook at the left corner of his mouth.

"What makes you think I'm a romantic?" he asked.

Rachel sipped her tea and smiled, and once again he noticed the dimple that gave her a little-girl quality. "You like romantic literature," she said, "and you like to rescue damsels in distress. I think you dramatize everything."

"No, that's not true!" he protested. "I'm very much of this world."

"No, I think you came to my rescue because you're a romantic. You see yourself as an Ivanhoe, and you came to the rescue of the Jewish maiden Rebecca." She laughed at his expression. "You shouldn't have told me you liked romantic novels like *Ivanhoe*. It tells me so much about you."

"Well, I suppose you're right. My father tried to get it all out of me when I was growing up, but he didn't succeed too well, I'm afraid."

Her companion seemed so strong, Rachel thought, yet she sensed that he was putting a damper on his youthful vitality. She noted that the corners of his lips had a tough, sharp set to them, yet behind the hardness was something else. Behind his light blue eyes lay an obvious compassion and interest in people. He seemed capable of looking deeply into others, and such a gift would bind people to him. There was also a deliberateness about him, and she knew he was a man who could spring into action. He had demonstrated that when he had come to her rescue.

Derek Grüber had a good sense of humor as well, sharp and sometimes self-ridiculing, which pleased her.

"You're looking at me pretty closely," he suddenly said. "What dark thoughts are running through your head now?"

Rachel returned his smile. "Whether to wear my blue dress or my green one tomorrow."

"I'd wear the green dress if I were you. It's my favorite color."

The two sat there enjoying each other's company, and Rachel knew this man had the ability to please women. Not that he appeared to be a womanizer, but he had a frank openness that invited female attention.

"What were you like when you were a little girl?" he asked.

"I was smaller."

Derek laughed. "I know that. But what were you *like*?"

Rachel sipped her tea and shrugged her shoulders. "They tell me the first thing I reached for was the moon, but I've never been able to reach it."

"Neither have I."

She smiled as she remembered something that had happened when she was a young.

"What are you smiling about?"

"I just thought of something I hadn't thought of in years. When I was a little girl of five or six, I asked my mom for a piece of—" she searched for the word in French and finally thought of it—"chalk and took a coin from my bank. I went out to the sidewalk and put the coin down, and then I drew a line all the way from the coin to the corner and down the other side. And then I wrote on the sidewalk, 'Money this way.'"

"Did you stay to watch someone go find the money?"

"No, I never did. It's fun to think about it, though." She shrugged. "What a foolish thing to do."

"Not at all. I did things like that. I used to put coins on the railroad track. The trains would pass over them and flatten them out, and I'd drill holes in them and string them together. I think I still have one of those strings somewhere."

She ordered more tea, and he got more coffee, and he asked about her family.

"My parents are getting on in years," she told him.

"They live in Czechoslovakia?"

"Yes. My father was a watchmaker, but he's retired now. When I finish my coursework, I'll go back—mostly to take care of them." She looked at him over her teacup. "What about your family?"

"My mother's dead. My father's in the army."

She heard the spareness of his reply. "What are you going to do?"

"My father wants me to go into the army."

His answer troubled her, but she did not let it show. "Will you?"

"I don't know. It's not what I want to do." He looked down at his hands as he answered.

"What would you like to do?"

"I'd rather be a teacher."

His answer surprised her, but when she gave it a moment's thought, it made sense.

"I'd like to be a writer too," he continued.

"I'd love to see what you've written."

"I don't feel comfortable showing my work to people."

Rachel lifted her eyebrows with surprise. "What good will it do if nobody reads what you've written?"

"It does *me* good."

She laughed. "I suppose that's enough, then." She looked at her watch and exclaimed, "I need to go!"

"There's a play on tonight that you might like to see. It's no fun to go alone. Would you go with me?" When she hesitated, he smiled. "I'm harmless, Rachel."

"Well then . . . I'd love to go."

"Good! I'll pick you up at six. We'll go out to eat, and maybe I'll let you read one of my poems."

"I'd like that very much."

They got up, and he walked her back to her apartment. As she went inside the building, Madame Billaud said, "You're with that German, I see."

"He's really very nice, Madame Billaud."

The woman did not answer. She had lost her father in the Great War and had never forgiven the Germans for it. "You'd better stay away from him. I don't trust that man Hitler. You mark my words. He won't be satisfied with any less than ruling all of Europe—and maybe the world!"

★ ★ ★

Rachel lay back on the green grass, enjoying the warmth of the earth. Overhead a number of sparrows were flitting from limb to limb, and she watched them with delight. She turned her head to Derek, who was sitting beside her reading from a book he had brought along. The remnants of a picnic lunch lay to her right, and there was a peace and quiet here from the incessant city noise. As they had eaten, they had debated the merits of various poets and quoted their favorite poems, but now Rachel was relaxing as Derek read.

May had come, and the hard winter was only a memory. She studied Derek, thinking, *It hasn't even been a year since we met, and I feel like I've known him all my life.*

Derek noticed that she was looking at him, and humor danced in his eyes. He put his book down and leaned closer to her. "You think I'm a handsome fellow, don't you?"

She did think him handsome but would not say it. "I think you're egotistical."

"Well, I think *you're* handsome." He reached out and touched the dimple in her cheek. "I wish I had dimples, one in each cheek, just like this one."

"I hated that dimple when I was a girl."

She sat up and stretched her legs out in front of her. "What are you reading?"

"A poem by a British poet, Thomas Hardy. It's called 'The Man He Killed.'"

"Oh yes. I've read a poem or two by Hardy. He writes long novels as well, doesn't he? Very gloomy."

He read the poem slowly. He was a good reader, and she loved the sound of his voice.

"Had he and I but met
By some old ancient inn,
We should have sat us down to wet
Right many a nipperkin!

"But ranged as infantry,
And staring face to face,
I shot at him as he at me,
And killed him in his place.

"I shot him dead because—
Because he was my foe,
Just so: my foe of course he was;
That's clear enough; although

"He thought he'd 'list, perhaps,
Off-hand like—just as I—
Was out of work—had sold his traps—
No other reason why.

"Yes; quaint and curious war is!
You shoot a fellow down
You'd treat, if met where any bar is,
Or help to half-a-crown."

"You like that poem? I wouldn't think you would."

"Why not?"

"Well, it's an antiwar poem."

"Yes, it is. That's why I like it." His eyes grew cloudy, and he spoke softly. "I feel like the speaker in the poem. Young men join the army for a lark. And when battle comes, they kill the soldiers in front of them—men who are like them in almost every way."

Rachel shook her head. "You're a mystery to me, Derek. The Germans are the most militaristic people on the face of the earth. Your father's a general, and yet you don't like war. I thought all Germans were warriors."

"I suppose there's a lot of that in my people, but that trait seems to have been left out of me."

"Read me something you've written."

"All right. I will." He did not take out a piece of paper but turned to her. To her surprise he reached out and took her hand. "This one's called 'To Rachel.'"

Rachel's face grew warm as she listened.

"I might have found beauty in the skies,
If I had never seen you.
But after I beheld your dark and lovely eyes
The heavens can offer nothing new!

"If I had never heard your voice,
The song of birds might have been sweet.
Now the mourning doves sound hoarse
And I live to hear my name your lips repeat.

"Before I saw your lovely face,
A new-sprung rose seemed tender and fair—
But once your skin beyond compare
I touched—I found the flower most rare!"

Rachel found herself unable to speak for a moment; then she whispered, "That's beautiful, Derek. Thank you so much."

Derek sat very still and watched her. She had not moved, and she was looking at him with her face lifted, her lips motionless. He saw the quick rise and fall of her bosom and the sunlight on her hair, and he drew her toward him in one quick gesture. He waited for her protest and was astonished when it didn't come. He had found this woman full of grace and beauty, and now the yearning of a lone man moved toward her like the needle on a compass.

She caught his gaze and waited, saying nothing but arresting him with a sweetness that fueled his intense feelings for her.

Derek touched his lips to hers and felt her surrender. He drew her closer, his heart aching with the feelings he had for her at this moment. She had the ability to touch him as no other woman he had ever met.

But then Rachel suddenly pushed him away, her expression disturbed. "We shouldn't have done that," she whispered.

"Why do you say that? You must know I'm falling in love with you."

"But you can't."

"Why not?"

Rachel looked at him directly. "What would your father say?"

Her words stopped Derek as if he had run into a door. He had no answer. She rose to her feet and he followed. "We can never be more than very good friends, Derek. That's all we can ever be."

CHAPTER EIGHT

THE PARTING

★　★　★

January 1937 brought sharp Arctic blasts to Paris and sleet that coated the streets with an icy sheen. As Derek walked cautiously along the street, the sidewalk under his feet was one solid sheet of slippery ice. He had already seen two people slip and fall as if their legs had been jerked out from under them. Keeping his head down, he thought about the months that had passed since the day he had told Rachel he loved her. That had been a fine day! Even now, surrounded by ice and snow, he could almost smell the fresh green grass and hear birds chattering in the trees overhead and see the gleam of golden red that tinted Rachel's hair in the bright sunlight.

He was savoring the memory when a dog appeared in front of him—an indeterminate breed, thin and with woeful eyes. It was a strange bluish-brown, and its ribs showed so plainly that Derek could count them. "What's the matter, boy? Are you hungry?" The dog eyed him apprehensively, but as Derek did not move, it began to wag its tail. "It's hard on fellows like you in the winter, isn't it?" Derek noticed that there was a meat market across the street.

"Wait here, friend. I'll be right back."

He disappeared inside the shop and came out almost at once. The dog was still there, and Derek opened the packet and took out a morsel of the meat. "How about this, fella?" he asked and extended the meat. The dog ducked its head, as if afraid of being struck, but when Derek silently stood there, it finally took the meat and swallowed it whole, then looked up eagerly, tail wagging again. "Here, you have a good breakfast, my friend." He put the meat on the sidewalk, then patted the dog, which gobbled the meat frantically. When it was through, it moved forward and leaned against Derek's legs.

"I'd like to take you home with me, but I'm leaving. I don't think there's any place for a French dog in the German army. Sorry." He walked away, and the dog followed him for a time. Derek turned around and said, *"Raus!"* rather sharply. The dog looked at him in a hurt fashion, then slunk away. "Well, boy, you've had one good meal today."

Derek continued his walk until he came to the small café where he had brought Rachel the day after they had met. It was so cold that no one was sitting outside drinking the strong coffee they served. As he opened the door, the tiny bell made a merry tinkling sound, and the owner, Monsieur Valdoux, came forward smiling and greeted him.

"Bonjour, Monsieur Grüber. Your lady, she is here before you today."

"Thank you, Raoul." He followed the pudgy owner over to the table in front of the window.

"I was starting to wonder if you were coming," Rachel said.

"Sorry." He sat down. "Just a Danish and good coffee, Raoul, if you please."

"Certainement!"

When Raoul left, Derek leaned forward and extended one of his hands. Rachel reached out and took it, holding it in both of hers. She was wearing a simple light green skirt with a darker green blouse that outlined her figure admirably. A chain of pearls and a pair of pearl earrings were her only adornment. She looked tired, and as she held his hand, Derek said, "I hate to go, Rachel!"

"I'll be grieved when you're gone." She released his hand and shook her head. "I like things to be simple, Derek. There should be beautiful simplicity in every life, but it doesn't happen, does it?"

Derek drank in her features, putting the memory of this moment into a safe deep within, knowing that he would go back to it many times and unlock the safe and remember her as she sat there. "I just know one phrase in Latin. I had to memorize many for school, but this is the only one I still remember."

"What is it?"

"Omnia mutrantur, nos et mutamur in illis."

"What does it mean?"

"All things are changing, and we are changing with them. That's true, isn't it? Nothing stays the same."

Tears brimmed in Rachel's eyes at the thought, and the two sat mostly in silence for a while. Conversation seemed to come hard.

Then a man entered the café who caught their attention, and both of them watched as he took a seat.

"He looks like a bank clerk who made off with his cash drawer," Derek commented.

"I would have said more like a cheerful embalmer. It's odd, isn't it, how we see people? Who is that man? What are his problems? Is he happy in his marriage? We see people constantly, and we know nothing about them."

"That's true, isn't it? Sometimes you go out to parties, and people are laughing and making a lot of noise, and they have smiles pasted on their faces, but you know they're not really happy. Nothing is sadder than watching people trying to enjoy themselves as much as they can but not really having a good time at all." Derek fidgeted with his napkin. "You're the only one I could ever talk to and say whatever came into my mind. I've always had to guard my speech because I have such wild thoughts."

"That's the poet in you. Your mind is full of imaginative ideas. I'll miss those crazy thoughts and the times we've had together."

Raoul returned with Derek's coffee and pastry and refilled Rachel's coffee cup.

Derek took a sip of his coffee and then held Rachel's hand. It was firm and strong, and he noticed the small half moons at the base of her fingernails. They were strong hands, not large but firm, and he loved them, as he loved all of her.

"Marry me, Rachel."

A cloud touched Rachel's eyes, and she shook her head. "We've been all over that. It's impossible, Derek."

"But I love you—and you love me, don't you?"

"Yes," she said quietly. "Very much. I know I will never love another man as much as I love you."

He was touched by her honesty and sincerity. There was a transparency about her that he loved, and still there was part of her he could never quite get at. He knew this was the Jewish side of her nature. Her heritage went back into history through long and bloody and terrible times. The times they themselves now lived in were ominous and uncertain, and he knew she dreaded what might come in the future to her and her family and her people.

"You'll be going home soon," Derek said finally. "Let me come and meet your parents."

"It would be useless, Derek."

"No it wouldn't. If I lose you, I could never find you again, Rachel." He took a bite of his Danish and chewed thoughtfully. "There's an old Persian myth about the creation of the world. It says that God made only one person—it was half male and half female. But when it sinned, God tore it apart as one would tear a sheet of paper apart. You know how that is. When you tear it apart, you can put it back together, for the pieces fit exactly. So . . . the creatures that were separated fit only each other."

"What does it mean, Derek?"

"According to the myth, these two creatures spent their

lives trying to find the one piece that matches. There are some that almost match, but only one will be the perfect match—the one it was separated from."

"That's a beautiful myth. I've never heard it before."

"I feel like that about you, Rachel. You and I match. I'll never find another woman I'll love as I love you."

"Perhaps not exactly, but you'll find someone."

"Don't say that. Please, let me come and visit you."

Rachel hesitated. She had steeled herself to this moment of parting, and now that it had come, she knew she could not do it. "All right." She smiled. "But my parents will be surprised when I bring home a goy."

"What's a goy?"

"Anyone who's not Jewish."

Derek ate the last of his Danish and looked at his watch. "I've got to go. My train will be leaving."

The two rose. Derek paid the bill and bade the owner good-bye.

"I'll see you soon, *non*?" Monsieur Valdoux asked.

"No. I'm leaving Paris."

"Oh, that is so sad! We will miss you, but you'll come back. Paris will draw you. You can't ever leave Paris. It goes with you."

Derek shook the man's hand and left. As they got into a taxi, he said, *"Gare Saint-Lazare, s'il vous plaît."* The two sat silently in the backseat. He put his arm around Rachel and held her close while she took his left hand in hers and held it as tightly as she could.

When they reached the station, the two got out, and Derek asked the cab driver to wait. The sky was overcast and gray, and a fine sleet was falling.

"It's a miserable day to leave," he said. "I wish the sun were shining."

Rachel simply looked up at him, and he took her in his arms. He held her gaze, then kissed her. When he lifted his lips from hers, he said huskily, "Things can change. Wait for me."

"God be with you, my sweet," she whispered, her

throat thick with hopelessness.

Derek released her and helped her back into the cab. He told the driver the address of her apartment, and after one last kiss through the window, he took up his suitcase and disappeared into the crowd entering the busy train station. When he reached the door, he turned to wave good-bye once again, but the cab was gone. An unhappiness and misery such as he had never known came over him. He set down his suitcase and looked out over the busy traffic, hoping to catch one last glance of the taxi that had taken his love away. With a sudden wrench, he walked through the entrance, knowing this was the lowest point of his life.

★　★　★

General Wilhelm Grüber could have posed for a picture of the ideal German officer. Tall and broad-shouldered, he exuded the strength and vitality of a man much younger than fifty. His uniform molded itself around his strong figure as if it had been painted on. His hair was iron gray with a curl, cut and trimmed with precision, and his trim mustache matched exactly. All of his features exuded strength, from his wide mouth to his deep-set, penetrating slate blue eyes, to the straight nose and high cheekbones. He sipped brandy from a snifter and looked at his son, who sat across from him in a maroon leather chair. There was a demanding quizzical look in Grüber's eyes, and when he spoke, his voice was filled with authority, exactly as if he were speaking to a subordinate officer instead of his son. "What's wrong with you, Derek?"

Derek sat stiffly in his chair, his legs crossed and his hands on the chair arms. He had become so accustomed to feeling defensive around his father that it had become second nature to him. "Wrong? Nothing I know of, Father."

"You're not yourself. You've been moping around ever since you came back from Paris." Grüber took a sip of his brandy. "That was a terrible waste of time, Derek. I told you it would be."

"I don't see it that way. I learned a lot."

"What did you learn?"

He had no ready answer. He might have said, *I learned to look at the sky and the trees in a way that I never did here in Germany. I learned that sometimes a man can be brought to tears over a French poem. A poem written a hundred years ago, and the hand that wrote it is now dead, yet it's still able to move me.* He could have given many answers like this, but he didn't dare. "I learned something about engineering."

"Well, that will be useful. Where did you stand in your class?"

"Very high, Father. In the engineering class, I was second."

"You should have been first."

Derek was accustomed to this. "I suppose so," he said. He knew there was no pleasing his father unless he was best in everything. It had always been that way—in sports, in his academic pursuits. Wilhelm Grüber wanted his son to be at the top of his class—exactly as he himself had been all of his life.

Since the death of his wife, Wilhelm had been a lonely man, and he had poured his energies into two things—his profession and his son. Embedded deep in his German soul was a desire to see his own life perpetuated in his son, and since he had no daughters and only one son, he had thrown himself into molding Derek into the model Aryan soldier.

Now, as he studied Derek, he was satisfied physically. Derek was strong, with quick reaction times. He was an expert with the saber and foil, and he was peerless with any sort of firearm. He was a handsome man too, but that meant little to Wilhelm. He took good looks for granted, his own and Derek's, for they came from a line of handsome men. Still, there was obviously something wrong with his son.

"You've come back from Paris like a whipped dog. I suppose you fell in love."

Derek could not conceal his shock. "I should have told you about it," he said. "I did meet a young woman while I was there. I became very fond of her. In fact, I'm going to visit her as soon as possible."

A tiny alarm went off in Wilhelm Grüber. He had carefully watched his son's choices in women. Some had come from good families and would have made suitable matches; one was even from the family of a prominent military leader. That match would have pleased Wilhelm, but Derek had shown no lasting enthusiasm for any of the women his father favored.

"What is her name? Where did you meet her?" Wilhelm demanded.

"She's a student at the Sorbonne." Then Derek hesitated, knowing that his next statement would bring an unpleasant response. "Her name is Rachel Mindel."

"Mindel? That sounds like a Jewish name!"

Derek steeled himself to meet his father's eyes. "She is Jewish, Father," he said quietly.

"A Jewess?" Angry words rose to Wilhelm's lips, but he saw something in his son that caused him to bite them off. Derek had been a good son, but Wilhelm was aware of the stubborn streak in him. He had always been glad of this, for he himself was a stubborn, proud man, and he knew that pride and an iron will were important traits for a German officer. He had been handling men all of his life, and he saw that this was no time to say what was on his mind. He took another sip of his brandy to calm himself down. "Tell me about this woman."

Derek told his father about how the two had met and about the course of study Rachel was taking. He even confessed that he had asked her to marry him. Derek was surprised at his father's restraint, but he saw the displeasure in his eyes and knew that the matter was not finished.

"Son, we will speak of this later." Wilhelm leaned forward. "And now about your future."

"I would like very much to be a scholar, Father—a professor and a writer."

"We talked about that before. I do not think it's best for you, Derek. You have a great heritage. Your grandfather and your great-grandfather were soldiers as I am. It is in your blood." He tilted his head, then shrugged and forced himself to smile. "I see no harm in your dabbling in such things. Write as you will, but your fate is with Germany. And Germany must have her place in the sun."

Derek had prepared arguments, but he saw that they would be useless. He sat silently as his father began to outline some of the great plans he had for his son, and a growing sense of despair enveloped him as he listened.

★　★　★

Derek's bedroom in his father's house was cold, but Derek paid little attention to it. February was almost over, and Derek had written to Rachel every week. She had not always responded, but he never gave up hope. Now he put the concluding words on his letter firmly:

> I've been expecting my father to say something about our relationship. I've told him that I care for you and that I've asked you to marry me. It surprised me that he said little, for he is a demanding man accustomed to having his own way. I keep waiting for him to bring it up, but he doesn't. I can't imagine going against him, for I never have. I think sometimes I gave too much thought in my youth to being a dutiful son and trying to please him and not enough to doing the things that I want to do. His only wish for me is to join the army and become an officer, but in this I have so far disappointed him greatly.
>
> I have good news. I am hopeful of getting an assistantship at the university here in Berlin in the Department of Literature. I can't tell you how I've hoped for this and prayed for it. It would be a dream come true. I have not yet been called up for the army, and I can only hope

that it will not come soon, if ever.

My other dream, my darling Rachel, is to be your husband. I will not cease to say this, for it is on my heart constantly. Write me back at once, for I treasure your letters. Let me—

An abrupt knock on the door interrupted his thoughts. "Come in," he called. When his father entered with a stern look on his face, he said, "Why, Father, what is it?"

"This just came for you. I thought you might want to see it now."

Derek took the envelope, which had been opened. "You opened it?"

"Yes, I did. I hope you don't mind."

Derek opened the envelope and took out a sheet of paper. One glance at it revealed his worst fears. It was his official order from the army to report for duty.

"You did this, Father?"

"I had nothing to do with it, but it had to come. All young men your age are needed to serve the Fatherland. You know that, Derek."

He did know this very well, but the thought of going into the army was like a shock of cold water.

"I have been ordered to go to Spain."

"Yes, I saw that. Actually, you will be on my staff."

Derek could hardly believe his ears. Surely it would be awkward to serve under his own father. He quickly reviewed mentally what he knew of the present political situation. He had followed the Civil War in Spain only in a cursory fashion. He knew that General Franco was trying to overthrow the present government. Franco was a fascist and had enlisted the aid of Mussolini, and Hitler decided that Germany must add her might in that struggle. On December 1, 1936, a battalion of five thousand German troops had landed at Cadiz.

His father interrupted his thoughts. "We'll leave the day after tomorrow. I suggest you get ready."

"Yes, sir, I'll be ready." He saw the look of satisfaction

on his father's face. *He thinks I'll forget Rachel, but he's wrong about that.*

"Good! We are going mainly as observers, however, that will probably change. In all likelihood you will see some action there." He put his hand on the doorknob. "A change will be good for you, Derek. You and I will spend some time together. We haven't done that for a long time."

We haven't ever done that, Derek thought, but he said, "Yes, sir, that will be pleasant." He watched as his father left the room, then picked up his pen again.

I have just received some terrible news. . . .

CHAPTER NINE

COMBAT

★ ★ ★

"Sit up, Dopey!"

The small fuzzy dog with mournful eyes promptly sat down and stared up at Derek Grüber. Its red tongue lulled out like a necktie, and its long skinny tail beat a tattoo on the floor.

Derek laughed and said, "Shake hands." He put his hand out, but Dopey simply licked it. "I said *shake hands*, you stupid dog."

The dog immediately lay down and rolled over and then came to its feet barking in a staccato fashion, pleased at what it had done.

"That's the dumbest dog I've ever seen, Derek."

Lieutenant Frederick Möhr was lying on his bunk looking at a magazine. He was a short, dapper individual whose uniforms were always spotless and pressed with razor-sharp creases. He disliked army life, for he had been born into a wealthy family and had enjoyed every pleasure that money could buy until he had been conscripted into the army. He turned his attention from a picture of a scantily dressed blonde to watch Derek attempt to teach the dog new tricks. "It always does some trick but never what you tell him to."

"It's not a German dog. That's for sure."

"That's right. If it were a dachshund, it would instantly obey every command." Möhr tossed the magazine on the floor and sat up, leaning on his elbows, his hand cupping his chin. He noticed Derek smiling rather wistfully and asked, "What are you thinking about, Derek? You don't smile all that often."

"Just about a good time I had once."

"With a girl, I bet."

He nodded.

"Tell me about her. Did she look like this?" Möhr grabbed the magazine and held up the picture of the alluring blonde.

"No, nothing like that."

"Too bad. This is what a woman should look like."

Derek laughed. Despite their differences, he liked Frederick. The two of them had come to Spain together and had both served on his father's staff for the past several months. Möhr was an amiable fellow, somewhat too in love with himself to please Derek, but the two got along well.

"You never saw a woman you didn't like."

"They're all beautiful," Frederick said. He stood up and walked to the window, then stretched and yawned. "I wonder if we'll go to the front today."

"I hope not."

Frederick turned and leaned back against the wall, crossing his arms. He found Derek Grüber a fascinating subject. He could not understand him at all. When they had been put together as roommates, he had blessed his stars. *What luck to be a roommate of the son of the commanding officer, General Wilhelm Grüber.* It had come as a shock to discover that Derek had no military ambition whatsoever. Derek simply fulfilled his duties. He never presumed upon his relationship to the commanding officer, and Möhr had not been able to profit by it. He liked Derek a great deal but had been unable to persuade him to go out and socialize with the willing young Spanish ladies. Many of them were loyalists and would spit when the soldiers of General Franco or his German and Italian allies passed, but some were more reasonable.

"Why don't we go into town and see if we can find some female companionship?"

"I don't think so. I'll just stay here and play with Dopey."

"You're gonna play with that stupid dog instead of meeting one of these beautiful *señoritas*? What's wrong with you? Don't you like women?"

"Not the kind we'd be likely to run into. Speak, Dopey."

Dopey promptly sat down and offered its paw. Derek laughed and shook it. "That's a good dog. You'll get it all straightened out one of these days."

Möhr ambled over and looked down at the dog. "That dog is a real loser, Derek. I don't see what you like about him."

"I rather like losers."

"You like *what*?"

"I like losers."

"You are absolutely out of your mind! Nobody likes losers."

Derek leaned back in his chair, and Dopey hopped up in his lap. He began to stroke the dog's head. "Sometimes people that seem to be losers are really winners."

Möhr shook his head with exasperation. "That's exactly the sort of wild thing you'd say! I never knew a poet before, and I don't want to know any others. Why don't you just say things that make sense?"

"You don't think some apparent losers are really winners?"

"No, I don't. You can tell a winner by looking at him."

"I can prove that you're wrong."

"Prove it, then."

"I don't know if you've ever read the Bible."

"Certainly I have! Do you think I'm an atheist?"

"You remember John the Baptist?"

"Of course I do."

"Do you remember Herod, the king who had him put to death?"

"Yes. I know that story."

"Well, everybody around at that time would have looked at John the Baptist, hauled out of prison to get his head cut off, and said, 'Man, that guy's a real loser!' And they would have thought that Herod was the winner, because after all, he got to watch the woman dance, and he got by with murdering John."

"And you're telling me that John the Baptist was the winner and Herod was the loser?"

"When they went to meet God in judgment, I wouldn't have wanted to stand in Herod's shoes. Would you, Frederick?"

Möhr stared at his roommate. He admired the tall, handsome young man who had everything—except common sense. "That's crazy."

"It's not crazy at all. The only difference is that Herod was the winner for a little while, but John the Baptist is the winner for all eternity. Poor old Herod! I would think he'd have a hard time explaining to God why he killed one of His servants."

Möhr shook his head and pulled a bottle of whiskey off of a shelf fastened to the wall. He took a healthy swallow and then gasped and stamped his foot. "Boy, that's strong stuff they make around here! You want some?"

"No, thanks."

Möhr laughed. He came over holding the bottle and sat down in front of Derek. He braced himself and took another large swallow. When he got his breath back, he said, "It's an education living with you, Derek. You could have anything you want. You're the son of our general! You could probably be a major by now if you'd put your mind to it."

"I don't care about being a major."

"You see? You're like Dopey there. You're not very bright."

Derek stopped stroking Dopey's head and put him on the floor. "Tell me, Frederick, do you enjoy what we're doing here?"

"Enjoy it? I haven't thought about it. I just try to get by."

"We've seen some pretty rough things. You remember Guernica?"

"Sure, I remember. What about it?"

"What'd you think about it?"

The question made Frederick nervous. "It was pretty bad, I'll admit." He took another drink. "I've thought a lot of times about those poor kids blown to bits by German bombs."

Guernica was a Spanish town of about five thousand people. It had become a military target, and the German air force dropped tons of bombs into the crowded city on a busy market day. The planes had kept coming until sixteen hundred people were killed, many of them women and children, and hundreds more wounded.

Derek had gone in after the attack with his company led by his father, and Möhr had been at his side. He had not been able to sleep for weeks thinking of those poor women and children and old people who had died for no reason.

"I wasn't proud of what happened at Guernica," Derek said. "I don't think anybody should be."

"Don't tell your father that!"

Derek stared at the smaller man. "I've already told him. As a matter of fact, I don't think we have any business being here in Spain at all."

The struggle in Spain had begun in 1936 when a fascist-led force commanded by General Franco had begun fierce fighting against the republic. The battle had seesawed back and forth. The common people of Spain had fought the fascists with every weapon they could find, though many had never used a rifle in their lives. Franco and those who came to help, including Germany and Italy, had not reckoned on the determination of the people to fight for their democratic rights. They had been shocked when anti-Nazis from all over the world, including twenty-seven hundred Americans, had come to Spain to form the International Brigade. They had fought valiantly, more than once stopping the fascists' advances, but the military might of the German and Italian forces had proved impossible to stop. The end was in sight, and now it was only a matter of time until Spain would become another totalitarian nation.

"I believe you're really for the peasants, aren't you, Derek?"

Lieutenant Möhr never knew what answer his friend would have given him, for at that moment the door opened suddenly, and Captain Fritz Heilman stepped inside, announcing, "We're taking the field. The enemy has broken through, and we've got to stop them. Come with me."

★　★　★

When Derek reached the line of battle, the machine-gun fire rattled, and the sound of artillery echoed with a dreadful finality. Möhr had taken the right wing, and Derek had stayed with Captain Heilman. Now he saw the German infantry falling back in a ragged fashion.

"We've got to stop them!" Heilman screamed, waving a saber. Derek wondered if he thought he could stop bullets and artillery with it. "Grüber, you take the right wing. Go to every man. If you see a man retreating, shoot him!"

"Yes, my Captain," Derek said. He had no intention of shooting any German soldiers, but he saw that the men were indeed in a bad way. The enemy was in force, and for the next half hour Derek moved back and forth, urging his men to conceal themselves to keep from getting mowed down by the machine guns. He heard the line of bullets around his head, and once he felt one of them pluck at the shoulder of his uniform. He looked down to see that it had ripped a neat gash, but it did not seem real to him.

Like most Germans, Derek had wondered how he would react in battle, if he would be one of those who would run. He hated military life, but he found that he could function, and in the heat of battle he remained cool.

"Lieutenant, the captain—he's wounded!"

A corporal was crouched behind a broken piece of concrete blown up by one of the mortar shells. His eyes were wild, and he was gesturing out in the open space where the action was hot and furious.

Derek turned quickly and saw Captain Heilman dragging himself along like a wounded insect. He was completely without cover, and bullets were kicking up dust all around him.

Derek did not hesitate. Leaving cover, he ran straight toward the captain, unable to hear the corporal shouting, "Lieutenant, you can't help him! He's gone!"

Derek ran, crouching low, firing his pistol, and saw two of the enemy drop. When he reached the captain, he saw that blood covered the front of his uniform, but he picked him up and started back. *I'll never make it!* He ran as fast as he could with the captain in his arms. He was strong and could carry the captain easily, who was rather small. He heard the bullets ripping, and once he felt as if someone had run a red-hot poker along his side, but he ignored it. When he reached the wreckage of the demolished barn, he dodged behind it and set the man down. He turned to find Colonel Dieter watching him with shock on his face. "That was a brave thing, Lieutenant Grüber."

"He's hurt pretty badly, Colonel. I'd better get him to the medics."

"Are you hit?"

Derek touched his left side and found it bloody. "It's not serious."

"Have them take care of you." He clapped Derek on the shoulder. "That was well done. I will see that your father hears of this!"

★   ★   ★

Derek felt ridiculous standing in the line of men receiving military honors. His father had gone down the line awarding medals, and now he stood before Derek. Derek heard him speak the words that went with the ceremony and felt his father's hands as he fastened the iron cross to his jacket. When his father put out his hand, he took it, and General Wilhelm Grüber suddenly stepped outside of the iron discipline he nearly always maintained. "I cannot tell you, my son, how proud I am of you."

"Thank you, Father."

It had been one of the greatest moments of General Grüber's life when he had discovered that Derek had performed not just as an average soldier but had gone beyond the call of duty to rescue his commanding officer. He tried not to show it, but those who served under him were well aware of his pleasure in his son's action.

Derek waited until the company was dismissed. He saw his father standing beside the general's staff, still watching him. He nodded, then left. When he got to his room, he pulled off his jacket and hung it up carefully, and going to the desk, he opened the drawer and picked up the letter he had received from Rachel—the only one he had received since he had been in Spain.

My dearest Derek,
   I pray for you each day. You make little of the danger there, but I know that in a war, soldiers get wounded and killed. I am praying that God will deliver you.

Derek reread the letter, which was three pages long, although he had committed it to memory. When he got to the last page, he slowed down and read it carefully.

   It is so good to be back in Czechoslovakia. As you know, I loved Paris but I missed my parents terribly. Now I am afraid of the political situation here. I must get my parents out of Czechoslovakia. Some say I can get them to Sweden. They would be safe there, I think.

I must close but not without telling you how I live upon the memories of the days and nights we had together. I love you with all of my heart.

Derek folded the letter, put it in the envelope, and returned it to the drawer. He took out the long letter to Rachel that he had been working on earlier when he'd had to leave for the ceremony. Now he picked up where he left off.

Do not worry, my dear, Germany will not attack Czechoslovakia.

Even as he wrote this, Derek felt uneasy. No one knew what Adolf Hitler would do. He had attacked other nations, and the talk at General Headquarters was that Czechoslovakia was on the führer's agenda. He continued writing:

Even if that should happen, I will come and get you across the border to a safe place. There are so many things I want to do that I can't. I read the other day that a big elm tree can make six million leaves in a single season. I can't even make *one*. That sounds crazy, doesn't it? But I do want to make something, my darling Rachel. I want to make a life with you. That's the height of my ambition. Right now, like the apostle Paul, I see through a glass darkly.

I was reading in the Bible last night about a man called Ezra, and when he got bad news, it said, "When I heard this, I tore my tunic and cloak, pulled hair from my head and beard and sat down appalled." I've been reading the Bible a great deal lately, especially the Old Testament, and I feel like Jacob at Peniel wrestling with the angel. Things seem dark now, but time will change those things. You and I will have many mornings and days and nights. Do not despair, my love. I read a poem once—can't remember who wrote it—but a line sticks with me: "God lies on his back under the world. I wanted to see him, but I kept seeing only the soles of his shoes, but even that is glory." Isn't that a marvelous line? I wish I could write like that!

He closed the letter, pledging his love as always, and then sealed it.

Later that day he was going to try to mail it, but he encountered his father, who stopped him.

After Derek saluted him, his father said, "Big things are brewing. I've just gotten orders to go home with all my staff. We'll be leaving at once."

"That's good news, sir."

Derek felt the letter in his pocket, and touching it, he thought, *I may get to see Rachel before this letter can get there. That would be all I could ask. The best thing I could think of!*

CHAPTER TEN

THE NET TIGHTENS

★ ★ ★

A faint blue haze of cigar smoke filled the room as four men sat around an ornate walnut table. General Wilhelm Grüber ignored the glass of brandy in front of him, for he was more interested in the man who sat across from him than in drinking.

It was his third meeting with Adolf Hitler, and as always, Grüber was mesmerized by the man who had led Germany out of a crushing depression to become a world power. To Hitler's left sat Heinrich Himmler, the head of the SS, and to his right Hermann Göring, minister of the economy.

As Hitler exchanged small talk with the others, Grüber allowed his gaze to rest upon Himmler, an ex–police chief from Munich. Heinrich Himmler was anything but an inspiring figure. He was an awkward man, regarded as a meddling but generally well-meaning fussbudget before his rise to power. He wore a heavy coat that overwhelmed his spare frame, emphasizing his narrow shoulders and thin chest. Himmler's pinched face with its modest mustache and thick round glasses displayed none of the fervor of a revolutionary. As usual, he wore an air of confusion and anxiety.

He may look like nothing, but he's a carnivore. Grüber knew the violence that lay beneath the mild manner of Himmler and was repelled by the cruelty of the man.

He shifted his gaze to the bulky figure of Hermann Göring. He was not the slim figure he had been while shooting down enough planes in the Great War to make him an ace. His body had thickened, his face had rounded, and rumors were circulating that he was a cocaine addict. He served as commander of the German infantry and was given to ornate ceremonies and fancy uniforms. There was something of a clown in him, but like Himmler, he was a deadly man and totally dedicated to his master, Adolf Hitler.

"Well, my führer," Göring started, "we have come a long way." He picked up his glass of brandy and drank it, his broad face beaming. "I think often of the days after the Great War."

"They humiliated Germany!" Hitler stated harshly, his eyes burning. Indeed, postwar Germany had been transformed into an economic wreck by the terms imposed at Versailles. The treaty made there had pared German territories down to the bone. Inflation had made the reichsmark absolutely worthless, so much so that women used the paper money to start their fires. The German people had felt ashamed and believed their punishment was undeserved. Hitler had fed upon their misery and desire to hold their heads up. He had screamed, "You are humiliated! You are degraded! Germany is a sick nation!" And he always blamed everything on people he called Jewish Communists.

Grüber knew that Hitler was basically a shy man and an awkward speaker. Grüber was aware that Hitler rehearsed long hours to bring the impact and impression of spontaneity to his speeches. Grüber thought it strange that now at the crest of his power, Hitler was still nervous. He twitched in his chair and wrung his hands together in an agonizing gesture as he spoke. But when he addressed masses of people, all this changed. He learned artfully honed gesticulations, imparting such force to his words that they became a raging torrent.

Hitler was not imposing physically. His small square mustache was his most noted feature. His straight brown hair was often unruly and sometimes fell over his fore-head. By no stretch of the imagination could he be called handsome. His eyes, however, could be as powerful and penetrating as a bolt of lightning. And even now, in the privacy of this secluded room, power seemed to emanate from him.

"All that is past," Himmler said nervously. "Need we speak of it?"

"You are right, Heinrich. We have risen out of the ashes, and now we must think of Germany." He looked down at his hands, and when he raised his eyes, they seemed to burn with a hidden fire. "We must talk of *Lebensraum*." The word, which meant simply *living room*, had become the key to Hitler's entire strategy. He had insisted that Germany be fenced in on all sides, so there was no room for growth of any kind. He had screamed at the masses at Nuremberg and other huge gatherings, "Germany must have room to grow to its full potential!"

Grüber listened as Hitler spoke erratically of his plans, as he often did. Obviously he intended to enlarge Germany's territory. In order to do this, he would have to occupy the nations that surrounded Germany. After Hitler mentioned Czechoslovakia, Poland, and Austria as being rightful German territory, Grüber spoke for the first time.

"And what about England, my führer?"

"They are of the Aryan race. If they will be reasonable, we will not invade them."

They all knew that Hitler admired the English. None of them really understood why, but Himmler and Göring simply accepted Hitler's dictum that Germans were the master race and all other races were inferior. Yet somehow he was able, in his thinking, to include England under that general umbrella. Göring continued to drink his brandy, and his face grew flushed. Finally he said, "We need to talk about Norway. I think we must have that territory, my führer."

Hitler shook his head. "I would prefer for them to remain neutral."

Göring rarely argued with his master, but he had obviously spent some time thinking about this. "We need Swedish iron for our war machines. We can only get it by passing through Norway. They can shut us down anytime they choose."

"Germany must have her day in the sun!" Hitler responded harshly. "The master race cannot be stopped by a tiny country like Norway."

Göring leaned forward. "Then you would not absolutely rule out occupying Norway."

"No. But it will be a last resort. Now, let the plans for the invasion of Czechoslovakia be set in motion."

Himmler shook his head slightly and protested. "There will be trouble over that with England and France."

"They are weak! We Germans are strong. We will take what must be ours so that Germany will one day be the premier nation on the planet!"

The meeting ended abruptly, but Hitler took time to come around and shake the hand of Wilhelm Grüber. He was charming when he chose to show it. He could be kind to dogs and peasants, could win their sympathies and their admiration. Now his grip was firm as he said, "We shall count on you, General Grüber, to help fulfill the destiny of Germany."

"I know my duty as a soldier, my führer."

"Good. You will receive your orders shortly."

Grüber left the room, not stopping to speak to Göring or Himmler. A strange thought crossed his mind. He knew that Himmler had developed techniques for racial selection, dreaming up pseudoscientific tests of the ideal Aryan look. The final product was a tall, strong, and handsome people with fair hair, not unlike most Germans. But none

of the three men who led Germany fit Himmler's own cri-
teria for what an ideal German should be. Göring was fat
and round-faced, a drug addict. Hitler was not even a
German but an Austrian—and certainly did not look like
the fair-haired, blue-eyed, tall, strong master race that
Himmler envisioned. Himmler himself looked more like a
bank clerk than anything else.

The thought discouraged Grüber, and as he left, he
thought about Himmler's pronouncement that it was the
patriotic duty of every man in the SS to sire at least four
children. He had flatly ordered all SS men to impregnate
their wives, and when possible, to serve as "conception
assistants" to childless women age thirty or older. It was
not the sort of world Grüber could admire, but he was a
faithful German and had given his life to the military. He
knew better than to question anything that went on with
these three men.

★　★　★

As Derek stepped outside headquarters, the brisk
March wind bit at his face. It had been a cold, hard winter,
and he imagined how welcome spring would be. But he
soon became gloomy once again as he thought back to his
interview with his superior officer, Major Hinton. Derek
had gone in to see if his request for leave had been
approved, but Major Hinton had smiled and said, "These
things take time, Lieutenant. You must be patient."

Now as Derek moved along the sidewalk, he struggled
not to feel angry with his father. When Hinton had first
refused his request, he had thought, *It's my father. He's
behind this.* He and his father had not spoken about Rachel
Mindel since their first conversation about her, but the subject lay like a wall between them, almost physical in its
enormity.

As Derek continued along the sidewalk, he passed a
group of six SS men, one of them a major. This in itself was

not unusual, but there were two civilians framed within the group, and both of them had placards with writing hung about their necks.

The woman was tall with blond hair and blue eyes. The man was short with protruding ears. He wore a gray suit and a neat blue bow tie, and misery was written across his face. Derek read the sign on the woman, which said, "At this place I am the greatest swine: I take Jews and make them mine." The man's sign said, "As a Jewish boy, I always take German girls up to my room!"

Instantly Derek understood that these two had violated the Nazi doctrine forbidding sexual intercourse between Jews and Gentiles. He watched as the SS men shoved them so that they almost stumbled and jeered at them, cursing and laughing. Other soldiers they passed took up the cat-calls, but Derek was disgusted. He tried to put the scene out of his mind but could not help wondering what would happen to the two. He suspected that they would be sent to concentration camps. This thought troubled him so deeply that his face assumed an iron cast. He had never been to one of the camps, but he had heard rumors about the inhumanities that went on there. Derek was a sensitive man, but clearly the German leadership was not. They seemed to care nothing about snuffing out the human spirit in the most degrading way possible.

When he reached his quarters, he picked up a pen and began writing a letter, dating it March 12, 1938.

> I hate this life, my dear Rachel. It is not what I want to do. I take every spare moment I can to read and write. I have started writing a novel, which I will probably never finish. Poetry comes so much easier to me. I'm saving all the poems I write so that when we meet again you can read them and I can watch your face.

He wrote page after page before he had said everything he wanted to say.

> I will not stay in the army longer than absolutely nec- essary. I have thought about going to Basel in Switzer-

land to continue my studies. You and your parents would like it there, and it is a neutral country. We could be happy and safe there.

The phone rang, causing him to start, and when he picked it up, he heard his friend Frederick's almost hysterical voice shouting, "Have you heard the news?"

"Don't deafen me, Frederick. What news?"

"It's Austria. She's given up without a fight. Now Germany has a foothold. Come and meet me. We're all going out to celebrate."

"I'm sorry, I can't do that, Frederick. You'll have to celebrate without me." He waited until Frederick expressed his displeasure, then hung up. Derek couldn't believe it. It sounded as if Hitler had taken Austria as easily as a man takes a piece of cake at a party. Austria had simply folded, unable to face war with the powerful German war machine.

"What will be next?" Derek whispered. He closed the letter, signed it, and ended by saying:

I love you, my dear Rachel, and I always will.

★ ★ ★

Derek did not get his leave, although he continued to reapply for it for months. In November, he was disgusted by what happened after a young Polish Jew named Hershel Grynszpan, an unemployed seventeen-year-old, shot and killed the third secretary to the Germany embassy in Paris. The boy's parents, Germans with Polish ancestry, had been among the Jewish refugees transported to and left at the German border a month earlier.

Adolf Hitler flew into a rage and vowed the Jews would pay. On his instructions, all German Jews were to be punished, and the German non-Jews responded with terrible enthusiasm. Within sixty hours of Hitler's orders, a wave of lethal vandalism swept through Jewish synagogues, homes, and stores. A virtual orgy of violence, it came to be called *Kristallnacht*, the night of broken glass, for the shards of glass that littered German streets. The Nazis killed thirty-five Jews, arrested many thousands, and levied fines against all German Jews that totaled a billion marks. They also wrecked seventy-five hundred shops and destroyed more than a hundred synagogues throughout Germany and Austria. Derek knew this marked a turning point in his thinking. There was nothing noble about this type of military action, and a bitterness grew in his heart.

Finally toward the end of November, he was promoted to captain, and his leave came through.

It came only because I told Father I was going to the mountains to hunt, Derek thought as he packed his things. But he was not going to the mountains. He was going to Czechoslovakia to see the woman he loved.

CHAPTER ELEVEN

IS ANYPLACE SAFE?

★ ★ ★

An eerie feeling came over Derek Grüber as he sat in the parlor of Rachel's home, facing Jacob and Sarah Mindel. It had something to do with the furnishings of the room, all of which appeared old and fragile. Age had brought a dull patina to their finish, and though they were in excellent condition, something about their aged fragility made Derek uncomfortable—for Rachel's parents also had a patina of age. Rachel had told him that they had been unable to have children early in life, but she came as a surprise when they had long since given up thinking about children. *"Your mother is like Sarah of old,"* Jacob used to tell his daughter. *"You were such a blessing to us in our later years."*

Both were very small people, especially Sarah. Both had silver hair, and neither of them appeared to weigh much more than an average twelve-year-old. Their bones were fine, and the age lines etched in their faces were pronounced. Jacob had a large nose, while Sarah's looked English—narrow and straight. They were gentle and gracious, and they spoke German quite well.

"Rachel tells me you are a scholar, Mr. Grüber, that you intend to become a professor."

Derek suddenly realized that Rachel had not told her parents he was a German officer. He had chosen not to wear his uniform on his visit to Czechoslovakia and was glad of it. The anti-German feeling was very strong in this country. Since the Nazi takeover of the Sudentenland, a portion of Czechoslovakia populated largely by Germans, the Czech government had been coming under great pressure from Hitler to give up their independence and be joined to the Third Reich entirely. The Czechs, however, were a proud, independent people, well armed for war, and as Derek had seen the tanks and armed men patrolling the borders, he knew that Hitler's army would have a tougher time with these people than with the Austrians, who had given up without a struggle.

"Yes, that is my hope, Mr. Mindel, although I'm not certain I have the mind for it."

"From what Rachel tells us, I'm sure you do," Sarah Mindel said. She was smiling gently and there was a warm light in her brown eyes. It was difficult for Derek to imagine that she had once been as rounded and lovely as Rachel was now, but he could see traces of her early beauty in her.

"What would you like to teach?" Jacob asked. He was sitting on the edge of his chair and turned his head to one side like a small bird. There were moments when he seemed to go off into a world of his own. *Advanced age. He cannot live long,* Derek thought. "I would like to teach literature, sir."

"Ah, literature! Then you and Rachel have much to talk about. She loves stories."

"Yes, I know. We've had a great deal of pleasure talking about literature at the university."

After the conversation went on for a short time, Derek realized that the aged couple were tiring. He stood up and said, "I must be leaving."

"You must come back tonight for dinner. Rachel is a fine cook."

"I would love to, but I'm afraid I can't. I need to get back to Germany. It's been a pleasure to meet you both." Derek bowed and left, and Rachel accompanied him to the door of the small house.

She put on her coat after handing him his, pulled a knit cap over her auburn hair, and said, "I'll walk with you for a way."

Derek was pleased. He had not had a chance to be alone with Rachel since his arrival, and now as they walked along the streets of the small village, he knew he had to persuade her to follow his plan.

The winter wind was cutting, and they ducked behind a wall to get out of it momentarily. "Rachel, I'm sorry we have so little time to be alone together."

"Can't you stay for a few more days?" Her face was turned upward to his, and he placed his hand on her cheek. She covered his hand with hers and said, "I haven't seen you in so long."

"I was fortunate to get away even for this brief time." He hesitated, enjoying the feel of her silky skin, and then he put his hand on her shoulder and squeezed it imperatively. "We've got to do something about your parents and about you, Rachel."

"What do you mean, Derek?"

He was certain that Adolf Hitler would not allow Czechoslovakia to remain independent for long, and urgently he said to her, "You must realize that Czechoslovakia will be invaded. Hitler will have all of it, not just the Sudetenland."

"Are you sure?"

"I have no proof, but I'm sure. Czechoslovakia stands in Hitler's way to the Balkans. You're going to have to leave with your parents for a safe place."

She lowered her head and said quietly, "There is no safe place in all of Europe for Jews, Derek."

"There could be. Marry me. I'll leave the army and

we'll take your parents and go away together, perhaps to Switzerland. If not there, we can go to one of the islands in the South Seas. I've always wanted to go there."

"Do you mean it, Derek?"

He felt like he was standing at a fork in the road. He had spoken from his heart, but now he realized that his whole life was at stake here. He thought of his father, and although he had never been on warm terms with him, in Germany fatherhood was a strong force. "I mean it," he said desperately, "but I'll have to go home first and talk to my father."

He saw something change in Rachel's eyes at those words. "What's wrong?" he asked.

"You must go, then, and talk to him."

"It'll be all right," he assured her. "I'll convince him."

Still Rachel did not answer, but she put her arms around his neck and pulled his head down. When she kissed him there was a fiery flavor on her lips, and it was as if she were saying good-bye. She clung to him as if she were a child, then released her grip and stepped back. "Good-bye, Derek. God be with you."

"It's only good-bye for a time, my love." Derek felt a sudden dread, as though something inside of him were terribly wrong. The world was going crazy in many ways, of course, but he had always felt he could conduct himself in a way that combined honor with his own desires. But at this moment he saw reflected in Rachel's eyes the impossibility of continuing his way of life. His inside world was collapsing as the love of his life walked away without another word.

"Rachel, I'll be back!" He called loudly, but she did not turn around. And as Derek stood, his eyes fixed on Rachel, he felt a dark despair. He was tormented with the desire to desert the army and flee with Rachel to a place where this madness could no longer touch them . . . yet he did not.

"I'll go talk to Father. I'll *make* him understand! He has to!" He turned and walked purposefully away, looking back once at the back of the woman he loved, knowing he loved her more than anything else in all the world.

CHAPTER TWELVE

WHEN THE HEAVENS ARE FALLING

★ ★ ★

The prime minister of England, Sir Neville Chamberlain, was a gaunt man, austere, unimaginative, and colorless. Chamberlain was neither a thinker, a writer, nor a soldier, but a businessman—and the biggest mistake of his entire career was that he tried to do business with Hitler.

In 1936, when Hitler marched into the Rhineland, Chamberlain persuaded the British parliament to do nothing, claiming that this would be the end of Hitler's raid on neighboring countries. When later that year Germany and Italy ganged up on helpless Spain, it was Chamberlain who persuaded his government to do nothing to help that country. In March 1938 Austria was taken without a shot by Hitler, and once again Chamberlain did nothing.

Finally, in September 1938, Hitler cast his focus on Czechoslovakia. The Czechs were a formidable barrier to Nazi expansion through the Balkans, and the very last bastion of democracy in central Europe. A line of fortifications comparable to the French Maginot Line stretched across Czechoslovakia's northern frontier, but her main defense was a pact of mutual assistance, and France and the Soviet Union and England were bound by a pact with the Czechs' defense. With these three great powers on her side, the Czechs felt no doubts about their abilities to stand against the armies of Germany.

Edvard Beneš, the president of Czechoslovakia, looked with pride at his country's four-hundred-million-dollar defense fortifications and proclaimed, "We shall never be an Austria. Hitler will not add us to his list of victims!"

But Beneš did not understand his enemy, and he overestimated his friends. Adolf Hitler moved toward Czechoslovakia, aiming first to take Sudentenland, a C-shaped territory in the western part of the country. On September 14, 1938, Prime Minister Chamberlain flew to Germany for a meeting with Hitler. He was desperate to keep the small British armed forces out of the hostilities.

Another meeting two weeks later, this time with the participation of France and Italy, resulted in the Munich Agreement, which turned Sudentenland over to Germany. When Chamberlain returned to England, he stood before the cameras of the press and pronounced, "It will be peace for our time."

In early October 1938 German troops marched into Czechoslovakia unhindered as huge crowds waved Nazi banners and cheered.

This was the beginning of the end for the last democracy in western Europe, which would finally fall to Hitler in March 1939, and the fault could lay, many argued, at the door of Neville Chamberlain.

★ ★ ★

Derek was sickened by Germany's invasion of the rest of Czechoslovakia in March of 1939, and it was with a heavy heart that he marched with his father's command into the homeland of his beloved Rachel. He sadly watched the brokenhearted Czechs standing in the streets weeping as the Nazis took over their country. Hitler's word that he would be satisfied with Sudetenland, and not attempt to take control of any more of Czechoslovakia, was not good, as Derek had feared.

The first night after arriving at their station, Derek was confronted by his father. The two men were in a hotel that had been commandeered for use by the German general's staff. Derek had been dreading this moment, and now his father faced him and demanded, "What's wrong with you, Derek? You act like a man who's half dead!"

Derek knew it was time to tell his father what had been burdening him like a millstone. "I have served faithfully in the army for two years, and I want out now, Father. I'm in love with Rachel Mindel, and I want to marry her and spend my life with her."

Wilhelm Grüber stared at his son in disbelief. "I can't believe it!" he shouted. "Have you lost your mind? You have a wonderful future in the military. Are you going to throw away everything for one woman—and a Jewish woman at that?"

"You and I don't think alike, Father." The words were hard to say, for in all of his life he had never stood up to his father. He had always simply caved in when there had been confrontations. But now he stood tall and straight, and he wished with all of his heart that he had taken Rachel and her parents when he'd had the chance and fled to some safe place. That was still in his mind, but he saw the anger in his father's eyes and knew he would never get a blessing from this man. "I'm sorry we see differently."

Wilhelm Grüber had been trying for weeks to convince himself that Derek had changed, that he had put his feelings for the Jewish woman aside. Wilhelm was a proud man, and the source of his pride was in the Fatherland. He had a heritage reaching back into history. The Grüber men had always served Germany, and now that the Fatherland needed every man, to hear of his son refusing to take his part, to speak of marrying a Jew, made his blood run cold. Forcing himself to control his anger, he said, "Derek, young men often make fools of themselves over women. I could tell you a story about my own youth when I had to make a decision. I very nearly threw my career away by choosing the wrong woman."

"Who was she, Father?" Derek was shocked. He had never heard his father speak of anything like this.

"It doesn't matter. She would not have been a proper wife for me, so I chose your mother."

"And in the same way, I'm choosing Rachel because I love her."

"Romantic love is nothing to build a life on! It is no foundation," Wilhelm said, biting his words off.

The two men stood face-to-face, the tension crackling in the room, and Derek knew his quest was hopeless.

Finally his father drew himself up and said, "What you ask is impossible. You are a soldier and an officer of the Reich. I will not allow you to abandon your responsibility to the Fatherland while this war is on." He softened for a moment and went on, "When this is over you will see things differently. Now, get back to your duties."

Derek did not answer. It was clearly useless to talk any further. As he left the room, he knew his life was falling to pieces and there was nothing he could do about it.

★ ★ ★

In the days that followed, Derek tried again and again to get time off from his duties so he could go find Rachel. He had witnessed the towns and shops and homes belonging to Czechs and Jews being vandalized and ransacked, and he grew sick at the thought of what might have happened to Rachel and her parents.

It was late one afternoon when they were advancing into a small town that his temper finally exploded. He was marching along at the head of a column, but when they met resistance, his men simply began shooting everyone they saw.

Derek tried to keep his men under control, but when he saw two of his men attacking a Czech girl no more than fifteen years old, his mind turned into a white rage. They were tearing at the girl's clothing as she sobbed and screamed for help. He pulled out his pistol and smashed one of them over the head. The soldier collapsed, and Derek whirled to face the other. "Are you a beast? You're not a man!" Derek shouted.

The private stared at him, his face pale. He saw death in his officer's eyes and could not speak.

"Take this one to the hospital," Derek said to two of his men who were watching, pointing to the man on the ground. "I hope he dies."

"Yes, Lieutenant," one of the soldiers stammered.

The terrified girl was cowering against a building, too afraid to flee. Derek looked at her kindly and motioned for her to run. With gratitude in her eyes, she jumped up and ran swiftly down the street.

A cold-eyed major approached. "Why did you do that, Lieutenant?"

"Did you not see what he was doing, Major?"

"That was not your affair. These people must be subdued."

"While I am an officer of the Reich, I will keep order with my men, Major. You must do as you please about that."

The major said nothing, for he was well aware of the dangers of getting involved in an argument with the son of his general. He turned and marched abruptly away.

That's not the end of that, Derek thought. But he found himself not caring.

Later that night Derek's father sent for him and

demanded to know the facts of the matter. Derek gave them simply, and his father said, "You struck one of your own men in defense of an enemy!"

"She was not an enemy! She was a mere child," Derek exploded in anger. "You've always told me that being a soldier is a noble thing. You call this noble, Father? Murder, rape, pillaging innocent civilians?"

Wilhelm Grüber could not answer. Above all, he was obedient to his government and his country. "Let this be the end of all this," he finally said. "I'm ashamed of you! You're dismissed!"

As Derek left his father's office, a door closed in his heart, and he knew he would never be able to be the man his father wanted him to be. An hour later, he left to go seek Rachel. He knew he would be severely punished and perhaps sent to prison, for General Wilhelm Grüber did not look kindly on men who left their post, but he had no choice.

★ ★ ★

As Derek entered the village where Rachel and her parents lived, he found it already full of German soldiers. No one questioned him or asked to see his papers, and he marched purposefully toward the small house where he had visited Rachel.

He knocked on the door, and when it opened, he was surprised to see a sergeant in a German uniform. "Yes, Lieutenant?"

Derek's heart sank, but he knew he had to find out the worst. "I am looking for the family that lived here."

"Oh, the old couple and the girl? They're gone, Lieutenant."

"Gone where?"

The sergeant, a tall man with a bland face, shrugged. "They left with others in the railway cars." The sergeant's eyes suddenly sharpened. "Do you know them, Lieutenant?"

"What railway cars, Sergeant?"

"Why, the ones headed for the camps."

Derek's heart went cold as stone. By now he was convinced that the stories about what happened at the concentration camps were the reality, but he had managed to bury the truth deep within himself. Without another word to the sergeant, he walked away, thinking of nothing but the last sight he'd had of Rachel as she had walked away from him down this very street. The memory was bitter and burned in his soul like acid. *I could have had her. Why did I run away? Why was I such a coward?*

★ ★ ★

Derek wandered in a daze for hours, and when he got back to his camp, Frederick Möhr immediately launched into a tirade. "Where have you been, Derek?" he demanded. "Our unit has gone into action!"

Derek stared at Möhr and found that he did not particularly care.

"I've been looking everywhere for you. You deserted your post. We've got to get back to our unit before anybody finds out!"

Derek allowed Möhr to hurry him along. He got into the truck that Möhr had commandeered and hung on as Möhr raced through the streets.

Soon they heard the crackle of gunfire and the roar of artillery shells. One shell went off almost directly in front of the truck, and Möhr was unable to avoid it. The left wheel hit the pothole, and the truck spun out of control and slid into a parked car.

"That was a close one," Möhr said, wiping his face as he inspected the wrecked truck. "Come on, our men are over here. Your father has taken command."

Dodging the bullets that whined around their heads,

the two soldiers advanced past several buildings that had been almost destroyed. The two men reached the house they were using for a command post, climbing over the debris left where a shell must have exploded.

As they approached, a colonel came out and saw the two men. "I have bad news for you, Lieutenant." His face was pale and tense with strain. "Your father has been wounded."

"Is it serious?"

"I'm afraid it is. Come on. I'll show you where he is."

Numbly, Derek followed the colonel and found his father on a bed. A military doctor was beside him. "Is it bad, Doctor?"

"I'm afraid so. The wounds are internal. He's bleeding to death and there's nothing I can do."

Derek knelt down beside the bed. He had never seen his father in a moment of weakness that he could remember, but now the pallor of death was on Wilhelm Grüber's face. "Father, can you hear me?" Derek whispered. He took his father's hand and found it cold. The others left the room as Derek knelt there, begging his father to speak to him. The eyes fluttered and the lips tried to move.

"Father," Derek said, his throat dry. He tried to think of something to say but could not.

Finally his father's eyes focused momentarily, and he said, "My son . . ." He tried to form words, and Derek leaned over, hoping that his father would say something about trusting in God. But the words that came were a disappointment. "I have . . . been faithful—to the Fatherland."

"Father, call upon God. Ask for mercy," Derek whispered.

But it was too late. His eyes fluttered, and then his body stopped moving entirely. Wilhelm Grüber relaxed and expelled one breath . . . and then lay in the awful stillness of death.

Derek stayed on his knees, unable to accept the reality. When his knees could take it no longer, he got to his feet and gazed down at the body of his father. There had been little warmth between them, but he knew a sense of loss that he could not put into words.

He turned and found the colonel waiting for him. "Your father was a great man, Lieutenant." He looked down at the still form. "We need every man we can get. I hate to call upon you at a time like this, but you must think of your men. They are being slaughtered."

"I will do what I can," Derek said stiffly. It was as if another man were speaking for him. "Give me my orders, sir."

★ ★ ★

Derek didn't remember a great deal of what happened in the action that followed his father's death. The shock seemed to block everything out. He had vague memories of returning to his men, moving carelessly through the hail of bullets. Many begged him to stay down, but he was beyond caring. His one thought was to save the lives of as many of his men as he could, and he performed his duties in a haze. It couldn't have been three hours later when he felt something terribly sharp strike him in the right shoulder, and he welcomed the darkness into which it threw him. His last thought as he lay with his life bleeding out of him was, *My father's dead, and I have lost the love of my life.*

★ ★ ★

Derek stood before the casket that held the body of his father. He had recovered from his injury enough to be released and had come from the hospital dressed in full uniform.

The church was filled mostly with soldiers. There were few civilians that Derek could see, but he could not make himself care. He had been confused when he had awakened in a hospital in Berlin, and now as he looked upon the mourners, he saw Göring and several other high-ranking officers. The words the pastor had spoken were meaningless to him, and he was glad when the service came to a close and the soldiers filed out.

As Derek stared into the coffin, he heard a voice and turned to see Hermann Göring dressed in a white uniform, which seemed strangely incongruous.

"I don't mean to interrupt your grief, Lieutenant, but I have news for you."

"Yes, my general?"

"First of all, your gallant action has done you and your family credit. You are being promoted to major, and you will receive the First Order of the Iron Cross."

The words, which would have meant so much to many Germans, meant nothing to Derek. He managed to nod and say thank-you.

"Your wound will keep you from a front-line combat command, but you will still be able to serve the Fatherland honorably. We have an important assignment for you, which will involve special training and studies in Norwegian. You will await further orders."

"Of course, my general."

Göring snapped his heels together and flung out his arm in a salute to the führer. "Heil Hitler!"

Derek returned the salute, but with a gripping despair at being held prisoner to such a madman as Hitler.

He watched Göring spin on his heel and stride away; then Derek turned back and took a last look at the casket. He felt sick to death, for life no longer held any meaning for him. He thought of Rachel—her loveliness, the excitement that would shine in her eyes, the pleased expression of her lips—but then he thought of what life in a concentration camp was like, and anguish clamped around his throat as if to cut off his last breath.

Desperately needing fresh air, he almost ran out of the

church and into the cold, drizzling rain. Not heeding it in the least, he walked down the street in a daze, the chilly air being no match for the bitter coldness in his own heart.

PART THREE

May–October 1940

★ ★ ★

CHAPTER THIRTEEN

A Salute for Nils

★　★　★

Mallory leaned forward in her chair and surveyed the dining area, where she sat across from Rolf and his young friend Nils Baalsrud. They had met for a noon meal at Restaurant le Canard, one of Oslo's more opulent restaurants. The room was brimming with eclectic antiques, Asian rugs, chandeliers, and Baroque paintings. It was housed in a looming brick mansion built at the turn of the century, with spires and wrought-iron decorations. The main dining room was spread throughout the first floor, and the place was half filled with white-jacketed waiters moving to serve the customers.

"I think I'll have duck," Rolf said, looking up at the waiter. "How do you prepare that?"

The waiter, a short, fat individual with rosy cheeks and bright blue eyes, bobbed his head. "The duck is roasted in honey and served with horseradish and a cognac sauce."

"That sounds like it will just about do me. What about you, Nils?"

He shook his head. "Too rich for my blood and too expensive. Just bring me some of that peppered baby halibut with asparagus."

"Of course, sir. And you, miss?"

"I think I'll have the chicken with eggplant."

"Yes, of course. Very good indeed. It comes with a sweet green shallot sauce."

The waiter took their orders for beverages and then left quickly.

"I feel like a condemned prisoner eating his last meal," Mallory said.

"Don't be foolish," Rolf said. "It's just routine."

"That's right," Nils said, nodding. "Everyone who's not a citizen has to report."

Mallory toyed with the heavy silver fork for a moment, not answering. The whole situation felt a little odd to her. Although she enjoyed the company of her companions, Nils, at age sixteen, was even younger than Rolf. Sometimes when Mallory was with the two of them she felt more like their mother than their friend. Dining in this fancy restaurant had been Nils's idea and was to be his treat. Apparently, money was not a concern for him and his family. The expensive restaurant did not seem a fitting place to eat just before she was to report to German headquarters in Oslo.

She had received her notice the day before, and although she was not given to worrying about such things, it disturbed her. "What can they want with me?"

"You know how the Germans are." Nils shrugged. "They're very methodical."

The sound of marching feet caught their attention, and all three turned to look out the large front window, where they saw a troop of German soldiers marching by in perfect order. Mallory watched them silently. When the footsteps had faded, she said, "I can't believe that Norway fell so quickly."

Her words put gloom on the faces of both young men, for there had never been any doubt about the outcome of the German invasion. The German air force, the Luftwaffe, had been the decisive factor that had permitted the Germans to keep pouring reinforcements into Oslo, and this had won the campaign. No one had been prepared for the closely coordinated operations of German air and ground forces. Within weeks the Germans had completely conquered Norway, and the ease with which they had accomplished it caused embarrassment to young men such as Rolf and Nils.

"They beat us so easily," Rolf said bitterly. He shook his head, his lips a thin, pale line.

"Well, it's no comfort, but the Nazis are taking Holland and Belgium even quicker than they took our country," Nils said.

"I can only hope that the new British prime minister can do something to stop Hitler," Mallory said. "If he can't, the situation looks hopeless." The British had grown disgusted with Prime Minister Chamberlain and forced him to resign.

"If anyone brought this war on, Chamberlain was the one," Rolf said. "He could have led his country to stop Hitler when he first began to attack the nations at Germany's borders."

The others nodded in agreement. Mallory took a sip of her coffee. She was deep in thought. "Sigrid is very anxious to get away but doesn't know how. Can we help her?"

"I plan to," Rolf said. "She needs to leave immediately." He reached over and squeezed Mallory's hand. "You need to leave too."

"Why, they wouldn't do anything to an American," Nils said.

"They'll do anything, these Nazis," Rolf insisted. "You really need to leave, Mallory."

"I can't do that. You know I have my work with the Lapps."

"If I were you, then, I'd go north to their part of the country. The weather's not so bad now, and I don't think the Nazis will bother them. They don't have anything the Germans want."

The three stopped talking when the waiter brought their food. Her meal was delicious, but Mallory ate without much pleasure. Nils and Rolf shared some stories about some mutual friends, but she was preoccupied with her interview at German headquarters and wondered if she would be deported.

After the meal was over, Nils left, but Rolf stayed, smoking a cigarette and contemplating his history with Mallory. When he had first met her and taught her to ski, he had enjoyed teasing her with his courtship, but his feelings for her had turned much more serious. He had learned to admire her beauty, the self-possessed curve of her mouth, her remarkably black hair that lay neatly over her head, and her graceful height and shapeliness that drew the eye of men everywhere. Her features were quick to express her thoughts, and her love of life seemed to lie behind her eyes and lips, waiting for release.

"You really should get away soon, Mallory." Rolf lowered his voice and leaned closer, whispering, "Things are going to get bad around here."

His mysterious expression drew Mallory's attention. "What are you talking about?"

"The Nazis are in for trouble. I can't say any more, but you need to get out of this place as soon as you can. Go back to Africa and wait until the war is over. Then you can come back."

"I can't do that, Rolf. You know I can't."

He sighed and sat back in his chair. "I knew you'd say that, but I really wish you'd change your mind."

"It'll be all right," she said. "I'd better get to the headquarters now and see what they want."

★ ★ ★

Headquarters for the Nazis had been set up at the *Radhuset*, the city hall of Oslo. Mallory walked down the broad street and then entered the redbrick building, noting the contrast between the dull brick exterior and the marble-floored interior. She glanced at the frescos on the walls, which were bursting with color. There were statues outside and inside, some of them depicting Viking gods and Norwegian literary figures.

The large room into which she stepped was crowded with desks, and German soldiers were everywhere, moving about or working at their desks. A hum of German voices filled the air, and she finally showed her summons to a sergeant seated at a desk near the front.

"You must see Lieutenant Stahl." He rose and led her across the room to an office off to the side. Mallory followed him into the office. He said in German, "This woman has a summons, Lieutenant."

"Leave her here."

The speaker was a short man with brown hair and narrowly spaced brown eyes. He wore the black ornate uniform of an SS officer and a revolver at his side. He waited until the soldier left, then said brusquely in Norwegian, "Sit down."

Mallory sat down in the chair opposite the officer's desk and watched as he took his own seat. He studied her papers, then said, "Your name is Mallory Anne Winslow?"

"Yes, Lieutenant."

"You are not a citizen of Norway?"

"No, I'm not."

"According to this, you are from Africa. Is that correct?"

"Yes, it is."

"What are you doing in Norway?" His tone was cold, but not as cold as his eyes. There was almost an aura of evil about this officer that frightened Mallory. She knew a little about the activities of the SS and had heard many horror stories of torture and beatings of the captives of the lands that Germany had conquered. She kept her head high and said, "I came as a missionary to the Lapp people."

"A missionary!" The thin lips curled, and he shook his head. "That doesn't sound too likely."

"It's true, though."

Uldrich Stahl laughed. "Just like you Americans. That's your nationality according to the papers."

"Yes, that's correct. I don't understand you, Lieutenant."

"Great things are going on in the world, and you waste your life preaching to a few Lapps. Why, they're primitive people. They make no contribution to the world."

"They are important to God."

His face grew tense. "I am not here to listen to your religious nonsense!" he snapped. "Here, you will fill out these papers. I will return and expect to see them done."

Getting up, Stahl left the office and moved across to the next door. When he entered, he found Colonel Ludwig Ritter studying a large map of Norway that was on his desk.

"Ah, Stahl," Ritter said, "I was about to send for you. We've got to do something about these villages up in the north. They're hotbeds of this resistance movement."

"Of course, Colonel. Have you ever heard of a woman called Mallory Winslow?"

"No. Who is she?"

"She's an American who is in Norway, but she comes from Africa, of all places."

"What's she doing in Norway?"

"She claims she's a missionary and she came here to preach to the Lapps, but she lives here in Oslo. I don't trust her."

Colonel Ludwig Ritter finally looked up from the map. He was a tall man, thin and spare, with icy blue eyes. "Why do you not trust her?"

"It's foolishness!" Stahl said. "You know how awful conditions are in the winter, but I have it on good authority that she actually lives with those people during the winter months. They live like pigs, Colonel."

"I've heard that, but do you have any evidence that she's an agent?"

"Not yet, but I'm suspicious. She's an attractive woman, and no attractive woman would throw herself away like that."

"Well, keep your eye on her."

"I may lock her up and interrogate her."

"No. If she's an American, that could cause trouble." He looked at his map again and traced his finger from Oslo north to Lapland. "Why don't you show her in. I want to meet her."

"*Jawohl*, Colonel."

Colonel Ritter's mind worked rapidly, for he had a superior intellect. He was a career officer and at heart was a greedy man. Unsatisfied with his pay, he made a habit of stealing treasures from conquered people. He had become a wealthy man by becoming one of the first men into Austria, where he had looted the museums, stealing priceless paintings. Some he'd had to turn over to the upper echelon, including Göring, who was completely greedy about such things. But he had managed to keep enough for his own private collection that he need not worry about money.

"This is the woman, Colonel."

"Ah yes, Miss Winslow. Will you sit down?"

Stahl left and closed the door behind him.

"Thank you, Colonel." Mallory sat down and faced the officer. His eyes were as cold as polar ice, and the smile on his lips did not reach them. She answered all of Ritter's questions, which seemed innocent enough, but finally he said, "I think it might be wise for you to leave Norway, Miss Winslow."

"I can't do that, Colonel. You see, I believe God has called me to be a missionary with the Lapps."

"You understand you can be forced to leave."

"That would not make a good impression on the United States," she said quietly. "The American press is not friendly toward you as it is. I'm not sure you would want it known that a simple missionary was prohibited from serving God."

A hot reply leaped to Ritter's lips, but he bit it off before it escaped. "Very well, then, but you will have to submit to the same regulations as the Norwegians."

"Of course, Colonel. There will be no problem about that."

"That is all."

As soon as Mallory left, Stahl came in. "What did you think of her?"

"I think she's probably what she says she is."

"Well, I'm not convinced!"

"Just keep an eye on her. If she gets troublesome, we may have to deport her. Perhaps we might have to take even stronger measures. But do nothing without speaking to me first."

"Yes, Colonel."

★ ★ ★

The shortwave radio that sat on the dressing table in Mallory's room crackled and popped for a moment, and then a British voice came in clear and strong. Mallory leaned toward the radio, listening intently. She had the volume turned down, for the Germans had forbidden any private citizen to own a shortwave radio. Her eyes narrowed as she listened to the announcer, who spoke grimly about the British position in France:

> ... and so the violence and the speed of the Nazi blow, which has broken through France, has taken the world by surprise. The Nazi forces have flanked the Allies at every turn, and Nazi bombers have attacked incessantly. British and French troops have been driven back during the onslaught of the Nazis until now they have reached the beaches at Dunkirk. They wait there in thin and winding but disciplined lines for small boats to take them to the transports and warships that wait offshore. Overhead the RAF fights valiantly against numerically superior Nazi air power.
>
> The evacuation fleet consists of practically every boat England and France have that can cross the Channel. There are ferry boats, small fishing trawlers, transports, and warships—a vast flotilla of small boats shuttled between the beaches and the big ships offshore. Day and

night now, for five days, the evacuation to England has continued while the Nazis push the heroic rear guard closer and closer to the ruined port of Dunkirk. More than three hundred thousand Allied soldiers have been heroically evacuated, but though the men have escaped, they had to leave all of their heavy armor, vehicles, and other equipment behind. Now that the British are gone, nothing stands between Paris and the onrushing German hordes—

The announcer's voice seemed to break; then he said, "France has fallen, for all practical purposes, and Paris cannot be saved."

For some time Mallory listened as the announcer reviewed some of what had happened in the last week or so, and she heard the hopelessness in his voice. Finally she turned off the radio and sat thinking. The news was discouraging, and she knew it would darken the spirits of Eva and Lars. They had been so kind to her ever since she had come to Norway as a stranger, letting her stay in their house time and again.

She knew she could not leave this radio in her room, for the Germans were now breaking into houses and ransacking them, searching for anything that was forbidden. Those who possessed these items were immediately arrested, and Mallory could not bear the thought of this happening to her host and hostess.

She hurriedly gathered up her equipment, which was considerable, and took it out to the small barn. The building was now used mainly for storage, and no animals were kept there. The upstairs could be reached only by a ladder fastened to the side wall and was crowded with odds and ends of furniture and other items from the past. It took several trips, but finally she had all of her shortwave equipment transferred.

She moved a pile of junk—old tables, desks, lamps, chairs, boxes, boards—out of a corner of the loft next to a window. Where all the stuff had come from, she had no idea. Perhaps Eva's grandparents had left it there. She carefully piled the stuff around the corner, making a small room with miscellaneous junk for walls. She set the largest of her radios on a small table that she had salvaged and dropped a wire out the window for an antenna. She looked around with satisfaction at her new communications center.

The radio worked even better than it had in the house. "There," she said grimly, "they'll never find this dream of a radio up in this old junk room."

She climbed down the ladder and went back into the house to get dinner started. Thirty minutes later when Eva came in, she told her the bad news about Dunkirk.

"I know. It's a bad day for France—and for the world."

"Can nothing stop the Germans, Eva?"

"They will be stopped, but it will take time." She had a worried look on her face. "We've got to get Sigrid out of here before she gets arrested for her writing."

"Do you have any ideas?" Mallory asked as she cut potatoes into chunks. "Can I be of any help?"

"I don't think there's anything you can do. Rolf and Nils have a plan to take her to Sweden."

"But Nils is only sixteen."

"When there's a war going on, a sixteen-year-old is a man, Mallory. Boys have to grow up quickly these days."

"What a tragedy! He's losing his youth."

"We are losing everything, but our day will come."

Mallory lit the burner under the pan of potatoes. "I moved all of my radio equipment out to the barn." Mallory went on to explain what she had done.

"That was a good idea! We'll be using that radio a lot."

★ ★ ★

Four days after Mallory had moved the radio, a squad of four privates led by a huge, hulking sergeant searched the house. They roughly shoved Eva and Mallory aside as the sergeant directed the men to search everywhere. "Turn up anything you can find that's against the Third Reich. We'll hold these women responsible for whatever you find!" He came over and put his hand on Eva's shoulder.

She slapped it away and turned to put her back against the wall. "Don't you touch me!"

The sergeant laughed. "Well, aren't you the high and mighty one! Maybe I'll come back later and you and I can talk about it."

The soldiers made a wreck of the house, and at one point the sergeant started to put his hands on Mallory, but she rebuffed him angrily. "You're brave, aren't you, with two women?"

"I'm a good man with women." The sergeant winked.

Again he attempted to put his arm around Mallory, and she snapped, "Maybe I'll have to report you to the American authorities."

"American authorities? What do we care about them?" The sergeant's round red face grew stern. "Do you have a radio in this house?"

"Yes, I do," Mallory answered at once.

"Get it."

Eva stared at her, but Mallory, followed by the sergeant, went to her bedroom and picked up a small receiving set she'd had for a long time.

"Radios are illegal," the man barked. "Do you have any more radios in this house?"

Mallory was glad he had added *in this house*, for now she could honestly say, "No. There's nothing like that."

After the soldiers had left, Eva said, "It's a good thing you hid the rest of your equipment. You're good with radios, and we need help."

"What can I do, Eva?"

"Lars and I are going to lead the resistance here in Oslo. We're going to need to contact England often. Agents need to come here, and we have to get information out." She collapsed onto the sofa. "None of us are good with such things."

Mallory sat down beside her but did not speak for a moment.

"Of course, this is not your country."

"It's not that, Eva. I-I'm just not sure what to do anymore. Let me pray about it."

"Pray quickly."

"I will. Is there any news about Sigrid?"

"No. It will be difficult for her to escape. They have thrown up more guards around Oslo and all up and down the Swedish border. It'll be awfully risky. They will all be shot if they're caught. You know that."

"I know. But it mustn't happen."

"It can happen, though. It's already happening all over Norway. They're taking hostages and shooting them without trials."

★　★　★

For several days Mallory struggled with the question of whether or not to help with the resistance. She had learned to love this country and the people in it, but she had not been able to reconcile serving in the resistance, which could mean violence. She firmly believed that her call was still to preach the Gospel to the Lapps. The problem perplexed her, and she prayed long and hard without arriving at a definite answer.

Finally she said one evening at supper, "I can't decide what to do about helping you with the radio, but, Lars, I can train you to use it."

"I am not good with such things," he said. "Actually none of us in the group are. Mechanical things are difficult for us."

"That's true," Eva agreed, "and you even make your own radio sets." The solution Mallory had offered did not seem practical.

Mallory was preparing for bed that night when suddenly she heard voices in the living room. She put on her robe and went out to find Rolf speaking hurriedly with Lars and Eva. "Did you get Sigrid away all right?" Mallory asked. "I'm so glad you're back." The hard look on Rolf's face made her ask, "What's wrong, Rolf?"

"The Germans almost caught us." His voice was spare, and anger glowed in his eyes. "We got Sigrid into Sweden, but coming back, we ran into a patrol. I got away, but they caught Nils." He looked up to the ceiling and exhaled loudly. "He's going to be shot in the morning, Mallory."

"Oh no!" she whispered. "He's only a boy."

"They're going to shoot him all the same." Rolf quickly left the room but not before Mallory had seen tears glistening in his eyes. She turned to face Eva and Lars, who stood silently before her. "Isn't there anything we can do?"

"There's no way to save him," Lars said, his voice as hard as granite. "We'll do the only thing we can."

"What is that?"

"The Germans are going to make a public spectacle out of it. We'll get as many people as we can to go."

"You mean to witness the execution?"

Eva said in a tense voice, "It's the only way we have to say good-bye to Nils."

★ ★ ★

The square where the execution was to take place was filled. Lieutenant Stahl had arrived at the center court, where the firing squad was already drawn up. He looked around at the crowd and said, "I didn't expect all these people here."

"It's good for them," Colonel Ritter answered. "Apparently, the boy was popular. It will teach them that they can't defy us."

"Have your men ready. There could be trouble."

"No, Colonel, they've got better sense than to attack us."

Mallory stood across the courtyard beside Eva and

Lars. Her head felt strangely light. She could not believe that the young boy so full of life and fun was going to die in a few moments.

"Bring the prisoner forward!" Colonel Ritter's voice bellowed, and a thick silence fell over the crowd.

Mallory dropped her head, not wanting to watch, but Lars said, "We must honor Nils and let him know that he's giving his life for his country."

"He's a Christian," Eva said. "You know that. So he's going to be with his God."

Forcing herself to look up, Mallory saw a squad of six soldiers bringing Nils out of the building down the street. They had to half carry him, and she heard Lars say bitterly, "They tortured him! He can't even stand up!"

"Tortured him? Why?" Mallory wailed.

"To try to make him tell who was with him, to give our names. He must not have talked, or we'd be under arrest right now."

Mallory watched as they tied Nils to a post. She heard Stahl ask him if he wanted a blindfold, but he said no.

Nils's voice was weak, but he held his head up. As he looked around, he saw the massive crowd that had gathered, and despite his plight, he suddenly smiled.

The soldiers who had tied him up moved away, and Stahl ordered, "Firing squad, take your positions!"

Stahl had no sooner spoken than a woman started singing the national anthem of Norway in a powerful operatic voice. Instantly hundreds of voices joined in, filling the bright, sunshiny air of May with song.

Mallory joined in, and despite the grief she felt, a strain of pride came to her for these people.

Ritter shouted, "Quiet! Lieutenant, stop them!"

Stahl marched back and forth screaming until his face grew red, but he could not make himself heard.

Finally in a rage, he turned and caught Ritter's nod. "Ready!" he screamed at the firing squad.

The voices in the crowd broke off as the rifles were

aimed, and then Mallory heard Lars cry out loudly, "God be with you, Nils!"

"Aim!" Stahl cried out.

And then, with tears running down her cheeks, Mallory stared at the face of the young man. His face was pale, but he suddenly smiled and cried out in a loud, strong voice, "God bless Norway—Jesus Christ is Lord!"

"Fire!"

Mallory dropped her eyes so she would not see the bullets strike, but silence fell over the crowd, and then another voice cried out, "God bless Norway!"

As others took up the cry, Ritter shouted, "Disperse these people, Lieutenant!"

The crowd turned and began to leave as the soldiers approached, shoving those who hesitated.

As Mallory stumbled away, she felt Lars take her arm to steady her. She looked up at him and said, "I want to be part of the resistance, Lars. Just tell me what to do."

Lars's grip tightened on her arm, but his face, which was dark with the scene he had just witnessed, said, "You might end up like Nils, Mallory."

She shook her head. "I must help in this work." She looked back over her shoulder at the awful scene. "Maybe that's one reason God brought me here to Norway."

CHAPTER FOURTEEN

AGENT IN PLACE

★ ★ ★

The Germans continued to sweep through France, and as they did, Mallory gave herself to the task of becoming an expert in radio communications. She was already skilled in the basics, but once she had made contact with England, she had to learn the codes that the resistance organization used. Information could never be given in common, ordinary language, for the Germans closely monitored the shortwave messages that could come from the resistance. They also monitored those that the resistance received that came from England and other places.

The codes were relatively simple, and Mallory mastered them quickly, winning the admiration of Lars, who shook his head with amazement. "I could not do that in a hundred years."

One Thursday morning Eva and Mallory spent over an hour in the makeshift radio room. They made the effort to disguise the room even better so that anyone sticking his head up into the loft would think the space contained nothing more than a jumbled mass of old furniture and junk. They had enlarged the room itself so that it was spacious enough to hold three or four people comfortably, and from the window, they could see the road so that any Germans approaching could be quickly identified. After the two women had listened to the news from France, filled with gloom, Eva found an English newscast coming straight from London. The announcer said:

> The English people are grieved over the fall of France. June 22 was a horrible day for Europe as France signed an armistice with Germany. Hitler's men now occupy the bulk of France, leaving only the southern third of the country under French control.

The two women discussed the situation in France, debating what could have been done differently to prevent the catastrophe.

"The more I think of what Hitler has already done, the harder I want to work for our cause," Eva said. "I want you to try to get in contact with Ajax." He was the British contact agent who directed all help that came to the resistance movement.

"I'll try."

"If you do get ahold of Ajax, tell him we need more arms immediately." Eva went on to describe exactly what Mallory was to relay to their contact. "I've got to go to town."

"All right, Eva."

After Eva left, Mallory went out to the barn and began to call Ajax. As she did so, she wondered if the Germans were tracing her call. She had heard they had equipment that could trace a shortwave broadcast to its source, and the thought worried her.

Finally, after forty-five minutes, a voice clearly said, "This is Ajax speaking."

"Ajax, this is Byron calling."

"Go ahead, Byron. I can hear you."

Byron was the code name Mallory used for her own signal. She had chosen the name in memory of Lord George Byron, the poet who had gone to Greece to fight for the independence of the patriots there.

For ten minutes, Mallory used code to give Ajax their request for more weapons. She also relayed some information that Lars and Eva had gathered that might prove useful to their English friends. She finally said, "Message complete."

"Now I have a message for you, Byron."

"Go ahead, Ajax."

Mallory quickly scribbled down the message, transposing it from code to plain English. Finally Ajax said, "Do you copy?"

"I copy. Signing off."

She immediately shut the radio down and left the barn. Glancing at her watch, she saw there would not be time to wait for Lars or Eva to come back. She got her bicycle and rode out of town, making her way down to the docks. She parked her bike and walked toward the ships at anchor. There were many of them, but she was looking for one man. It was late afternoon now, and for a time she grew frustrated. But finally she saw him—a man of medium height wearing a blue-and-white checkered shirt. He was sitting alone on the docks smoking a pipe, a small suitcase at his side.

She walked up and said, "Do you think it will rain tonight?" This was the test question, and the answer was important.

"It will always rain somewhere."

This was the correct response, and Mallory said quickly, "What's your name?"

"James St. Cloud."

"I'm Mallory Winslow. Come with me."

Without a word, the man picked up his suitcase, and Mallory went to get her bike. The two moved away from the docks, passing some German soldiers who were supervising the unloading of a craft. Mallory saw that the Englishman watched them carefully but said nothing.

When they cleared the dock area, she turned to him. "Did you have any trouble coming over?"

"No. They stuck me in the hole with a bunch of fish. I must smell terrible."

"You are rather rank." They walked down the road trying to look like they belonged there. "You'll be staying with the Sorensens, Bernhard and Einer," Mallory told him.

"Do they know I'm coming?"

"No. I didn't have time to tell anyone. I'm going to ask Ajax to give us a bit more warning next time. If I hadn't been on the radio, you might have sat on that dock for a long while and you might have been caught."

"It was a bit sudden. I'm sorry."

James St. Cloud was not a man who would attract a great deal of attention. He had mild blue eyes and lank brown hair. He spoke in a voice that indicated he was highly educated.

They sat under a trio of distinctive trees, waiting for their contact who would give them a ride to the Sorensens' place. "What's your part in all this?" James asked. "You're not Norwegian."

"No, I'm an American." A truck pulled up near them, and the driver and Mallory exchanged code sentences. Mallory was grateful Ajax had managed to get her message through to the driver. He dropped them off at the Sorensens in the country, then disappeared back toward town.

They were met as the door opened, and Bernhard Sorensen stepped outside. He stared hard at the two and asked, "What can I do for you?"

"Mr. Sorensen, you remember me. I live with the Klovstads, Eva and Lars."

"Yes, I remember. Who is this man?"

Mallory lowered her voice. "This is James St. Cloud. He's just come over from England to help us with the work."

"Do you have proof of that?" Sorensen was a huge, bulky man with a shock of straw-colored hair and sharp eyes. "Where did you run into him?"

"He came in on a fishing boat."

"How do you know he is who he says he is?"

"He knew the password."

"We'll have to have more proof than that." Sorensen reached beneath his coat and pulled out a pistol. "You may be who you say you are, but I'll have to have more proof before I risk my wife's life."

James sighed gustily. "This is no way to run an operation!" he protested.

"I'll have to hold both of you until I can talk to Lars or Eva."

"But you know I stay with them," Mallory said.

"I don't know anything except that I'm not taking any chances. Follow me."

Mallory saw that it would do no good to protest. Bernhard Sorensen was obviously a stubborn individual, and she said no more as he directed them into a shed outside. They made themselves comfortable on boxes and crates. When the door shut, they heard the lock fasten on the outside. She turned to James. "I guess we'll just have to wait."

"This is a pitiful way to run an operation."

"We're doing the best we can. If you had given me more time, Lars would have met you."

"I suppose that's true." He surveyed their surroundings. "What are you doing here in Norway?" He listened as she told him of her work with the Lapps, and finally he shook his head and laughed. "That's a very bad cover story."

"It's not a cover story."

"A missionary to the Lapps?"

"It's why I came here." She wiped her sleeve across her forehead. "How did you get into this business?"

"I was in the army, but I took a bullet in the knee. You may have noticed I limp a little. I'm not much good as a soldier, but I'm good enough for this sort of thing."

"Do you have a family?"

"Not now." He hesitated, then said, "I was married once, but my wife is dead."

"I'm sorry."

"Not your fault." He shrugged. "What about you?"

"My family's all in Africa."

This seemed to interest James. "Africa's a long way from Norway. You're not married?"

"No."

Amusement danced in his eyes. "Why not?"

Mallory was surprised at his direct questions. "Because I haven't found a man yet that I want to live with for the rest of my life."

The conversation eventually trailed off. They were getting thirsty in the stuffy little space, but they had no success at attracting anyone's attention. Although James banged on the door several times, he got no answer.

Finally, after what seemed like a very long time, they heard voices. "Well, I hope we're out of this place," he said.

"I think so. That's Eva's voice."

"Who is she?"

"Eva Klovstad. She and her husband, Lars, head the resistance in Oslo."

The door opened, and Eva stood there. She listened as James explained his mission, and finally she said, "He's all right, Bernhard."

"Good to get a little recognition finally," James said wryly. "But we'd better get our stories straight."

"Why exactly have you come?" Eva asked.

"There are going to be a great many supplies coming in—guns, ammunition—and our timing to pick them up needs to be exact. We've got a new aircraft that will serve admirably, but it can't stay on the ground long."

"Yes, the timing will be important. Mallory's our best radio operator. You'll have to work with her."

"Fine. When can we start?"

"You will stay here as a farmhand," Eva said. "When you want a message sent or you need to receive one, you must come to Oslo."

"That sounds too awkward and dangerous."

The two argued for a while, and Mallory finally said, "I

have enough components to make another radio. We can set it up here. Do you know how to use a shortwave, Mr. St. Cloud?"

"Just James is fine. No, I'm not much good with things like that."

"Then I'll come out and teach you."

"That would be better," James said. He took a deep breath and looked around at the small group. "I hope I can be of some help."

"If you can get us some supplies," Eva said grimly, "that will be a help indeed."

"I'll do my best." James St. Cloud smiled and seemed a very ordinary man. "If we're caught, we'll all be shot together, I suppose."

"Exactly," Eva said, nodding. "So be careful."

"I'm always careful. It's other people who get me into trouble." He smiled lightly and nodded toward Mallory. "But this young lady and I will work well together, I think."

★ ★ ★

James St. Cloud was sitting beside Mallory in the corner of the library as they listened to a discussion about recent events in France on the radio. The announcer said with great sadness in his voice, "France is no longer a republic but a puppet under the Nazi regime."

"Well, I guess it had to happen," he said.

"What does it mean, James?"

"It means that unless the Americans help us out, Hitler will have his way."

"But America will never do that unless she's attacked."

"Yes, you're right. The only other force that could stop Hitler is Russia."

Mallory was surprised at his answer. She had worked with him now for weeks and found him to be knowledge-able and well educated, and she had learned to trust his judgment in political and military matters. "But Russia's their ally."

"On paper."

"I don't understand."

"Russia will do whatever she thinks is for her own good. Hitler's the same. The first time either one of them sees a chance to attack the other one, they will. That's what I'm hoping for. It's the only thing I can see that will stop Hitler."

"But you've told me that the Russians are poorly armed."

"That is true, but Germany can still never defeat Russia."

"Why not?"

"It's simply too big, Mallory. When an army goes into a country, they have to have supplies. Can you imagine how long a supply line would have to be to reach all the way from Berlin to Moscow? If they tried it, they'd be cut to pieces by partisans just like us. And even if they weren't, the winter would kill them." He puffed on his pipe and shook his head thoughtfully. "Napoleon defeated every nation he ever faced until he tackled Russia, and it was the Russian winter that defeated him. The same thing would happen to Hitler. I wish he *would* attack the Russians! That would take the pressure off the rest of the world."

The two sat there speaking quietly, drinking coffee out of a Thermos jug that Mallory had brought. Finally he turned to her and said, "I'm thinking about what it would be like to hold you close."

Mallory's face flushed. He had said things like this before, and worse, and she had vowed not to let it bother her. James St. Cloud was a worldly man who had no belief whatsoever in God. She liked him very much but knew that nothing could ever come of a serious relationship between them.

"You just stay in your own place, James."

"Have you ever had a man?" he asked casually.

Mallory felt her face burning. "You ask the most awful

questions. It's none of your business."

"Well, I believe every woman needs a man." He reached out and took her hand, and when she tried to pull it away, he held it with a surprisingly strong grasp. He lifted it to his lips despite her efforts and kissed it. "I hate to see a woman wasted."

He grinned at her, knowing that she disliked this part of his personality, but he could not resist the urge to tease her incessantly about her lack of a love life.

It was true enough that Mallory did not like his amorous comments, but she found him to have a warmth beneath his somewhat mean streak. "I'm glad you're here, James," she said, hoping to change the subject. "These people need all the help they can get. Sometimes I wonder if we're doing any good here, but I suppose we are."

"Of course we are."

She hesitated, then said, "I still think of Nils almost every day."

"Your friend who was executed?"

"He went out with a beautiful smile on his face. I hope when it comes my time to die, I can face it as he did."

"I don't think about death that much. I've gotten used to this old planet. I've decided that this old world can be cheerfully enthusiastic or cheerfully cruel. It doesn't seem to make much sense."

"You'll never make sense out of the world if you leave God out of it, James."

"Now, don't start your preaching. I don't think men catch grace from preaching."

"How do you think they get it, then?"

"Well, maybe by reading the Bible for themselves."

Raising an eyebrow, Mallory said, "You read the Bible, James?"

"Why, yes. It's a wonderful book, at least a lot of it."

"I'm surprised you would say that."

"One of my uncles is a rector in the Church of England. I have a great deal of respect for him. He started me reading the Bible."

"What part of it do you like the best?"

"I'm fascinated by the character of Jesus, but His words don't seem to work for today. I think there's a lot more evil in the world now than when He came to save it."

"It's not over yet, though."

"No, it's not over yet." James started to say something else but was interrupted as Bernhard Sorensen came lumbering into the library. "What's the matter with Bernhard, I wonder," he whispered. "He looks scared."

"Someone shot a German soldier," Sorensen panted. "The Germans have taken five hostages."

"They're going to shoot them, I suppose," James observed calmly.

"Yes, and one of them is Willi Shardorst. He's only seventeen years old, and he's not right in the head. He wouldn't harm a fly."

"Surely they wouldn't shoot a person like that!" Mallory protested.

"They'll shoot anybody. In Belgium they used bayonets on babies and held them up to the sky."

A chill ran over Mallory. At the same time a grim determination seized her. "I've got to go talk to the commandant."

"It won't do any good. It will just draw their attention to you."

"I've got to try anyway. It probably won't do any good, but I couldn't live with myself if I did nothing to try to stop this."

★ ★ ★

"Colonel Ritter is not available, and he will not be for a week. He's gone to the north."

"But I must see someone."

"Tell me your business."

Lieutenant Uldrich Stahl had suspicion in his cold blue eyes.

"I want to talk to someone about one of the hostages."

"You may talk to me."

Stahl listened to Mallory, then shook his head. "We make no exceptions. That is my final answer. You may go."

Mallory knew it was hopeless. As she left his office, a new wave of grim determination swept over her. She approached the sergeant who kept watch at the door of the headquarters. "Sergeant, is there a senior officer here? Someone higher in rank than Lieutenant Stahl?"

"Ja, Colonel Ritter's new assistant, Major Grüber. He's in that office over there."

"Thank you."

Avoiding Stahl's office, Mallory made her way through the crowded area until she came to the door the sergeant had indicated. There was no name on it, but she knocked anyway. A voice spoke up, *"Kommen Sie herein."* She opened the door and saw a tall man dressed in the uniform of a major standing by the window. He was holding a book in his hand, and he lowered it, looking at her with surprise. He spoke to her in Norwegian. "What is it you want?"

"I . . . I need to talk to you, Major."

"Come in and close the door. What is your name?"

As Mallory took her seat and gave her name, she had an opportunity to see the book, which the man laid down. She was surprised to see that it was a book of English poetry called *The Poetry of George Herbert*. Herbert was a favorite Christian poet of hers, and she was shocked to find a German officer reading it. "Major, there is going to be an execution. One of the people captured is a boy named Willi Shardorst. . . ." She spoke passionately about the wrongness of killing such an innocent and ended by saying, "Surely you wouldn't make war on such people as this poor boy. What harm can he do you?"

As she spoke, she studied Major Grüber carefully. He was a fine-looking man, extremely tall, at least two or three inches over six feet, and compactly built. He looked like an athlete, and his movements were smooth and easy. She expected him to order her out of his office, but he said, "I'll go see this man. You come with me."

Strolling out of the office, he opened the door for her and accompanied her outside the building. "I am new here, but I understand that the prisoners are kept in the local jail."

As they moved forward, he turned to glance at her. "You're not Norwegian, are you?"

"No, I'm not, Major. I'm from Africa, but my family is American."

"And what are you doing here?"

"I am a missionary to the Lapps."

"An interesting people. You have been with them long?"

"I've spent two winters with them. My work here is just beginning."

The two entered the prison, and the corporal in charge brought Willi Shardorst in. "My name is Major Derek Grüber. What is your name?"

"Willi."

"Tell me about yourself, Willi."

"I'm Willi."

The boy was not able to communicate more than this. The major tried asking some other questions, but Willi just smiled at him. The major had the corporal return the boy to his cell.

"You can see he's retarded," Mallory said.

"Yes, he's mentally defective. I will have him released."

"Thank you, Major," she said breathlessly. "I'm surprised."

"You probably think we Germans are monsters." He saw her searching for a proper reply and said, "Don't try to answer that. Just let me know if I can be of any help to you."

Mallory watched him go, wishing she had said more. She started to go home and then straightened up and went back to his office. He was surprised to see her again, but she said immediately, "I feel that my thanks were not what they should have been. I am very truly grateful to you, Major Grüber."

He looked surprised. "This wasn't necessary."

Mallory found herself speechless, then saw that he was holding the book of poems by Herbert again. "I see you are reading one of my favorite poets."

"You like George Herbert?"

"Yes. He was a man of a lovely spirit."

"I like English poetry and am especially interested in the metrics of his poetry."

"He's very original, isn't he?"

"Yes. I try to write a little myself, and sometimes I use him for a model."

He invited her to sit down, and for the next twenty minutes they talked about the poetry of George Herbert. Finally he leaned forward and said, "I'd like to meet some of your Lapps. Maybe I'll write a poem about them."

"They are lovely people once you get to know them."

"When will you be going back to them?"

"I'll probably be joining them again late in the fall."

"Keep me posted. I'd like to know how the work goes."

When Mallory rose, he came over to her, still holding the book in his left hand. Impulsively she put out her hand, and when his hand closed about hers, she noticed how large and strong it was. Also, she had to look up at him, which was unusual for a woman of her height. "This whole situation is difficult, but you've made it somewhat easier."

"Try not to hate us too much, Miss Winslow."

★   ★   ★

Eva listened as Mallory described her visit with Major Grüber. "He was so different from any German I've ever met."

Eva said slowly, "You got along well with him?"

"Yes, I couldn't believe it. And he let Willi go."

"Ritter never would have done that—or Stahl."

"No, I think not. But this man was different. He was reading a book of English poems by a Christian writer, George Herbert."

Eva cocked her head to the side. "We can use this, Mallory."

"Use it? Use it how?"

"I want you to see if you can become close friends with him. He's left the door open. I can tell that."

"I'm not a spy!" Mallory said sharply.

Eva Klovstad was thinking bitterly of her countrymen who would be executed. In a harsh tone, she said, "We are whatever we have to be, Mallory!"

CHAPTER FIFTEEN

A STRANGE SORT OF NAZI

★ ★ ★

Hearing a honking sound overhead, Mallory looked up and was pleased to see a V-shaped flight of geese high in the sky. She had been interested in geese ever since she had first learned that they mated for life. She had read an article about them that described their undying fidelity. When one of a pair died, the remaining goose would grieve and mourn much like a human being, usually refusing to take another mate.

That thought had pleased her, and she watched the formation cross the sky like a miniature flotilla, finally disappearing into the east. A large pothole caught her almost unaware, and she grunted as the front wheel of her bicycle struck it. With a wild gesture, she grabbed at the large leather case in front of her and managed to keep it from falling. She glanced back at the saddlebags that straddled the rear wheel and was relieved to see that she had lost none of her equipment. Doubling her effort, she raced along the narrow road that wound between fields that were now covered with stalks like dry, brown skeletons, and twice she crossed narrow arching bridges, noting that a thin crust of ice was glittering on the surface of the water. The September air was sharp and would be bitter by the time the sun went down, but Mallory was starting to become accustomed to the biting cold of the north country. She thought for a moment of the blazing sun over the veldt of Africa and of her parents and of Ubo, the Masai whom she had missed greatly since leaving that far continent.

Traffic was sparse along the road, but suddenly she heard an engine behind her. Glancing back, she saw a truck coming, and her heart gave a lurch as she recognized the German vehicle. Quickly she moved off the road, hoping she would be ignored. Her hope was denied, however, for the truck rumbled to a stop, and a corporal got out and strode over to her.

"Let me see your papers," he said in heavily accented Norwegian.

"Yes, Corporal." Mallory fumbled in her coat pocket for the papers, which she always carried in a sturdy envelope. She handed it to the corporal, who carelessly opened it, examined the papers, and then put his cold eyes on her. "What is in your basket? What are you carrying here?"

"This is a portable phonograph, Corporal, and these are some things I'm taking to my friends in the country."

"Who are your friends?" he demanded. He picked up the phonograph, opened the top, then slammed the lid shut and jammed it back into the basket.

While she explained that she was going to the Sorensens', he rummaged through the items in the back, picking up a brightly colored birdhouse. "What is this?"

"Just a birdhouse. I made it and am taking it to the country."

The corporal grunted and picked up a can. "And this? What is it?"

"It's a can of varnish they asked me to bring."

Mallory's heart was beating like a trip-hammer, for she knew she stood on the brink of discovery. She wished fervently she had waited until after dark to go to the Sorensens', but it was too late now. Finally the corporal tossed the items onto the ground and laughed when she stooped to pick them up. He muttered something in German, which Mallory took to be a rude remark, then turned and got back into the truck.

As the military vehicle roared off, Mallory found that her hands were trembling. "Here," she told herself sternly, "you can't let a thing like that disturb you." She looked up to the sky and forced a smile. "Thank you, dear Lord, for keeping me safe." She waited for a moment until her fear passed, then resumed her journey.

Fifteen minutes later she pulled into the farm, and Einer Sorensen, her round face flushed, met her as she dismounted in front of the house. Einer was wearing a gray wool dress with a scarlet wool kerchief tied under her chin.

"What are you doing here this time of the day?"

"I need to see James."

"He's fishing down at the stream. Do you want to come in and get warm?"

"No. I need to see him, but I'll come back and maybe get some coffee before I go back to town."

"We have some fish soup. It will put meat on your bones."

Mallory smiled but shook her head. "I'm not sure I need meat on my bones, but the soup sounds good." Turning her bicycle around, she rode across the field until she came to a line of trees. She spotted a bright flash of color and moved along the small stream until she found James, who had stood up and was watching her approach. "Catch any fish?" she called out.

"No, not yet." He came toward her and held out his hands, and when she took them, he squeezed them and said, "It's good to see you again. It gets lonesome as the devil out here." He shook his head, and a mournful expression crossed his face. "I'm just not cut out to be a farmer."

"Here. I've got some things to show you. You want to go to the house?"

"In a minute. What do you have?"

"I got the radios you wanted for your connections. Let

me show you." Putting the kickstand down, Mallory fished the varnish can out of the back. "How about this?"

"What—varnish?"

"Watch." Mallory released a catch, and the body of the can lifted. Underneath was a radio that fit perfectly inside. "This is just a receiver, but I don't think they'd ever find it."

"You're clever," James said, smiling. He watched as she replaced the can and then picked up a birdhouse painted red and white with blue trim. "Is this a radio too?"

"Yes. I don't think the Germans would ever expect such a thing." She opened the bottom, and they examined the primitive receiver she had built inside. "And I'm really proud of this one," she said, handing him what appeared to be a box of matches. She opened it and showed it to him. "This doesn't have much of a range, but you can pick up things that are very close."

"Fascinating! What's in the large case?"

"Why, it's a portable phonograph." She put it on the ground and took a record out of the saddlebag. He squatted beside her as she put the record on the phonograph and turned the crank. She put the needle on the record and smiled as the strains of a jazz band broke the stillness of the air. "I hope you like jazz," she said with a laugh.

"Very much. Did you bring some more records? I suppose this is to entertain me."

"No. Look at this." Mallory removed the turntable and opened what appeared to be the foundation of it. Underneath was a mass of wires, and in a small, perfectly constructed place, a pair of earphones. "This is my masterpiece," she said proudly. "It's a powerful transceiver called a Type 3 Mark II. It'll carry a signal more than six hundred miles."

The two examined the radio, and Mallory's face flushed as James commended her warmly. "You're a genius! Smart as well as beautiful. One woman shouldn't have all of those good qualities."

"Well, I've enjoyed tinkering with equipment like this

for a long time." She started packing everything back onto her bike. "Let's go back to the house."

James reeled in his fishing line, and they made their way back toward the house. "It's a good thing you weren't stopped with all this gear," he said when they were half-way there.

"Well, as a matter of fact, I was."

"They didn't examine any of this?" he asked, wide-eyed.

"Actually, a corporal picked up every piece. Thank God he didn't look inside any of it!"

"This is too dangerous. You shouldn't be risking your life carrying stuff like this around."

"It's what I can do to help. I want to help in the resistance. There's so little that most of us can do really."

The resistance, at first, had been merely a matter of symbols. Norwegians took small stones and put anti-Nazi signs alongside the road or wrote on walls. During the warm summer months, Mallory had seen two Norwegian women sunbathing with a message written on their backs in lipstick—*Down with the Nazis*—along with the initials of Haakon VII, the king of Norway. Mallory had no idea if the Germans had seen the sight and worried for the women if a soldier saw them.

Now, the resistance fighters had determined to sabotage Nazi efforts at every opportunity, and it had become well known that every time a German was killed by a partisan, there would be hostages shot immediately in retaliation.

When James and Mallory reached the house, they quickly hid the radios, which would be passed on to others. Afterward they sat down to some of Einer Sorensen's delicious fish soup. Mallory enjoyed James's company, and when he pressed her to stay for the rest of the afternoon, she was tempted but had to decline.

"I've got to be getting back. I'm going to meet with Major Grüber."

"I don't think that's a good idea, Mallory."

"It puts me in place to hear what's going on. Just being in headquarters, I hear things that could be helpful. It's what Eva instructed me to do."

"Eva shouldn't be putting you at risk like that."

The Sorensens had been listening to this mild argument, and now Bernhard shook his head. "I've heard talk about you, Mallory."

"What sort of talk?"

"That you're fraternizing with the Germans. You know how bad that can be. People hate those women who go out with German soldiers."

Mallory knew that this was one of the dangers, and she had talked it over with her friend. "Eva thinks it's worth the risk," she said.

"Well, I don't think so," Bernhard insisted. "I'm going to talk to Eva and Lars about it. You're too valuable to risk."

Einer shook her head in concern, her lips firmly compressed. "I hate to see you having anything to do with a German officer. We understand what you're doing, but other people don't."

"It's just a job that has to be done," Mallory said. "It can be explained when the Germans are driven out."

She finished her meal, and when she left, James followed her out and made one more plea. "I wish you'd think about this. There's plenty of work you can do without risking being tied up with that Nazi."

"This is just something I have to do, James. Don't worry about it."

James reached out and put his hand on her cheek. She stood very still, her eyes opening wide. He said quietly, "I don't want anything to happen to you."

She felt the warmth of his hand on her cheek and covered it with her own. "Don't worry," she said. "I'll be very careful."

James watched her as she pedaled away. When he went back inside, he said to Bernhard, "It's a bad idea."

"I think so too, but you know how Eva is. She's hard-headed, and so is Lars."

"I'm going to talk to them all the same."

"Talk all you please. When those two get an idea in their heads, it can't be blasted out with dynamite. Besides, they're right. This is a good way to gather valuable information."

"You know how the Germans are with these easy women," James said. "He'll want to sleep with her."

"You don't have to worry about that," Einer said strongly. "She's not that kind of woman."

"I know that, but I still don't like it!"

★ ★ ★

Mallory walked along self-consciously with Derek, aware that several civilians they had passed had glared at her. She thought of James's concern about her fraternizing with the Nazis, but she still felt this was something she had to do. She stopped suddenly and asked, "Do you know this building?"

"It's a museum, isn't it?"

"Yes. Have you been through it?"

"No, I haven't had time."

"Come along. I want to show you something."

The two entered the museum and stopped before a Viking ship and other ancient Nordic artifacts. "These were probably some of your ancestors, Derek."

"I've always admired the Vikings."

"They were a brutal race, though. Medieval prayers always ended with, 'And God save us from the wrath of the northmen.'"

Derek inspected the magnificent restored ship and shook his head. "I guess people are still praying that prayer, only now they're saying 'Deliver us from the wrath of the Germans.'"

The statement shocked Mallory. It was not something

the average Nazi would say. She turned to look at him and saw the strength of his jaw and the clear light of his blue eyes. She could not think of a proper answer, so she said, "Come along. There's something else I want you to see."

She took him to the back of the museum, where there was an African ethnographic exhibit. "There," she said, pointing to a map of the continent. "That's the country I grew up in—Kenya."

Derek was fascinated by the exhibit. Mallory showed him a life-sized picture of a Masai warrior, complete with his shield and broad-headed spear. "You really knew people like this?"

"One of my best friends is a Masai. His name is Ubo."

"What are they like, the Masai?"

"They are strange. Fierce yet gentle. They are very poetic people too."

"Do you know any of their poems?"

"Oh yes."

"You speak their language?"

"Of course. I learned it when I was a child growing up."

"What does their poetry sound like? And their language? Say one of their poems for me."

"All right. This is a song, but I'll just say the words instead of singing them." She began to speak, and Derek listened carefully, his eyes fixed on her. *"Abuaki emutu iyai endarona nab uaki alapa dleepo. Peemejo Engai nemejo engoop kalo ele lembwAak ebewaki."* She continued on for a moment before stopping.

"It's a strange-sounding language," Derek said. "What does it mean?"

"It means 'I pray to evening, and I pray to dawn, and I pray to the moonrise, so that God and earth may not say, "Who is this who never prays while others are praying?" I, whose misery weighs heavily on my neck with a herd of less than fifty. I want a bull.'"

"That's beautiful, Mallory. I'd like to hear more about the Masai."

"Well, some other time. I'm hungry now."

"Come along. I've found a good place to eat." They left the museum and he took her to a restaurant called Babette's Jestehus, explaining as they were seated, "The food is Scandinavian here but with a French twist."

"I'll let you order, Derek."

Derek ordered garlic-marinated rack of lamb in rosemary sauce, and for her he ordered pan-fried breast of duck with creamed spring cabbage.

At his insistence, Mallory told him about the Masai and her life in Africa as they ate. She took another bite of her creamed cabbage and made an appreciative sound. "What kind of poetry do you like best, Derek?"

"It's hard to say. I enjoy all kinds of poetry—German, French, and English mostly."

"You speak Norwegian and English very well. Do you speak French too?" Mallory wondered.

"I studied Norwegian for about a year before I was stationed here. I lived in Paris long enough to get comfortable with French, and I've been reading and speaking English ever since I can remember. My father insisted on it as part of my education." He cut a bite of lamb. "There's an English poet named Housman that I like a lot. Have you heard of him?"

"Yes, I have. But his poetry is rather sad, I think."

"Well, the world is sad."

"What's your favorite poem by Housman?"

Derek slowly quoted a poem that Mallory knew very well: "With rue my heart is laden for golden friends I had. . . ."

When he finished the first verse, Mallory said, "I know the second verse." She smiled and quoted it softly, especially the parts about broad brooks and sleeping girls.

"I've always loved that poem," he said.

"I think it's beautiful, but it's sad. Housman was that way, wasn't he?"

"I think he was right that the world's a sad place. Everywhere I look I see loss about me."

They talked for some time about the nature of poetry as

they finished eating, and finally he quoted a poem almost spontaneously:

"When you in heaven find peace
And think no more of me who loved your beauty,
I will still keep one thing at least
The memory of one that I loved more than duty.
Not all the dusty years of time
Can erase your soul—that I still call mine."

"Why, that's beautiful, Derek! Who wrote that?"

"Oh, a very mediocre poet."

Derek's expression gave him away. "You wrote it yourself, didn't you?"

"I suppose I did."

"It's a beautiful poem," Mallory said simply. He didn't answer. It almost looked like he had dropped off into a deep reverie. Without thinking, she leaned forward and said quietly, "You must have loved her very much, Derek."

He almost flinched at her shocking words. He had not intended to reveal so much of himself. "It's just a little poem." Quickly he changed the subject. "Now, you said earlier you were heading north later this week to join the Lapps."

"Yes, I'm leaving the day after tomorrow. I finally got enough gas for Lars's truck. Since the summer, the Lapps have been camping close to Narvik, so I want to make a trip up there to take them some books and Bibles, as well as some food that's hard to come by up there."

"I need to make a quick trip up to Trondheim," Derek said. "If you would allow me to accompany you, I'd like to see your Lapps."

Mallory heard the voice of Eva Klovstad urging her on. *"Go on. Take advantage of this."* But along with this, Mallory realized she actually wanted him to accompany her. It surprised her to have to admit that she was enjoying her time with Derek Grüber.

"All right, Derek. I'd love for you to meet my little flock.

But I'd like to leave nice and early so I can get a full day in."

"Where do you stay on your trips up there?"

"I know of several hyttes along the way where we can stay very cheaply. You'll have to share a room with several other men."

"I guess I'm pretty used to that," he said with a teasing smile. "What about the Lapps? Will they mind my coming?"

"Oh no," Mallory said. "They're very hospitable when they know you, and they will welcome any friend of mine." She smiled suddenly, thinking of what this tall, distinguished man was going to think crowding into one of the reindeer-skin tents along with a whole family of smelly Laplanders. But she kept this information to herself. "I think I can promise you an experience you won't soon forget."

"You're laughing at me," he said. "I can always tell when you're doing that."

"How can you tell?"

"That little dimple right here." He touched his finger to her cheek. "It always shows when you're up to some devilment. What are you planning for me?"

"Nothing. I'll plan to see you the day after tomorrow at dawn."

★   ★   ★

Derek found himself enjoying his trip north more than he had thought possible. Ever since he had come to Norway, a heavy curtain of gloom had fallen across his spirit. He still thought constantly of Rachel and slept poorly. He had lost weight, and the work he did had no meaning for him. Meeting Mallory had been a breath of fresh air and a chance to stop brooding over the love he had probably lost forever.

He had quickly made arrangements for his absence at

headquarters, telling Lieutenant Stahl he would be gone several days. Stahl had been relieved that Derek was going to Trondheim. Stahl had been afraid he would have to make the trip himself but preferred to keep an eye on things in Oslo.

Derek and Mallory had loaded Lars's truck with all of the cartons of books and food she wanted to take to the Lapps. He enjoyed the trip immensely, laughing more than he had in years, for he had discovered that Mallory Winslow was a very pleasant companion.

They had brought food along for the road, for there were few eating places on the way. They made their stop in Trondheim so Derek could take care of army business, and they spent the nights in the simple rustic hyttes Mallory was used to staying in on her trips north.

When they got to Narvik, Mallory did not stop to see the Bjellands, for it would only confuse them to see her driving around the country with a German officer. They continued north from Narvik, and in about twenty miles, they found what they were seeking.

Derek stopped the truck in front of an enormous reindeer herd and watched as Mallory got out and ran to meet a family whose tent rose up out of the ground like a mushroom. Derek got out slowly and waited for Mallory to wave him over to meet her friends. He noticed that the Lapps were all very short and most of them were wiry, although some of the men were quite husky.

He first met Jagg and Remu and their younger daughter, Mayda, and their son, Lorge. Orva made her way over when she spotted the truck, and Derek was especially interested in meeting her, for Mallory had told him her story in some detail. As he greeted her, he noticed how intently she studied his uniform, which he had worn to allow them free access around the country, and she met his eyes with a veiled antagonism.

I suppose even these people hate us, Derek thought. But he had no more time to worry about Orva, for Mallory had put her arm around the shoulders of the young man.

"I'm very proud of Lorge," she said. "He's going to be a fine minister and a great preacher."

"I'm glad you're back," Lorge said. "Everyone's been waiting for the Jesus woman to come."

"I'm glad to be back too, but I'm afraid I need to head back to Oslo tomorrow."

A short time later, when they had a few moments alone, Derek asked, "Did he call you the Jesus woman?"

Embarrassed by the title, Mallory shrugged her shoulders and gave him a half smile. "That's what they call me."

By the time Remu had fixed a meal of reindeer steaks, darkness had fallen. Derek sat down crossed-legged in the circle around the fire and listened attentively as Mallory encouraged the others to tell her all that they had been doing. He watched her face by the flickering light of the fire. She had worn reindeer boots made by the Lapps and a reindeer jacket with the fur turned inside. Her eyes danced as she laughed at some of the misadventures that Lorge told her about, and several times she spoke to Orva in an affectionate manner.

The reindeer steak was surprisingly good, somewhat tough with a wild flavor, but Derek was hungry and ate well.

"Tomorrow we will have a service," Lorge said, "and you must preach."

"No, you must preach," Mallory said. "I need to hear a good sermon."

"You can both preach," Orva said. She looked at Derek and said, "Are you a Jesus man?"

Derek was taken aback by the question. He saw that there was a little animosity behind it, and he felt the eyes of everyone as they turned to him. "I'm not a good Christian like Mallory," he finally said. "But I hope to be someday."

"Maybe tomorrow you will be saved," Lorge said. "The Scripture says, 'Believe in the Lord Jesus, and you will be saved.' That's in the book of Acts," he said proudly.

"I brought you as many Bibles as I could lay my hands

on," Mallory said. She had also brought some food to break the monotony of the diet, and for dessert that night they had chocolate pastries Mallory had picked up at a small bakery in Narvik. Soon everyone was savoring the sweet desserts, and Derek laughed at the chocolate on his fingers.

"It's not just your fingers—it's in the corner of your mouth too! Here, wipe it off." Mallory handed him her handkerchief and giggled as he cleaned his lips.

As the evening wore on, many of Mallory's friends stopped by to enjoy some time around the fire with the family. After the last visitor left, Mallory yawned and said, "I'm exhausted."

"You must go to bed," Orva said. "Come, everyone."

Derek was startled. He had given little thought to where he would spend the night, and now he said awkwardly, "I'll sleep in the truck."

"It will be too cold," Jagg said. "You will sleep with my family. Come."

Derek turned to see that Mallory was laughing at him. "You didn't tell me about this!" he said good-naturedly.

"It'll be something for you to put in your memoirs, Derek."

He felt lighthearted. Life had been so hard for so long that he suddenly felt a release in his spirit.

He entered the tent and found that a fire burned inside the tent. Some of the smoke escaped through the hole in the ceiling, but it was still thick inside. There was little ceremony about settling in for the night. "You can sleep here, Derek, next to me," Lorge said.

Derek was startled when he saw the others simply lying on the ground between their blankets. Remu handed him one and he lay down, feeling incredibly awkward. Before he knew what was happening, he found himself wedged between Lorge and Mallory. It gave him an odd feeling of possession somehow as she pressed against him. The others were chattering, and he listened for a time. The smell of unwashed bodies was pungent.

Mallory suddenly reached out and touched his face,

and when he turned quickly to face her, she whispered, "I'm sorry to put you through this. It was mean of me not to tell you."

He was very aware of the pressure of her body against his, but he shook his head, saying, "It's a night I'll never forget."

"Go to sleep now. You've got to listen to lots of preaching tomorrow."

★ ★ ★

Derek slept surprisingly well. He got up at the first stirrings of the camp and joined the family for breakfast as they watched the sun rise. After breakfast he saw that other Lapps were coming, and Mallory said, "The service will start soon, but you don't have to stay if you don't want to."

"I'd like very much to stay," he said and surprisingly found himself eager to observe the kind of service they would have.

He discovered it was quite primitive. A group of about twenty-five people had gathered to listen to the Jesus woman preach. She handed out the gifts she had brought—Bibles for some, small packages of food, and other things the people could use.

The enthusiastic singing impressed Derek. He did not know most of the hymns, but he was surprised when they sang "A Mighty Fortress Is Our God," written by Martin Luther.

"You didn't think we knew any German hymns, did you?" Mallory whispered with a smile. She was sitting beside him as Lorge got up to preach first.

"No, I didn't. It sounded good, though."

Mallory saw that Lorge had developed great confidence. He delivered a simple message on the death of Stephen, whom he called Steben.

"Steben was a great lover of Jesus," Lorge said. "He

was not afraid to die, for he knew he would be with Jesus forever." He went on to trace the story of Stephen, quoting many Scripture verses.

Derek whispered once, "Is he one of your converts?"

"Oh yes, my very first one! Isn't he good?"

Lorge finished his sermon and then said, "Now we will hear from the Jesus woman."

"Well, here goes. Don't be too critical."

"I couldn't be that."

Derek listened with interest as Mallory spoke. She had a Bible in her hands, and the cold had turned her cheeks pink and her lips red. Her dark eyes flashed as she passionately spoke of the love of God. Her message was to love one another as God loves us. After she had spoken for about fifteen minutes, she said, "If any of you here want Jesus to come into your heart, we will pray with you and for you. And if you will open the door, He will come in."

Derek bowed his head, and during the prayer he felt a strange stirring in his heart. He felt a million miles from God, but he had seen the reality of God through this woman who had entered his life so unexpectedly. He had seen it in the love that these simple people showed to her, and even in Orva, who did not bow her head, he noticed, but stared straight at Mallory as she prayed. Even this hard woman had some sort of love in her. Derek felt a great longing for Mallory, but what could he do? He was caught in a world that was completely hateful to her, and it grieved him.

When the service was over, Mallory said to him, "I hope you enjoyed the service."

"Very much."

"I hate to go, but I guess it's time."

"Yes, I suppose so. I can't stay away from my post for too long."

He watched as the congregation crowded around Mallory, and he stood off to one side. He was surprised when Orva came and stood in front of him silently. "It's been good to meet you," Derek said politely.

"You are not good for Mallory." The words were flat, and Derek blinked with surprise. He could not think of an answer, and the woman turned and walked away without another word.

"What was Orva saying to you?" Mallory asked after they had gotten into the truck and started back toward Narvik and their long drive south.

"Oh, something about you."

"She's had a hard life. I'd give anything to see her come to know God. She needs peace in her heart."

"Don't we all."

She looked at him and said, "Yes, we all do."

CHAPTER SIXTEEN

A MAN'S STRENGTH

★ ★ ★

The night had closed in quickly, and Mallory sat half asleep in the seat beside Derek. They had run into bad weather on the last part of their trip south and been unable to travel very far before darkness fell. Now a turbulent keening wind jostled the heavy truck from side to side, and Derek was having trouble keeping it on the road.

Suddenly the engine clanked loudly and began to whir.

"What's wrong with the truck?"

"I don't know," Derek said, "but something is." He steered the truck to the side of the road, where the engine gave a final loud cracking noise and fell silent.

"Just what we needed," he said grimly. "A breakdown in the middle of nowhere at night in this weather!"

"Will it start?"

"I don't think so." Derek tried the starter but got no response. "It's not something I'd be able to fix, especially in this weather. We'll have to wait until a vehicle comes along and we can get a ride to the next village. Maybe there'll be a phone there."

"The temperature is dropping. We'd better bundle up."

They both got out their heavy-duty overcoats and mittens, but with no heater, even the inside of the truck began to grow unbearably cold. Derek stared outside, then turned to look back down the road. "Not a soul. There's not likely to be anyone out on the road either, I'm afraid. Maybe we ought to try to walk to get help."

"No, don't do that," Mallory said quickly. "Do you know where we are?"

"Let me see." Derek grabbed the map that was on the seat beside him and turned the light on overhead. He traced the map with his finger and said, "I think we're somewhere about here. It's at least fifteen miles to the next village."

"You can't walk that tonight. We'll just have to wait and pray that somebody comes by pretty soon."

"I don't know," he said, shaking his head. "Not too many people are going to venture out in a storm unless they have a good reason."

The two fell silent, and for a time the only sound was the whining of the wind and the sleet striking the truck.

"That wind sounds like an angry beast trying to get in," Derek said.

"It does, doesn't it?"

They sat in silence for several more minutes. "Well, we're going to have to use our body heat—just like the Lapps do in their tents." Derek smiled despite the difficult situation.

"I didn't mean to laugh at you the other night," Mallory said.

He moved over and put his arm around her, and she leaned against him. "It didn't hurt me. I'd never seen anything like it, though. I guess all Lapp families are really close. They have to be."

"They're lovely people. They have a keen sense of humor. I think they were enjoying your discomfort. You looked so funny."

"I *felt* ridiculous too," Derek said with a laugh, "but I enjoyed meeting them." He adjusted his arm behind

Mallory. "I think I understand a little better now why you left your home to come to these people. I didn't before."

"Most people don't understand at all, but I think you have to remember that God doesn't have any favorites."

"What an odd thing to say!"

"Well, we all have favorites. We think kings are more important than chimney sweeps, but they're not. Not in God's sight."

"You're a strange woman, Mallory Winslow."

"Not so strange."

Even in their thick winter coats, Derek was very conscious of Mallory's body pressed against his as they huddled together in the cold. "Here," he said. "Let's get the other blanket." He struggled to turn around and pull the extra blanket they had brought and arranged it over them. He carefully tucked it in and then settled back with his arm around her again. "Is that better?"

"Yes. I'll be all right. Don't worry about me."

Derek found himself unable to think of anything except the closeness of this woman. Since he had lost Rachel, he had been a lonely man, and now his attentions were drawn to Mallory almost as if she were an angel sent to save him. He turned, and she caught his gaze and held it, her eyes as direct as his own. He became vividly aware of the good and warm things he felt for her. She had a woman's spirited fire beneath the soft depth of her femininity. He knew she would not reveal these things deliberately and thought that it must be his own desires that made them so plain.

Mallory smiled frankly at him, and it gave him a feeling of pride that she showed no fear of him. As they gazed at each other, he felt a powerful warmth in her presence and saw that she felt the same. He couldn't be sure in the darkness, but it looked like her cheeks were redder than usual. He pulled her close, and as she lifted her face to his, he felt a great rush of desire. The touch of her lips was like a wild sweetness, stirring him deeply with his longing for her. He did not want this moment to end, and he was shocked when she abruptly pushed him away.

"You shouldn't have done that, Derek."

He was flustered at her reaction. Hadn't she wanted him to kiss her? "No . . . no, I know I shouldn't. I'm sorry." He blamed himself for misreading her like that. He watched her as she drew back, leaning against the door of the truck. "Do you hate us so much—the German people?" he asked.

"No, I think your country is wrong, but I don't hate you." Mallory was disturbed by what had just happened and didn't want to talk to him just now. "I think we'd better try to get some sleep." She turned away from him, drew the blanket closely around her, and shut him out. She did not, however, go to sleep, for she was deeply shaken. She knew he had not kissed her against her will. She had been more than willing to receive his kiss and had in fact invited it. But this wasn't love, she insisted. It couldn't be. She didn't want to fall in love with a German officer. Yet what they shared was the beginning of *something*. She simply could not understand what. Desperately wishing she hadn't kissed him, she told herself vehemently, *No matter what I'm feeling, nothing good can come of this!*

★ ★ ★

Derek got out of the truck and reached up to hand Mallory down. She took his hand and stepped out without speaking.

"Thanks for the ride," Derek said to the driver of the truck that had picked them up at dawn. He had hitched up the broken-down vehicle to his own and towed them all the way back to Oslo.

"That's all right, Major," the driver said. "I hope your truck's not broken completely." He got out to unhitch Lars's truck and leave it outside the Karlstads' place.

"It'll be all right, I'm sure. Thank you."

The truck had come along as the storm was winding down, and thankfully the driver had spotted them and stopped. He didn't seem to have much to say, and during the long drive back to Oslo, the three had spoken very little.

Derek watched as the truck pulled away, then turned and said suddenly, "I behaved badly, Mallory."

"We both did."

"No, the fault was mine." He struggled to find the words that would explain himself but could not. Finally he shrugged and said, "I'm a lonely man, Mallory. I hope you can forgive me."

"Of course, Derek."

"May I see you again?"

She hesitated. She had not been able to get her mind off of that moment of intimacy they had shared. She could not understand her response to him. She had been kissed several times before but had never felt as she had at that moment. It had touched a deep well in her that had suddenly overflowed. She realized that she longed for such intimacy as much as anyone else, and that if the conditions had been a little different, she might have surrendered more of herself. The thought troubled her, but knowing that the fault was at least half hers, she forced a smile and said, "Yes, of course you may see me again."

★   ★   ★

Colonel Ludwig Ritter sat bolt upright behind his desk looking up at Derek, who had come to give a report. Ritter had been waiting for an opportunity to dress him down, and now he said, "I'm disappointed in your work, Major."

"What bothers you in particular, Colonel?" Derek asked quietly. He knew he did not have the heart for what Ritter required of him, but he met the man's eyes squarely. Most people collapsed under Ritter's iron scrutiny, but Derek stood upright and challenged his superior officer.

"This resistance. It's getting out of hand, and you're not helping a great deal."

"I'm sorry you think so, sir."

"You've got to crack down. These people don't understand softness. You've got to put the fear of God in them—or at least the fear of Germans."

Derek never dropped his gaze, and finally when Ritter dismissed him curtly, he wheeled and left the room without another word.

Ritter was irritated, his feelings bruised by the dressing down he himself had received from headquarters in Berlin. He was a hard man, demanding instant obedience, and Derek Grüber's insolence angered him. If he had been just another officer, he would have cracked down harder, but Grüber's father was a national hero. One did not strike out at men like that with impunity!

The door opened, and Stahl entered with a sheaf of papers. "These just came in from Berlin."

"What are they?"

"The usual demands. They can't understand how stubborn and bullheaded these Norwegians are."

"I'd like to see Herr Göring in charge here for a week. Then he would see what it's like."

"What about Major Grüber?"

"He's soft, Stahl. Not like his father."

"No, sir, I don't believe he is." He hesitated, then said, "He's been seeing that American woman Winslow. I don't trust her."

"Do you have any hard evidence against her?"

"No, but I've got a man watching her. Sooner or later she'll make a slip." He snorted and shook his head violently. "All this nonsense about preaching to the Lapps! She's a liar, and I'll expose her sooner or later!"

Ritter nodded but had turned his focus to the papers. "Have you read these?"

"Yes, sir."

"We've got to implement this." He tapped the paper on top. "We're ordered to deport all Jews. Ordinarily I'd ask my second-in-command to take care of this, but I don't trust Grüber to do it. You and I will take care of it."

Stahl was pleased, for he disliked Grüber. "I'm glad you trust me, sir, and believe me, it will be a pleasure to get rid of those filthy Jews!"

★　★　★

Mallory carefully packed the battery units into what appeared to be a wicker-covered carboy. It looked, for all practical purposes, like a jug to hold liquid, usually wine, but when the top was removed, an oversized battery was fitted into it. She closed the top carefully, then turned to the large brown leather case. It looked rather like the case a lawyer or an accountant would carry, but she lifted the top and checked the wiring of the large radio concealed within it. Anyone opening the case would know at once it was a radio, but she trusted that no one would think to do that. She turned then to the book, which, according to the cover, was a cookbook. But when she opened it, she gazed with satisfaction at the revolver that lay inside. She had carefully cut out the pages using a razor blade until finally there was a hollow space just large enough to contain the revolver. She picked it up, checked the load, and put it back down again. Her last encounter with the gestapo had made her more careful and apprehensive.

Closing all the cases and the book, she moved outside and saw that it was starting to rain. She had covered the case with the radio and the carboy with an old raincoat and stuffed them all into the wicker carrier she had made for the back of her bike. The rain began coming down harder, and it was starting to freeze. She had not gotten clear of town and was thinking of the project that she and James St. Cloud were working on. The new radio was more powerful than any she had been able to build, and now it was becoming more and more necessary to have more radio contact with Ajax. She heard a vehicle approaching and pulling over to one side, but when it stopped, she saw it was a German army vehicle and she thought at once of the revolver. She stopped and sat on the bicycle as the cold rain sifted down. She debated how she might get out the revolver if necessary.

Then she saw that it was Derek who was driving the vehicle. He came around, wearing a slicker over his uniform, but the rain immediately soaked the black peaked cap he wore. "You're going to freeze to death in this weather, Mallory," he said. "Come on. Where are you going?"

"I'm going out to see my friends, the Sorensens."

"Get in the truck."

"I can't leave my bicycle."

"We can put it in the back. You get in. I'll handle this."

Mallory tried to think of some way to object, for the radio was heavy, but nothing came to her. "All right," she said. "Here, let me take these things out of the carriers." Quickly she picked up the case and the carboy and watched as he lifted the bicycle and placed it in the trunk.

"Do you want to put those things in front so they won't get soaked?"

"Yes, if there's room."

"Plenty of room. Come along."

Mallory quickly opened the door and got in. She placed the case on the seat beside her and the carboy down on the floor.

"What's all that?" Derek asked as he got behind the wheel and slammed the door.

"Just some things I'm taking out to the Sorensens. They don't get into town very often."

"You'll have to tell me how to get there."

Mallory sat tensely in the seat directing Derek, acutely aware of the incriminating radio and the concealed battery. She was planning ahead how she would run inside with them as soon as she got there and was only partially listening to Derek.

"There it is right over there. The stone farmhouse."

"Who are these people?" Derek asked as he turned and headed for the house.

"Just some friends of mine. They've helped me a great deal with my work with the Lapps—raising funds and things like that."

Derek stopped the truck, and Mallory promptly jumped out and grabbed the case and the carboy.

"I'll help you with those things."

"No, if you'll just get the bicycle out, I'll be ready."

"Don't be foolish. That looks heavy."

Mallory turned, but Derek was already beside her, and she could not, without making a scene, help but surrender the case. He picked it up, and his eyes widened. "It's heavy."

"Yes, it is. But I can take it."

"What is it—wine?"

"Oh, just something they asked me to pick up for them," Mallory said evasively. The two walked toward the house, the rain soaking them. Derek's cap was sodden, and the kerchief that Mallory used to protect her hair was also soaking wet. The door opened as they approached, and Einer Sorensen stepped outside. "Why, I didn't expect you, Mallory."

"I thought I told you I'd be here. I brought the things you asked me to get." She handed the carboy to Einer and then said, "This is Major Derek Grüber. Major Grüber, this is Mrs. Sorensen."

"This is rather heavy. Shall I put it inside for you?"

Einer shot a quick glance at Mallory, who nodded imperceptibly, then said, "Come in. You're both soaked."

When they stepped inside, Mallory found Bernhard and James St. Cloud sitting at the dinner table. James had on a black-and-red checkered wool shirt with the tail out. She knew he had a pistol under it and said quickly, "Let me introduce you, Major. This is Mr. Sorensen, and this is Mr. St. Cloud."

"I'm happy to know you."

"Here. Let me take that," Einer said quickly. She had put the carboy over against the wall and now came to take the case.

"I'm afraid it's gotten a little damp. It looks like fine leather. Water sometimes spoils good leather like that."

"I'll take it and dry it off," Einer said, hurrying from the room, much to Mallory's relief.

"I was about to get drowned when Major Grüber saw me on the road and gave me a ride."

Mrs. Sorensen came back and said, "We were just having dinner." She hesitated, then said, "Would you care to join us?"

"Oh, that would be an imposition!" Derek protested.

"Not at all," James said. "There's plenty here." He was wearing a black stocking cap on the back of his head and looked somewhat like a farmer. Mallory had noticed before how smooth his hands were, not the hands of a farmer, and hoped he'd have sense enough to keep them concealed.

"Sit down, Major," Bernhard said.

"Well, if I won't be any trouble."

"No, there's plenty," Einer said. They all sat down, except Einer, who served them all. The meal consisted of *kjottkaker*, Norwegian meat balls, served with creamed cabbage. There was also a nutty Norwegian bread to go with it, and Derek ate more than the others. "This is very tasty, Mrs. Sorensen. You're an excellent cook."

"Thank you. I learned to cook when I was a little girl."

"What do you hear about the war?" James asked. "We get very little news here."

Derek looked up and studied the man, wondering about him. He did not look particularly Norwegian and seemed rather thin to be a farmhand. "About as usual," Derek said noncommittally. "You farm this land quite a bit?"

"Lately I have."

"What kind of crops do you find grow best here?"

Mallory was stiff with fear, for she knew James hated farming and cared nothing about crops. She spoke up quickly, "If you want to know about farming, you should ask Bernhard. Everyone says he's the best farmer in the country."

Derek turned his attention to Bernhard, and the distraction gave a great relief to everyone else.

When the meal was over, Derek thanked the Sorensens and then said to Mallory, "It's still raining hard. Are you going back to town?"

"Well, eventually. It'll probably stop soon."

"I doubt it. Why don't you come with me. It'll be no trouble. I'm going back anyway."

The others watched as the two put on their coats, and as soon as they left, James removed the pistol from where it was stuck in the waistband of his trousers. He walked to the window and looked out, muttering, "I don't like this. That man's no fool."

"What did she bring in the case?" Bernhard asked.

"A radio, I think. She was supposed to be getting a very powerful one, and that's probably the battery for it."

"If he had opened that case, she would have been exposed," Einer said, fear gleaming in her eyes. "She's playing a very dangerous game."

"She is, and I don't like it. It's putting us all in jeopardy." James shook his head and moved out of the room. "I've got to check that radio."

★ ★ ★

As Derek and Mallory pulled out of the drive and headed back toward town, Mallory breathed more easily. "What have you been reading lately?" she asked.

"I'm interested in an American female writer now— Emily Dickinson."

"Yes, I've read some of her things. They call her the 'Nun of Amherst.'"

"Why do they call her that?"

"Because she never married. She lived in the little town of Amherst, Massachusetts, and led a very cloistered life, so they say. Supposedly, she fell in love with a man, but they didn't marry, and she spent her life grieving over him."

"Look. I brought the book with me. Open it where I've got the bookmark and read the poem there."

Mallory picked up the book that was on the seat and opened it to the marked page, then read slowly out loud,

"My life closed twice before its close;
It yet remains to see
If immortality unveil
A third even to me.

"So huge, so hopeless to conceive
As these that twice befell.
Parting is all we know of heaven,
And all we need of hell."

She shook her head. "What a sad poem."

"Yes, it is." He quoted the first line. "'My life closed twice before its close.'"

"I think that might have been the death of her father and the loss of the man she loved."

"Those last two lines are powerful. 'Parting is all we know of heaven and all we need of hell.' I know what *that's* like."

"What is it, Derek? I know you suffered a tragedy."

"I guess I'm like Emily Dickinson. I've had two losses." He did not speak for a while. He peered out into the rain that slanted down across the road. "I suffered a great loss when my mother died."

"You were very close to her, weren't you?"

"Yes. I think I might have been different if she had lived, but she died when I was very young."

"Sometimes it helps to talk about these things."

Derek turned and said simply, "I've had no one to talk to, Mallory."

"Not your father?"

"Especially not him. He was a great soldier, but we were not close."

"What does this poem mean to you?"

"The first time I read it, those last two lines went through me like a knife. 'Parting is all we know of heaven and all we need of hell.' It reminds me of the line from *Romeo and Juliet*, 'Parting is such sweet sorrow.'"

"That's true, isn't it? Parting *is* a sweet sorrow."

"Sometimes when I read the Bible, I find certain verses jumping out at me like that," he said. "Does that surprise you?"

"It does rather."

"Well, I read a lot of it and it means nothing. And then suddenly I'll read a verse and it's like a . . . it's like a bayonet driven through my heart."

This was a side of Derek Grüber that interested Mallory intensely. "I know a little something about that. I think it's the Holy Spirit that quickens those little verses." She turned in her seat a little. "What was your mother like?"

Derek began to speak about his mother as he pulled up in front of the farmhouse where Mallory lived with the Klovstads. The engine was running, but his voice had grown soft, and she could see the pain he felt in his expression.

"I loved my mother very much," he said simply.

"What about your other loss?"

"I . . . I've never talked about her to anyone." The rain made a symphony on the hood of the truck as it came down in long, slanting lines. Everything outside was gray, but inside, the heater had warmed the truck, and Derek sat quite still for a time.

Finally he said in a spare tone, "Her name was Rachel."

"I've always loved that name."

"She was beautiful—and a Jew. . . ."

Mallory listened as Derek spoke. His voice became thicker, and he had more and more trouble speaking. More than once he had to stop to get control of himself, and after he told her how they had parted for the last time, he gave a sudden helpless cry and leaned forward, resting his forehead on his hands where they gripped the steering wheel. "And I lost her, Mallory! It was my fault!"

Mallory was shocked at the intensity of his emotion. His shoulders were shaking as he sobbed. Her heart went out to him in a way that it had rarely gone out to anyone. She reached out without thinking and pulled him toward her. Even in the darkness, she saw the tears streaming down his face. His features were contorted as he struggled to control himself.

"Maybe I can help," she whispered. She pulled his head down, and he buried his face against her shoulder and collapsed, shaking with sobs he could not control. She held him tightly, stroking his back and patting him as if he were a child. A torrent swept him, and she knew this was probably the first time this strong man had ever given way like this. She made no attempt to get him to stop but quietly soothed him. She put her hand on the back of his head and held him tightly.

Finally the torrent ceased and Derek stiffened. He straightened up and put the heels of his hands over his eyes. Clearing his throat, he finally said, "I . . . I haven't cried since my mother died."

"We all need to cry, even strong men. My father's the strongest man I've ever known, but I've seen him weep."

Derek withdrew a handkerchief from his pocket, mopped his face, and cleared his throat. "You're a loving woman, Mallory. You have love even for an enemy."

Mallory reached out and touched his cheek. "I don't think of you as my enemy," she said quietly. She opened the door and got out and then waited until he got out and lifted the bicycle to the ground. "I'm sorry about your losses, Derek."

He stood there in the falling rain as she turned and made her way to the house. Finally he got in the truck and drove away. His face was still contorted, and he could not believe that he had broken down. "I've never wept like that—not before anyone!" Still, he knew the weeping had been a catharsis, and he felt that at least some of his burden was lifted.

★ ★ ★

Mallory's mind was occupied with the scene that had just happened, so she was startled when she stepped inside and saw Eva standing squarely in the hallway with a gun in her right hand. Her glance shifted into the room on Eva's right, where she could see two people, a man and a woman, both appearing to be in their late twenties. She stepped forward and saw that they had two small girls, who looked to be about ages three and four or five.

"Ritter's rounding up all the Jews, Mallory. They're going to be deported." Eva's face was fixed with grim determination. "This is Abraham and Leah Goldstein, and these are their children, Thora and Abigail. We've got to keep them here until we can get them to Sweden."

"Of course." Mallory smiled at the family. "We'll make a place for you. I'm sure it will be all right."

"The attic will have to do. It's too small to stay in there all the time, but it'll give them someplace to go when there's trouble," Eva said.

Mallory and Eva worked together to clean up the attic and put together some makeshift beds. When they had gotten the children settled and the Goldsteins were in bed, she and Eva collapsed in front of the fire, and Eva's shoulders sagged. "It's going to be hard. I don't know if we can do it, Mallory. The Germans are going to be searching every house."

"We can do it."

"What were you doing coming home with that Nazi? You're not still seeing him, are you?"

"He picked me up when I was riding my bike to the Sorensens', and he insisted on bringing me back. There was nothing I could do about it."

"I wish he were dead like all the rest of them."

Mallory shook her head vigorously. "He's . . . he's not a bad man."

"Not a bad man! What are you talking about? He's a Nazi."

"There's good in him. I can see it and I can feel it, Eva."

She snorted. "They say Mussolini made the trains run on time, but he's a butcher. Hitler is fond of dogs, so they say, but he's still a killer."

"Derek is different."

Eva straightened up and turned her eyes fully on her friend. "I can't believe it!"

"Believe what?"

"You're falling in love with that man." She saw the truth in Mallory's eyes and reached out and grabbed her shoulders. "You're falling in love with a Nazi! Wake up! He's like all the rest of them."

Mallory tore herself free from Eva's grasp. "No he's not! He's not!" She fled to her room, and as soon as the door was closed, she ran to her bed and fell across it, burying her face in the covers. She lay there for a long time thinking of how Derek had clung to her, and then she found herself beginning to weep in her confusion.

CHAPTER SEVENTEEN

MEETING AT NIGHT

★ ★ ★

From July to October 1940, the Battle of Britain raged over the skies of England. The Royal Air Force fought valiantly and prevented Adolf Hitler from taking England, as he had taken so many other countries. Day by day, at all hours, Mallory monitored the radio, passing the news along to the others of the valiant stand of the RAF against the Luftwaffe.

Hitler had been confident he could conquer England. The problem was that the German navy was not equipped for the feat. There were no landing craft, and the sea was rough. The British Royal Navy was the strongest in the world, and the only way an invasion was feasible was for the Luftwaffe to control the skies so the Germans could send barges towed by ships across the English Channel.

Hermann Göring had assured the führer that there would be no problems, but indeed there were. Days passed, and the thin ranks of RAF pilots fought off the swarms of German fighters and bombers that attempted to wipe them out. Göring targeted the airfields, trying to destroy planes on the ground. He sent fighters to shoot them out of the air, but he did not succeed.

Along with the rest of the world, Mallory listened and prayed that the RAF could fend off the onslaught. Day by day she tallied the totals of enemy planes shot down, as well as the British fighters lost, and somehow England held on. Prime Minister Churchill had risen to the occasion and become the symbol of freedom for the English-speaking peoples of the world. He went on the radio time and time again, his strong voice urging the people of England on to new efforts. They withstood the bombings even when the population of London was forced to go into the subways as their homes were destroyed.

Eva had put a stop to Mallory's continuing to see Derek, and sadly Mallory had had to tell him it would be best if they stopped seeing each other. She missed him terribly, but she kept her mind occupied not only with her radio duties, but also with taking care of the Goldsteins. It had become the fixed purpose of her life to protect them, and she guarded them almost as fiercely as did Lars and Eva. She became very attached to the girls, entertaining them and finding she had a gift for taking care of children.

One of the things she did was to read the girls stories from the Old Testament. She was careful always to use the Old Testament rather than the New.

Abraham Goldstein observed all this. He was not yet thirty-five, and his wife Leah was five years younger. The scholarly man rarely spoke, but he loved to listen.

One day after Mallory had read the story of David and Goliath as dramatically as she could and kept the girls enthralled, Goldstein did speak to her. When the girls had left the room, he came to stand beside her where she was gathering up the books the girls had used to draw pictures on and said, "Leah and I appreciate the time you take with our daughters."

"They're beautiful girls. I know you're proud of them."

Goldstein hesitated, then went on, "I've been waiting for you to tell our girls stories about Jesus. I know you are a Christian missionary."

Mallory looked up quickly. She wanted to be absolutely honest with this man. "I've wanted to, but it wouldn't be right. It would be taking advantage."

"I appreciate that." He sat down, and for a while the two talked about the girls, and then Goldstein shook his head slightly as if puzzled. "I can't reconcile the love that I see in people like you and so many of the Norwegians and the hatred I see in some others. So many of you are risking your lives, but there are others who are killing our people by the thousands, and yet they call themselves Christians."

Carefully Mallory said, "Not everyone who calls himself a Christian is actually a follower of Jesus."

Goldstein stared at her. "Tell me how you feel about Jesus."

She was uneasy about coming on too strong about her faith in Christ, for this man was a devout Jew, but she knew the time had come for her to share her faith with him. She told him how she had accepted Jesus in Africa when she was very young and how she had learned to walk in His commandments. "One of the things that drew me to Jesus was a passage out of the Old Testament."

Goldstein immediately grew interested. "And what was that, Miss Winslow?"

"It's in Isaiah fifty-three, beginning at the third verse." She began to quote slowly, and her eyes were warm as she did:

"He was despised and rejected by men, a man of sorrows, and familiar with suffering. Like one from whom men hide their faces he was despised, and we esteemed him not.

"Surely he took up our infirmities and carried our sorrows, yet we considered him stricken by God, smitten by him, and afflicted.

"But he was pierced for our transgressions, he was crushed for our iniquities; the punishment that brought us peace was upon him, and by his wounds we are healed."

By the time she finished, there were tears in her eyes. "I can't help weeping every time I read those words of how Jesus suffered for my sins."

"You really believe that the death of one man two thousand years ago has something to do with your soul?"

"Oh yes! Before Jesus came into my heart, I was troubled and had no peace, even though I was very young. Since that time, I've seen so many others find that same peace. What do you make of that Scripture, Abraham?"

"I do not know. The Old Testament seems to present two Messiahs. Indeed, some scholars think there will *be* two—one a suffering servant as you have just read, but the other a victorious leader who will give Israel a place in the nations of the world."

"But it's the same Messiah," Mallory said. "I think the book of Isaiah speaks of two comings of the Messiah—one to suffer for the sins of the world and the other when He returns to set all wrongs right. He will bring justice to the world in a way man could never do."

The two spoke for almost an hour, and Goldstein finally shook his head. "I honor your love for my people, and I think you indeed love all people. I've been touched as you have spoken of your work with the Lapps."

"Let me read you one verse out of the New Testament," she said. "It's only one verse, but it has meant a great deal to me."

"I would be pleased to hear it."

"It was written by a man called John."

"John the Baptist? I've heard of him."

"No, there were two men named John. One of them wrote what we call the Gospel of John, and I'd like to read you this one verse out of that Gospel, which means 'good news.' It's found in the first chapter, verse twenty-nine. John the Baptist had been baptizing," she explained, "and the Scripture says, 'The next day John saw Jesus coming toward him and said, "Look, the Lamb of God, who takes away the sin of the world!"'"

"What a strange thing to say! Whatever does it mean?"

"You could teach me a great deal about the sacrifice of lambs, Mr. Goldstein, for the Old Testament is full of them."

"Indeed it is. From the Passover and even before, the Jewish people often sacrificed lambs."

"Do you believe that killing a lamb would wash away anyone's sins?"

"Why, no. It was merely a symbolic act."

"I agree with you exactly. John the Baptist knew that very well, and I think he was saying in effect, you have been sacrificing animals for years. Thousands and thousands of lambs have died, but none of them ever saved anyone. Not one sin was ever wiped away by their blood, but now the real Lamb has come, the one God has chosen. It was He that all the lambs slain on Jewish altars pointed toward. That is why it says back in Isaiah fifty-three, 'Yet it was the Lord's will to crush him and cause him to suffer, and though the Lord makes his life a guilt offering, he will see his offspring and prolong his days, and the will of the Lord will prosper in his hand. After the suffering of his soul, he will see the light of life and be satisfied.'

"That's the way I think of Jesus. God was holy and righteous, and none of us could ever find our way to Him because we're all guilty of sin. But Jesus bore those sins, and when He died on the cross, that was when we saw the real Lamb of God."

Abraham Goldstein suddenly removed his glasses and rubbed his eyes. He was obviously moved. "I must think on this," he whispered. "Thank you for sharing it with me, Mallory."

★ ★ ★

"A plane is coming in with a shipment of arms."

James St. Cloud had been working over the transcription of some signals. "When?" he asked.

"Tonight," Mallory said.

"It will be dangerous. We need more time."

She shook her head. "Ajax says it's already set. They'll be coming in on the field where we got the two agents last month over by the river."

"Well, that's private enough, all right. I don't think anyone would ever think of a plane landing there."

"Listen, James, I have an idea. Why don't we make arrangements for the Goldsteins to fly to England rather than trying to get them to Sweden? They'd be safe there."

"I don't know if that plane could hold that many passengers."

"They're small people. The girls weigh practically nothing."

"It might work," he said. "Let's contact Ajax. We can at least ask."

Ten minutes later the two were sitting in front of the transmitter. "Ajax . . . calling Ajax. This is Byron calling Ajax."

"Ajax . . . this is Ajax. What is your message, Byron?"

"Four units need to be moved. Can you arrange to have them shipped tonight?"

A long pause ensued, and then the British voice said, "Ship the units tonight. When the supplies are unloaded, simply load the units in. Congratulations." Then the voice grew warmer. "Good work, Byron."

"Quick," Mallory said, "we've got to get ready. It's going to take close timing."

"I'm taking Rolf with me," James said. "I don't want anyone else to go."

"I'm going."

"No you're not. It's too dangerous."

"I'm taking the radio. They may need help, and you and Rolf will have all you can do to take care of the supplies. Don't argue with me, James. I'm going."

He smiled despite himself. "I knew we'd have trouble with women once we let them eat with us and taught them how to count money!"

* * *

The arduous rounds of stops around the country that Derek had made had done little to drive his problem from his mind. He had volunteered to make a circuit of all the German headquarters scattered over Norway, thinking that staying busy might give him some peace. He had been wrong, however, for though he worked hard at his task and seemed to be accomplishing something, all he could think of was Mallory Winslow.

Now as he sped along the narrow mountain road, guiding his motorcycle around potholes amid the gathering darkness, he was completely frustrated with himself.

Why can't I forget her? he thought. The October wind was cold, and the Norwegian winter lurked just over the mountaintops, ready to descend and kill every living blade of grass in one lethal moment. Derek's mind was not on the weather, however. He was thinking about how Mallory had embraced him and held him as if he were a child when he had broken down. His mother had been gentle like that, but that had been long years ago. It was the first moment of genuine tenderness he had known from anyone, and it seemed to be burned into his memory. Night after night he would lie awake thinking about it, and he knew he would never forget it as long as he lived.

I should have been ashamed, but I wasn't. I just felt the love flowing out of her, and it seemed to soak into my soul.

He sped on, driving the motorcycle as fast as he could go safely, and finally he realized that the night had indeed fallen. "It'll be two o'clock in the morning, at least, before I get back to Oslo." He found that that didn't matter to him, for his mind was still preoccupied with his grief at not being able to see Mallory anymore.

* * *

"Come along, girls. We're going to take a trip."

Thora and Abigail both looked scared. They had learned to live with fear, but now as Mallory bundled them into warm coats, she kept up a cheerful stream of conversation. "It's going to be fun. You get to go on an airplane. Have you ever been in an airplane before?"

"No," Abigail whimpered. "I'm afraid."

"A big girl like you mustn't be afraid," Mallory said. She hugged the girl and kissed her cheek, trying to sound as confident as she could. "We're going to leave here in a truck with Mr. St. Cloud and Mr. Bjelland, and we're going to go to the mountains. A plane is going to come out of the sky, and you and your mother and father are going to get in it, and they're going to take you to a place where you'll be safe forever."

"Really?" Thora said. "We won't have to hide anymore?"

"No, darling. You won't have to hide anymore. Come along now."

Mallory led the girls out and found that Abraham and Leah had already carried out their meager belongings. "The girls are all ready," she said. "I've told them that they're going to have an airplane ride and at the end of it they'll be safe."

"That's right. Miss Mallory is right," Abraham said cheerfully. He picked up the two girls, holding one in each arm, and then shook his head. "You're getting to be such big girls. I won't be able to do this much longer."

"I guess we're all ready." Rolf appeared out of the darkness, and the Goldsteins noticed that he had a revolver in a holster on his hip.

Then James arrived, also armed with a revolver in a holster and looking tense. "We're all ready. We're taking the strong radio, aren't we, Mallory?"

"Yes. I'll be able to contact the pilot well before he gets overhead. That way I can guide him in."

"Well, let's get on our way," Rolf said. "It will take at least two hours to get there."

The truck was crowded. Rolf drove, and the two women, each holding a girl on their laps, sat in the front seat. James and Abraham sat in the back, bundled up as best they could against the chilly air.

"It's going to be all right. You'll see, girls," Leah said. She reached over and took Mallory's hand. "You've done so much for us, Mallory. Abraham and I will never forget it."

"I'll never forget it either," Thora said.

"Neither will I," Abigail echoed. "Tell us a story while we're going, Miss Mallory."

"All right. I'll tell you the story of King David and how he killed a lion and a bear. . . ."

★ ★ ★

"We ought to be hearing from them soon," James said nervously. He was walking back and forth staring up into the clear night sky. The stars were glittering overhead, and the moon was bright. The pasture that lay beyond the grove of trees where they had parked the truck was level and flooded with the silver moonlight. "I think you can try to contact him now."

"What's his code name?"

"Condor."

Mallory had set up the radio, and now she began transmitting. "This is Byron calling Condor. This is Byron calling Condor. Do you read me?"

For ten minutes Mallory tried fruitlessly and began to get nervous. "He should be close enough by now. What time is it?"

"Almost five minutes after two," Rolf said, holding a flashlight to his watch. "Try again."

"This is Byron calling Condor. This is—"

"This is Condor. I read you, Byron."

"We are waiting. What is your ETA?"

"Fifteen minutes." The pilot's voice crackled, and he

said urgently, "Make the turn-around quick."

"We'll be waiting, Condor."

"Well, everything looks good," Rolf said. "But he's going to need a signal. There are lots of pastures around here. I'll tell you what. Why don't we go down to each end of that pasture, James, and when we hear the engine, we'll turn our flashlights on. You'd better tell him about this, Mallory."

"All right."

The two men waited until finally Rolf said, "Listen. You hear that?"

"I hear it. It's the plane. Let's go," James said. "You'll soon be safe," he said to the Goldsteins, and then the two men left.

"It won't be long now," Mallory assured the family. "You'll be in England and won't have a thing to worry about."

★ ★ ★

The road had gotten rougher, for Derek had taken a shortcut off the main road. He was weary now, and his wrists ached with the strain of keeping the cycle on the road. The night was bright enough that there was no danger of running off, and there was no traffic on this back way.

He suddenly turned his head to one side, for he thought he heard something over the roar of the cycle. He stopped and pulled to one side, put the kickstand down, and killed the engine. He stepped off and stretched his weary legs and flexed his fingers.

"There it is. It's a plane," he muttered. He searched the sky and couldn't see a light, but he heard a plane. "What's a plane doing down here, especially this low?" Suspicion coursed through him, and suddenly the roar of the plane became very clear. Something caught his eyes, and he turned to see two bright pinpoints of light down the side of the mountain in what appeared to be a valley.

"Agents coming in," he muttered. He pulled his Luger from his holster and began running down the mountainside. He half fell, half slid, scraping the skin off his knuckles, but when he reached the bottom, the moonlight was bright enough that he could see that a plane had landed. He wished he had help with him, but he of course had not anticipated this.

"There can't be that many of them," he said grimly. He ran forward and soon he saw the outline of a truck and several figures. When he got closer, he shouted, "All right! Stop where you are!"

One of the figures whirled, and he heard the explosion of a gun. He thought he heard a twig overhead fall from a tree, and he shot back, firing three times. He saw the man go down and then he threw the beam of his flashlight on the group. "Stand where you are or I'll shoot you all!"

Derek knew he was in a bad position. He saw someone bending over the fallen man, and another man with a gun in one hand was staring into his flashlight. "Drop that gun!" Derek ordered. "Throw it on the ground!" He waited until the man obeyed.

Derek moved closer, keeping a wary eye out. At first he thought there were only two men, but then as he got closer, he saw two more figures. He threw the beam of light on them, expecting more men with guns. Instead he saw a couple, a man and a woman, both dressed in dark coats and each of them holding a child.

"What are you doing here?" he asked. They did not answer, but then he noticed the peculiar round hat of the man, and the truth dawned on him. "You're Jewish." The fear in the faces of the four Jews told him all he needed to know. He heard the plane's engine revving up, and then the man who had thrown the gun on the ground said, "I'm sorry it has to end like this, Mallory."

Mallory!

Derek whirled and turned the flashlight and found that it was a woman bent over the wounded man. When she turned to him, he recognized her instantly. *It* is *Mallory!* He did not speak the words aloud, but they echoed in his mind.

Derek Grüber had never been so shocked in his life. Mallory did not rise. She was holding the wounded man in her arms.

Derek walked over stiffly. "Is he dead?"

"No, I'm not dead, you filthy Nazi!"

"Be quiet, Rolf. You're hurt," Mallory said.

"Where are you hit?" Derek asked roughly.

"What difference does it make?"

"He's been shot in the leg, and he's bleeding badly."

Mallory got to her feet. Derek lowered the flashlight and saw that the moonlight coated her face with silver. Her eyes were wide and her lips tremulous. Derek heard the noise of the airplane behind him. "Who are these people?" he asked.

"They're Jewish people, Derek. We're trying to keep them alive."

Derek turned and looked at the four figures. He saw the terrible fear etched on the faces of the couple, and the children had turned and were clinging to their parents, unable to face him. He had seen it all before, and he knew well what would happen to them. He had seen the trains leaving for the concentration camps, and he was not blind to the terrible things that went on there.

"Please, please have mercy on my children!" the woman cried.

Derek saw that the woman's lips were trembling, and in that moment, he realized that she closely resembled Rachel.

Mallory saw Derek hesitate. He was standing with the pistol pointed at the ground, not moving. She wanted to beg for their lives but knew she could not. She held her head high and said nothing.

James also saw that something was happening to the German. He recognized an opportunity to take advantage of the situation, and he crouched and prepared to launch himself. He knew he had little chance of success, but it was better than nothing.

Derek saw the move and turned to face James, holding the man with his glance. Derek looked back at the woman and saw that she was crying, her shoulders heaving.

Suddenly Derek Grüber turned to James and said, "Do you believe in God?"

James hadn't expected anything like this, but he answered honestly. "No, I don't."

"You're a dead man, you know that?"

"Go on. You can kill us, but there'll be others."

Derek walked over and leaned down to pick up James's pistol. "You'd better get these people on that plane," he told James and Mallory. The only sound was that of the engine of the plane, which revved again. "God is with you," Derek said. Then he turned and walked away into the darkness.

James was stunned. He could not believe what had just happened. As soon as Derek disappeared, he said hurriedly, "Let's go. Mallory, get the medical supplies out of the truck and tend to Rolf. We've got to unload the plane and get these people on."

Mallory did as he asked and put a tourniquet on Rolf's leg. He gritted his teeth against the pain, but Mallory held on to him. "You're all right. We'll get that bullet taken out." The men helped her get Rolf into the truck, and then the rest of them climbed in.

"This is one of your miracles," Abraham told Mallory, "and I will never forget it."

The next moments were confusing. The pilot was angry because of the delay, but when he saw the wounded man, he became almost frantic. "Let's get this stuff unloaded!" Leah and Abraham helped unload the supplies into the truck; then Abraham picked up Thora and Leah picked up Abigail. They stopped for a hasty good-bye, and Abraham said, "I will never forget you for this. God's blessing be on you."

The pilot was impatient. When the door was shut he

roared off, and Mallory stood looking up in the sky until the plane disappeared.

"Why did he do it?" James asked Mallory.

When she did not answer, he said slowly, "I think he did it for you, Mallory."

"No, it wasn't for me. It was something he saw in Leah."

"In the Jewish woman?"

"Yes. When he looked at her face, he couldn't do it."

"What was it? What in the world made him do it?"

"I think it was God."

James lifted his eyebrows and looked off in the direction Derek had gone. "Come on. We've got to get Rolf to a doctor."

CHAPTER EIGHTEEN

OUT OF THE PAST

★ ★ ★

As winter fell across the land, Derek came to know the country well. He was driven by a deep-seated and inexplicable unhappiness and volunteered to travel a great deal. He not only came to know the southern part of Norway, where Oslo was located, but traveled along the coast to the north and never ceased to be fascinated by the beautiful fjords. These vertical walls of rock, very steep in places, were impressive, and he became familiar with the small red barns perched on the steep slopes. His vivid imagination took him back in time to where he could almost see the fierce Viking pirates, setting forth from the jagged mountain creeks, called *viks,* to conquer and plunder new lands. More than once the thought crossed his mind, *Once these people went out to conquer others, but now they've been invaded by men far more cruel than any Viking was.*

He learned that the country north of Trondheim was far more wild and desolate. The Arctic Circle cut straight across central Norway, and here began the Land of the Midnight Sun, where for two or three months in the summer the sun never set. The extreme northern section of

Norway made up part of the area called Lapland, which included parts of three other countries: Sweden, Finland, and Russia. Lapland would be totally covered with ice and snow if it were not for the Gulf Stream. This ocean current carried the warm waters from the Gulf of Mexico right up to and across the Atlantic, and as a result the sea never froze. He discovered that Hammerfest, the northernmost town in the world, was often warmer than Oslo due to the Gulf Stream.

Many of the small villages and hamlets were little affected by the war, and Derek found that he was not greeted with the fear and terror he knew in Oslo. He formed the habit of stopping at small, isolated houses and found the people to be warmhearted and hospitable. But he also found out that in spite of its breathtaking beauty, life in Norway was hard, opportunities were few, and the people there were molded by the difficult conditions. The short summers of Norway drew people from cities into the mountains and to the sea, and most town dwellers got away to the secluded fjords and windswept mountains for vacations. During the brief summers, they enjoyed skiing, hiking, and swimming. Almost every man, woman, boy, and girl was good at all of these. Many of them lived in the furnished hyttes during their holidays, located on far-away islands or in remote valleys.

But despite his interest in the country, Derek's spiritual and emotional life became almost as frigid as the wild mountainous regions through which he traveled. He grew more silent and attended to his duties in a perfunctory fashion, but his nights were filled with disturbing dreams, and he slept little. Everywhere he went he took books with him, usually of poetry, and found himself reading from his German Bible more than he ever had in his life. From time to time he would stop and enter a small church. He always felt self-conscious, but for the most part he was ignored. He would listen to the sermon and leave, usually without speaking to a soul, but such visits seemed to make him even more despondent.

One Sunday he arrived at a small village called Karas-jôk in the far northern section of the country. It was a stave church, beautifully constructed of wood. He knew that Christianity had established itself in Norway in about 1030 and that over the next three hundred years, a thousand stave churches were built. He had also learned that only about twenty-five remained, the rest having been destroyed by fire or decay.

The pastor of this church was a tall, broad-shouldered man with blond hair, looking very much, Derek supposed, like one of his Viking forebears. He did not single Derek out, for which Derek was grateful, but he preached a good sermon about the humanity of Jesus of Nazareth. Derek listened intently as the pastor said, "During the history of the Christian church there have been many attempts to disprove that Jesus of Nazareth was divine. He himself distinctly claimed to be the Son of God. On many occasions He said such things as, 'I and the Father are one.'

"Naturally the enemies of the church would attack this doctrine, and theologians have defended it ably. And I say to you this morning that Jesus is the Son of the living God. The book of John tells us that all things are made by Him, and without Him was not anything made that was made. So He is the great Creator. He is also the Sustainer. The book of Colossians tells us that it is Jesus' power that keeps the universe running, and the entire New Testament points to the time when Jesus will come back and receive the living saints, and those who are dead will rise from their graves. So Jesus is the Alpha and the Omega, the first and the last."

The pastor masterfully wove a texture of Scripture around the doctrine of the divinity, but only briefly. "I would have you know this morning," he said, looking squarely at each individual in the sanctuary in turn, "that our Lord Jesus, although He was very God, was also born of the Virgin Mary, a very human woman indeed. The Gospels record that the coming of Jesus was announced by the angel to Mary, and when Mary could not understand how she could have a son, not having known a man, the angel simply told her that the child would be born of the Holy Spirit.

"So Jesus came into the world, and we must never forget that He laid aside His divinity. He did not come in the form that He would later assume, but for thirty-three years He inhabited earth as a man. First as a child, a helpless baby nursing at his mother's breast, as all of us did, then as a young boy, running, I would suppose, and playing in the streets of Nazareth, then as a young man growing up and learning the carpenter's trade. The Bible teaches us that Jesus experienced and overcame every temptation we have, but it was not an easy thing, as some suppose. We must never say that because He was God He never knew temptation."

Derek leaned forward, and for the next thirty minutes listened as the pastor spoke of how Jesus grew hungry, how He grew thirsty, how He grew so weary that He could fall asleep in a small boat in the midst of a raging storm. The pastor also indicated that the temptations that Jesus endured in the wilderness were representative of all those things that torment man.

"I do not pretend to know the nature of all the temptations that our Lord endured, but I have known temptations as a man, and sadly I must confess that I have not always been victorious, but I believe that the Lord Jesus endured every temptation I have ever had and endured them victoriously."

The pastor closed his Bible and stood silently for a moment. "Jesus is the Son of Mary, and He is the Son of the Eternal God. Once when things were going badly, He asked His disciples, 'Will you also go away?' And my answer is the same as Simon Peter's when I sometimes feel doubt or despair, when my heart is heavy and it seems that there is no way out." He smiled. "You didn't think your pastor felt like that? Well, he does. And so does every man and every woman here, I believe. What did Simon Peter answer? He said, 'Lord, to whom shall we go? You have the words of eternal life.'"

Derek felt those words enter his spirit, as Scriptures or certain poems did at times, and he felt that the pastor was directing them at his own heart. When the service was over, he left at once without speaking to anyone, but for the rest of the day and for three days afterward, he relived the words of the pastor's sermon. They seemed to be engraved on his mind, and always like a refrain came the question of Simon Peter, *To whom shall we go?* These words troubled Derek greatly, for he felt his frailty, and the depression and despondency that settled onto him was darker than anything he had ever known.

Three days after the sermon, he arrived at Harstad, a small fishing village not too far from Narvik, and found a mere handful of soldiers controlling the territory. They had commandeered a house, and the sergeant in charge had seen to it that Derek had the best room and the best bed. He inspected the scanty effects of the barracks and spent a brief hour with the sergeant in charge, then went to bed early.

He was too tired to undress, but even so, sleep eluded him that night. He read until his eyes burned, moving restlessly between the Bible and three books of poetry he had brought with him. He finally grew so weary he could barely contain himself, and still, though his body ached with fatigue, he knew he would not be able to sleep.

He took one of the poetry books with him and went to the kitchen and heated some coffee. Taking the cup to the office, he sat down at the desk and opened the book, a small volume of George Herbert's poetry. He was tired of reading and weary of his own company, but the silence of the room seemed to intimidate him. He opened the book at random and read the first poem that his eyes touched. The title of it was simply "Love."

Love bade me welcome, yet my soul drew back,
Guilty of dust and sin.

But quick-ey'd Love, observing me grow slack
From my first entrance in,
Drew nearer to me, sweetly questioning
If I lack'd any thing.

"A guest," I answered, "worthy to be here";
Love said, "You shall be he."
"I, the unkind, ungrateful? Ah, my dear,
I cannot look on Thee."
Love took my hand, and smiling did reply,
"Who made the eyes but I?"

"Truth, Lord; but I have marr'd them; let my shame
Go where it doth deserve."
"And know you not," says Love, "who bore the blame?"
"My dear, then I will serve."
"You must sit down," says Love, "and taste my meat."
So I did sit and eat.

At first Derek felt dull and lethargic, and the words seemed to mean very little. But then as he read it a second time, he found himself becoming more interested, and finally on a third reading he found the poem to be fascinating.

He had a quick ear for good poetry and had no trouble understanding it. The poem was really about a man's attempt to draw nearer to God, and in poetic fashion had set forth the man's argument that he was unfit to come close to God.

"Well, this Englishman knew what it was like to feel like a dirty beggar," he muttered. "He calls himself unkind and ungrateful, and that's exactly the way I feel."

The sound of his own voice was somewhat startling, but he continued to read the lines over, and finally he read the last three lines aloud:

"'My dear, then I will serve.'
"'You must sit down,' says Love, 'and taste my meat.'
So I did sit and eat."

Suddenly tears came to the eyes of the tall, erect soldier who sat beside the feeble lamp.

He felt somehow that he was in a holy place. This crude, plain room seemed filled with the presence of the Lord. It was an experience he had never had before, and he sat gripping the book until his knuckles grew white, and more and more he realized he was not alone. He studied the last three lines where the poet said that God insisted that the poet sit down. That God himself would serve him.

This broke Derek's heart. He had not knelt to pray since he was a boy, but he knew he had to humble himself. Putting the book down, he knelt, placing his elbows on the chair, and began to pray. "Lord, I'd give anything to know you. But I can't find you." He prayed in a hoarse voice, stammering at times and at other times unable to say anything. Then the words began to flow. "What is it, Lord? Are you there? Is it all just fiction? A dream? Please, if you are there—if you are here with me—let me know it!"

And then something happened to Derek—something he knew he would never be able to explain to anyone. He had always felt that words sometimes failed, that an experience could be so extraordinary that words would not capture it. Now as he knelt, he *knew* he was not alone in the room. He saw nothing with his eyes and heard nothing with his ears, yet he was intensely conscious of a presence. The moment seemed eternal, having nothing to do with time, and he cried out, "Lord God, I am so lost! Please—help me! I know that Jesus is your Son, and I ask you to forgive my sins in His name!"

After a long time, a great peace came to him. He was exhausted physically and emotionally, and finally he began to grow sleepy. He left the office and went back to his bed, pulled off his boots, and pulled the covers over himself. He still had the impression that God was very near, and he remembered the words of Jacob from Genesis: "Surely the Lord is in this place, and I was not aware of it."

"But I *know*, God, that you have been in this place—and I know I can never be the same man that I have been!" He spoke these words aloud, then went to sleep praying.

Later in the night he had a vivid dream. He was walking down a road and came to a fork. He looked to his right and saw a smooth road with no dangers. Beautiful trees arched over it. It would be an easy road to take.

Then he looked to his left, and he saw that the road became little more than a footpath, leading to rough and savage country. It passed through a dark forest filled with wild beasts, and the road was broken and led over dangerous passes and through raging streams.

In the dream Derek knew he had to go on, and he told himself, "Only a fool would take the way that leads through such terrible dangers. I will take the easy way."

But then he felt himself halted, and in the dream a voice said to him, "If you take the easy way, my son, you will be forever miserable."

Derek woke up abruptly and sat bolt upright in bed. The dream had been so clear and so real, he knew he would continue thinking about the voice that had spoken. He lay down again, but sleep would not come, and until dawn he thought about the two ways that lay before him, wondering what the dream meant.

★ ★ ★

Derek sat at his desk going over the mountain of papers that had accumulated while he was away on his travels. He was weary, for he had slept very little, and he had lost weight. He had been back on the job in Oslo for a week and had said little to anyone. He had made no attempt to contact Mallory, but he still could not get her out of his thoughts. He thought about his dream every day and night, and it troubled him greatly.

"A woman to see you, sir." Corporal Schultz had knocked and opened the door. "I don't know what she wants. She won't say. She's not from here."

"Let her come in, Corporal."

"Yes, sir."

Derek tossed the papers down and put his pen on top of them. He flexed his fingers, and when the woman came in, he stood to his feet. "Good afternoon," he said. "I'm Major Grüber."

The woman who stood before him was not pretty in any sense. She seemed to be around forty years old and was thin, and her face was full of lines that bespoke a hard life.

She wore a plain dress, and her hands, Derek noticed, were hardened with work. "My name is Marzina Klimek," she said in German.

"Won't you sit down? How may I help you?"

She did not speak but nodded and took her seat. Her gaze was very direct, and Derek was puzzled. "You're not from this country, I take it, Mrs. Klimek?"

"No, I am a Czech, but I was married to a Polish officer."

"You're a visitor here?"

"I came to Norway to see you, Colonel Grüber."

He blinked with surprise. "To see me? What business do you have with me?"

She was studying his face with a clinical interest. Her eyes were intelligent, and she must have been a pretty young woman, but life had been hard on her, Derek saw.

"I knew a very good friend of yours."

He could not imagine whom this Czech woman could have known.

"Her name was Rachel Mindel."

The world seemed to stop for Derek, and he could not speak. All that existed for him at that moment was this poorly dressed, worn woman.

"You knew Rachel?" he whispered.

"Yes. My husband and I were sent to Dachau."

Derek almost flinched at the words. He knew that many Poles had been slaughtered when the Germans had overrun that poor country. Many others had been sent to the concentration camps. He found his mouth dry, and it was difficult to speak. Finally he managed to say, "You . . . you knew Rachel at Dachau?"

"Yes, we were very close. In that place you needed someone to lean on. Those who had nobody did not last long."

Of all things that Derek Grüber did not want to know, it was the details of the horrors of Dachau, yet he found himself saying, "Tell me about her, Mrs. Klimek."

For the next twenty minutes Derek listened as the woman told of the struggle to live in a Nazi concentration camp. She spoke calmly, but the memories that came to her showed in the darkness of her eyes. Derek was sure she left off some of the more horrible parts of that life, but he heard enough that he seemed to shrivel up as he thought of the gentle Rachel going through such things.

"Rachel and I were like sisters, although I was older than she. We shared everything with each other, and one of the things she shared with me was how much she loved you, Major Grüber."

Derek could not say a word. He could only sit there as if hypnotized. "She knew she was going to die, and she gave me this letter and asked me to try to get it to you if I survived."

Derek watched as the woman produced a small envelope from her purse. She extended it to him.

He did not take it but said, "Aren't you afraid of a German officer? A Nazi?"

"No, I'm not afraid. God was with me throughout the years at Dachau. He set me free. But while I was there, I was able to share Christ with Rachel. She accepted Jesus as her Messiah and knew such joy!" She looked straight into Derek's eyes. "Perhaps God got me out of Dachau just for this. I loved Rachel, and this is all I can do for her. Here, take it, Major."

Derek took the letter and noticed that his hand was not steady. He knew the woman saw this also, and he met her eyes and could hardly speak. "You won't believe this, Mrs. Klimek, but I loved Rachel."

"I know. She told me. It was the joy of her life, the love that you and she had." She rose to her feet. "I must go. I pray for you every day, Major Grüber. You may think that impertinent, but I am a Christian, and I believe that God is going to do something with your life."

He could not answer. He looked down at the letter and then lifted his eyes. "I will give you a pass that will get you out of here without any trouble, Mrs. Klimek." He took a sheet of paper, wrote a few lines, signed it, and then stood up and came over to her. He handed her the paper and said, "I thank you for coming."

"Good-bye, Major Grüber." She turned and went to the door, but before she left, she turned back and said, "Sometimes a simple thing will make us take a new way. I hope this letter from our dear Rachel will help you to choose the right path. Good-bye, my friend."

Derek stood there as the door closed, and her words brought back memories of his dream and of the voice. *"If you take the easy way, you will be forever miserable."* For a long time he stood there not moving, and then finally, with unsteady hands, he opened the envelope. It was a few paragraphs on a single sheet of rough paper. The sight of Rachel's handwriting hit him like a blow, and his eyes so burned that he could not see to read for a time. Finally, getting control of himself, he read the letter. He could almost hear her voice. She did not speak of her sufferings at all, and in the last paragraph, she said,

> I have only loved one man, and that is you, my dear Derek. And now I go to meet God, and I treasure the time we had. God bless you, my dear. Serve Jesus and love Him.

Derek turned blindly and made his way back to his desk. He sat down, put his head on his arms, and struggled with the emotions that rushed through him like a mighty waterfall. He could not find the strength to get up for a long time, but when he heard a knock on the door, he quickly sat up and said, "Come."

The door opened, and Corporal Schultz said, "Colonel Ritter wants to see you, sir."

"Very well. Thank you, Corporal." Getting up, Derek took a handkerchief out, cleaned his face, and then set his jaw. He left his office and went at once to meet Ritter. As soon as he entered the colonel's office, he saw that Ritter was triumphant.

"I knew you were wrong about this American woman!"

"Sir?"

"This Mallory Winslow. Look here. She's a Jew."

Derek took the magazine that Ritter thrust under his nose. "There's a story here about Mallory's mother. She was quite a celebrity, it seemed. Escaped from going down on the *Titanic*. But look what it says. Her father was a Spanish Jew. That means that Mallory Winslow is a Jew. Go arrest her. She'll go to Dachau with the rest of the filthy Jews!"

Derek automatically said, "Yes, sir," then turned and left the room. He was unconscious of the laughter and the talking in the outer office, and instead of going to his own office, he walked straight out the front door. He felt like a man who had been badly wounded as he walked mechanically down the street. It was covered with snow, and large flakes were drifting down to add a new layer. He had not worn his hat, and the flakes bit at his flesh with a fiery fervor.

Everything seemed strangely quiet on the streets of Oslo. The snow muffled the sounds of traffic, and there were few pedestrians in this bitter weather.

Derek Grüber suddenly put all the pieces of his life together. He had thought it was all terribly complicated, but now it was simple enough.

I lost Rachel because I was a coward, but now I've got another chance. I told her I would marry her and take her and her parents to safety in Switzerland, but then I had second thoughts and worried about what my father would think. He began to pray, but there was no confusion in his mind now. "God," he said, "I believe this dream is from you, and I believe you sent this woman. I am going to take the hard way, Lord. If it costs my life to save Mallory, then so be it!"

Derek walked the streets for a long time, unaware of

the bitter cold, and finally he found himself standing before the cold, gray sea. Ships were bobbing up in the harbor, but Derek paid them no heed. He was praying in a way that he had never prayed before.

"Lord Jesus, I want you in my life. It doesn't matter what it costs. If I must die, then so be it. But I need you. Like Simon Peter, I have no one else to turn to. I am at the very bottom of my whole life's experience, and I'm asking you to come into my heart and show me the way to go."

The snowflakes, some of them as large as a fingernail, drifted down, adding a layer of glistening snow on the streets of the city. The tall man stood there, his hair turned white by the flakes but not feeling them. His lips moved, and finally he uttered out loud in a voice tinged with triumph, "Thank you, God! I love you with all my heart!"

PART FOUR

November–December 1940

★ ★ ★

CHAPTER NINETEEN

A MATTER OF FAITH

★ ★ ★

Outside, the wind was sweeping around Lars and Eva's house. It seemed to claw at the windows like a beast trying to gain admission. At least so it seemed to Mallory, who was sitting in the living room at a small desk she had drawn up close to the fire. November had brought with it terrible weather, and she thought of the Lapps, concerned about how they were faring. It was a useless worry, of course, for this hardy people had survived hundreds of years of harsh Norwegian winters.

A log settled in the fireplace, making a hissing sound and sending a myriad of sparks flying up the chimney. They swirled as they rose, golden flecks of fire, and the wood popped and crackled vigorously. Mallory had always liked the smell of woodsmoke, and she hypnotically watched the fire, grateful for its radiant heat.

The room was murky, for she had only one small light on the desk, which did little to illuminate most of the room. Again the wind sighed and moaned, and the whole house seemed to shake with the violence of its power.

Mallory rose and went to peer out the window at the

night sky, but she could see nothing, for the storm that had gripped the land for the past two days had shut out the heavens. *The stars are still out there*, she thought, *and in Africa I know they can see them, but here, it's like being buried underground*. She could make out nothing but the swirling of the icy snowflakes, which made a sibilant sound as they brushed the glass, driven by the moaning wind.

No planes can fly in this weather, she thought as she turned and walked back toward her desk beside the fire. She sat down, held her hands out, and luxuriated in the warmth. *I always took warmth for granted in Africa. How many times did I complain about how hot it was? Well, I don't have that problem here.*

The place was quiet, for Lars and Eva had gone on a mission. They were often gone, for it was their strength and determination that kept the resistance in this area tied together. They lived a precarious existence, unsafe and in danger every day. Of course Mallory knew that she was at risk herself, but she had learned to live with the fears that would sometimes rise in her.

A sound caught her attention then, and she turned to see the Klovstads' large gray cat named Michael as he jumped from the table and walked across the floor. He was a huge animal with large golden eyes, rather aristocratic and hard to get to know. Mallory had won him over with frequent offerings of tuna and had discovered that he seemed to like olives. One had fallen to the floor, and he had pounced on it immediately and devoured it. "You want an olive, Michael?"

Michael looked up and said, "*Yow!*" and turned to pad back toward the refrigerator. Laughing at the antics of the huge cat, Mallory went to the refrigerator and fished out three olives out of a can with her fingers. She put one on the floor, and Michael ate it and then meowed again. He repeated this twice more, and then without a meow of gratitude, he turned and walked away, headed for the fire. He curled up, and Mallory made a face at him. "You're welcome," she said. "If there was such a thing as a cat charm school, I'd send you to it!"

Going back to the desk, she sat down and took up the letter she was writing to her parents. She had written them several times, on each occasion finding a way to smuggle the letter back to England, but it was a one-way communication. She had received no mail from her parents for over two months. She suspected that the battle in the Atlantic had something to do with this, for the mails depended upon the shipping lanes, which were dangerous, with German submarines prowling incessantly, looking for their prey.

She had a hard time concentrating on her letter as her thoughts kept turning to Derek. She missed seeing him and kept wondering if they could ever have a relationship. That was hard to imagine as long as the war was on. Derek just didn't seem like a Nazi to her, although Eva kept reminding her that of course he was. But to Mallory, he seemed much too gentle and kind to be a Nazi in his heart.

Even as she thought this, Mallory felt a deep conflict going on inside her heart. There was a gentleness in Derek Grüber she did not see in any of the other Nazis she'd had to deal with. She sensed it and had also seen it in his quick agreement to release the retarded boy. No other Nazi she knew would have done that, but Derek had done it readily. She could not picture his being a part of a wicked system that shot hostages mercilessly. "I mustn't think about him anymore," she told herself and went back to her letter.

> I carry a revolver now, which is something I thought I would never do. Eva insisted on it, and I always keep it concealed. The question that comes to me over and over again is, "What would I do if I had to use it? Could I actually shoot someone—take a human life?" I don't think I could, but it satisfies Eva.

She finished the letter, signed it, and sealed it in an envelope, then stood and stretched. It was getting past eight o'clock, and she was a little concerned about Eva and Lars, but they had told her not to be worried if they did not get home before ten o'clock. She turned abruptly, went to her bedroom, and came out bearing a radio she had put into working order. It had been damaged in transit from the last plane that flew in, and it had been difficult to repair. Now, however, it was working perfectly.

She set it on the table while she put on her heavy coat and pulled a black wool cap down over her ears. Picking up the radio, she opened the door and stepped outside. As always, the biting cold hit her like a fist and she gasped, keeping her mouth closed, for she had learned how cold the air could feel in the lungs. She thought of the Lapps as she made her way back around the house and headed for the barn. She had seen Lapp children playing in weather not much warmer than this with lightweight clothing on. That was their heritage, but she knew she herself could never endure it. The wind pulled at her and was strong enough to actually propel her forward.

She had almost reached the barn when suddenly she heard a voice call her name. She whirled around and saw a tall figure, and for a moment she could not tell who it was in the darkness. Then he came closer, and she said, "Derek!"

"Hello, Mallory."

She stood transfixed. The radio in her hand was enough to send her to a firing squad! She ordinarily was a very quick thinker, but the suddenness of his appearance and the abruptness of his greeting stopped her mental processes. The only thing she could think of was, *I'm caught! I need to do something*.

"Can I help you with that?"

Derek reached forward and took the radio; then she saw his head drop as he stared at it. In that one moment Mallory made a heartrending decision. She reached inside her coat and pulled the thirty-eight from the band of her trousers. He straightened up and his eyes widened.

"I wish you hadn't come here, Derek. You don't give me any choice."

Derek Grüber silently looked not at the gun but into her

eyes. She could not read his face, so intense was the blackness of the night.

"You're going to shoot me?"

Mallory knew she could do no such thing. Still she had to do something! "Go back to the house," she said curtly.

Derek turned and walked alongside the house. Mallory stayed behind him, the gun held tightly in her hand but pointed at the ground. When they reached the front door, she said, "Go on inside." When he entered, she stepped inside after him and shut the door. "Put the radio down on the table, Derek."

He did so and then turned to face her. The snow had dusted across the shoulders of his black overcoat, which was belted with a black leather belt. The peaked officer's cap was also coated with white. He pulled off his hat and laid it down beside the radio. The silence in the room was broken only by the popping of the wood in the fireplace.

"Sit down." He opened his coat, and when he did, she saw his Luger in the black holster. "Take off your coat and put your pistol on the table." She waited until he had done so, still without saying a word. He sat down in the chair and watched her. His face was leaner than it was when she had first met him, and she knew he had lost weight. The clean line of his jaw and the strong lines of his face bespoke the strength that was in him, and he sat there clasping his hands and making no move to say anything.

Mallory had regained her swiftness of thought, but it troubled her that he showed no surprise and certainly not any fear. He was simply watching her, ignoring the gun. "Why did you come here, Derek?"

He did not answer her directly but said, "What about the Jewish family? Did they get away safely?"

The question caught her off guard. She was so startled she could not answer for a moment, but then she nodded and said, "Yes."

"That's good. I'm glad."

"Why did you let them go?" Mallory burst out. She had wondered this ever since that night in the mountains, and now her voice was sharp, yet there was a trace of something else in it. "We expected you to turn us all in. Why did you let us all go?"

"I saw something in the Jewish woman's face, and I couldn't do it, Mallory," he said, his voice full of unconcealed emotion.

"Why not? What did you see?"

"A woman came to my office a few weeks ago. She had known Rachel." He related how the woman had led Rachel to the Lord and how the woman had brought him a letter from Rachel, in which she declared her love for Derek and expressed her faith in Christ. He hesitated, then shook his head. "It did something to me, Mallory. The woman looked a little like Rachel. You know how I felt about her death. You knew that the night I broke down and wept. But then to find out that she loved me in spite of my betrayal and went to her death loving me . . . I . . . I couldn't take it all in. It doesn't seem possible."

"I'm glad she came to know Jesus, Derek. That should be a comfort to you. You can be sure she's in heaven now."

"Maybe it should be a comfort, but it isn't. All I can see is my failure. I'll never be able to think of her without tearing myself apart inside." He dropped his head, and his voice was almost imperceptible. "Some things never die, do they?"

Suddenly Derek looked up and said, "I have to tell you something—but you won't believe it." She stared at him, but before she could speak, he said, "Not long ago I was alone in a room in a little village called Harstad. . . ." His voice was quiet, but his face was different—more peaceful than Mallory had ever seen it.

"I know exactly where that is. It's not far from Narvik."

"Yes that's right." He related how he had asked God to forgive his sins. "It sounds like a story a man would make up to get a woman to put her gun away, doesn't it? But since that moment, I've been different, Mallory. You spoke once of the peace of God, and I had no idea what you meant. But now I do."

Silence filled the room, and then Derek said, "I was tearing myself apart over my guilt over Rachel. I didn't think God could forgive a thing like that—but He has."

Mallory had forgotten the gun now. She still held it loosely, but it was hanging down at her side. "What would you do if you could do it all over again?"

"I'd save her or die trying."

At that moment Michael stretched and looked up at the man sitting in the chair. He did not like strangers, and he walked away to disappear into the darkness of the other room.

Derek suddenly leaned toward her with a look of urgency on his face. "You've got to get away from here, Mallory."

"What are you talking about?"

"Colonel Ritter read a story in a magazine about your mother. I don't know who sent it to him, but it says that she's half Jewish."

"That's right. Her father was Jewish, although her mother wasn't."

Derek's voice was grim. "You must leave right away. Ritter sent me here to arrest you, and you know what that means. It'll be a death sentence. They'll either send you to a concentration camp, where you'll die like Rachel, or they'll hang you here on some other pretense."

Mallory felt a tinge of fear. She did not fear death, but she did fear going through some of the things others had endured at the hands of the Nazis. "How can I believe you, Derek?"

"You don't have any choice, Mallory. If I don't bring you in, they'll send somebody else. You can believe that. But that must not happen." He got to his feet and stepped closer to her. She did not lift the gun. She had forgotten it. "Let me help you get away," he said urgently. "There's little time."

Mallory did not know what to think. The revelation had come so suddenly! She was still thinking when she heard a car engine, and she was spared the necessity of making an instant decision. "That's Lars and Eva."

"What will you tell them?"

"I'll tell them just what you told me." She turned to face him squarely. "They'll have to decide what happens to you."

They heard the footsteps and voices as the two approached, and then the door opened. Shock washed across both of their faces as they saw Derek standing there in his uniform. Instantly Lars reached inside his coat for his revolver, and Eva said, "What are you doing here, Major?"

"I was sent to arrest Mallory," Derek said evenly.

"Well, you're not going to do it!" Lars shot back. His voice grated, and he lifted the pistol and aimed.

"Wait!" Mallory said. "You haven't heard all of it." She looked at Derek and saw no fear at all in his face. "Derek let the Goldsteins and all of us go because of something in his past. He came here to warn me, not to arrest me."

"Did he tell you that?" Eva said, her voice cold and her eyes filled with suspicion.

"Yes. He says that I've got to get away."

"I know you don't believe any of this, but it's true. Colonel Ritter will be expecting Mallory to be under arrest tomorrow morning. When he finds she's not, and I'm missing, he'll know something's wrong."

"He's just trying to talk his way out of this," Lars said.

Eva shook her head. "I'm not sure. Why did he let our people go? I've been thinking about that ever since."

"You have no reason for believing me," Derek told them, "but I'm leaving the army. There's no excuse for what Hitler's doing. I've known it for a long time. A lot of us have, I think. We Germans have a talent for following the wrong leaders for the wrong reasons. And you won't believe this either, but I've given my life to God. I don't know how I can possibly convince you of that. Do what you will with me, but I beg you to get Mallory out of here. And you'll have to leave too. They know she's been living with you, and they won't let you go free."

Mallory suddenly believed that Derek was speaking the truth. She put the pistol back in her belt and said, "We have to trust him."

Derek nodded his head and said, "Thank you, Mallory. I wouldn't have you hurt for anything in the world."

Lars and Eva silently struggled with their options, and finally Eva made up her mind. "I don't know why I should believe anything a Nazi says, but I do somehow." She turned to Mallory. "Can we get a plane in to escape?"

"No. Everything's grounded."

"When I said get Mallory away, I meant *now!*" Derek said. "Ritter has already doubled the guards along the Swedish border and along the coast."

"There's no way out then," Lars said. He too replaced his revolver. "We'll just have to make a run for it."

"I think there's one way that might work," Derek said. "I think if you and Eva can hide out with friends for a couple of weeks, they'll stop looking for you. As for Mallory, I know that the guards are placed thickly along the Swedish border in the south, but in the mountain country in the north they're spread out pretty thin. There just aren't enough men to cover it. I know where they're located, and I think I can thread the needle."

"You mean go north and then turn east and go to Sweden that way?"

"That's the only chance I can see."

"But how will we get there?" Mallory asked.

"We'll take the truck I came in. I'll keep my uniform on. There's no alarm out yet, so if anybody stops us, I can use my rank to get us through. By tomorrow it will be different. I'll have to put on some other clothes."

"I think you could wear mine," Lars said with a nod. "They'll be a little small on you, but it'll be better than that uniform."

"We have to go now. Right away," Derek urged.

"All right. Let's just load everything you can use," Eva said quickly.

The next thirty minutes was taken in loading the truck.

At Derek's suggestion, they took skis in case they would have to go across country. Mallory took a small radio and batteries so that they could trace any calls Ritter would send out, and of course, they took warm clothes and blankets.

Finally they stood outside in the darkness, and Mallory embraced both Eva and Lars. "You've got to get away," she said. "They'll be looking for you."

"Don't worry about us. We have plenty of places to hide," Eva said. She turned to Derek and said, "I never thought I'd trust a Nazi."

Derek shook his head, and the shadow of a smile touched his lips. "You're not trusting one now."

"You'd better get going," Lars said. "Go as far as you can tonight, but if I were you, I wouldn't travel in daytime. It'd be easy for a plane to spot you."

"I think you're right." Derek put out his hand. "Thank you for trusting me," he said simply. The two men shook hands, and then he turned to Eva. "I'll take the best care of her I can."

"See that you do."

The two got in the truck, and as it moved down the street and disappeared into the darkness, Eva turned and put her hand on her husband's arm. "Did we do the right thing, Lars? It's so hard to know."

He put his arm around her, and the two embraced. "I think it is. I think the man is what he says."

"I think he's more than that. I think he's in love with Mallory—and I think she's in love with him too."

"Well, they'll need each other if they make it out of this mess. Come on. We've got to get out of here ourselves!"

CHAPTER TWENTY

"We'll Hang Her in the Square"

★ ★ ★

Leaning forward and narrowing his eyes, Derek peered into the darkness. The snow had stopped for a time, but with no moon and no stars, he could barely see five feet ahead of the truck.

"If I go off the road, we'll be in real trouble," he lamented over the sound of the laboring engine. "And there's not much road to go over."

Even as he spoke, Mallory glanced over to her right, where she saw a sheer wall of rock that seemed to plunge into a bottomless pit. The mountain road Derek had chosen was not one often traveled. She could well believe that and couldn't help but imagine the horrors of falling off such a road. They were headed for the crest of the mountain, and the road was only wide enough for one vehicle. "What happens if we meet somebody coming down?" she asked.

Derek did not take his eyes off the road but laughed softly. "Somebody would have to back up a long way—or else get pushed over the edge."

"How much farther?"

"We ought to get to the top in another fifteen minutes, but the road down is even worse, if I remember correctly." He turned the wheel slightly, and they spun on the packed ice and snow. "I'm surprised we can even get up this incline. One good thing about it, though. There won't be many people out looking for us."

They had been on the road for two long days. The farther north they went, the less daylight they had to worry about, and the longer they spent driving. Now the first hints of daylight were beginning to appear, so they needed to find a safe place to pull off the road so they could get some much-needed rest.

"When do you think they'll discover that you're gone?" Mallory asked.

"By ten o'clock, I suppose. Then they'll send someone to find you. With both of us gone, Ritter or Stahl will put two and two together."

"I hope Eva and Lars got away."

"I'm sure they did. They're pretty shrewd operators."

"What will we do in daylight?"

"I'm hoping we'll get to the farthest mountain before it's too light. Then we can pull off and hide."

"There aren't many trees to hide in."

"No, and we'll leave tracks in the snow. We'll just have to hope for the best, I guess." They were silent for a time, and then he said, "You know, I was just thinking, there aren't many things you can lock up and put away and believe that they'll always be safe."

"That's true, isn't it? Life is pretty uncertain."

"I read a poem once that said, 'Hopes are like children who go out to pick flowers in the field—and never come back.'"

"I don't like that. It's too gloomy. But I guess life is pretty gloomy. All the people I love best have shoved off from my life like lifeboats leaving a ship." He suddenly turned to her and laughed. The pale light that was beginning to light the east illuminated his face. "Sorry. I didn't mean to be so mournful."

"Make up a poem for me, Derek."

"A poem about what?"

"Oh, about how good things come."

"All right," he said. "Let's see . . .

"Your heart counts the good moments like a bank teller.
There's a rustling of paper and the ringing of gold
And then the flesh and blood rejoice
As if a fugitive had come home after long years away."

"How do you just make up things like that?" she asked.

"I don't know how I do it. It's like your working the radio. I've worked at studying poetry until finally I know a bit about how it comes together."

"It's not like a radio. That's technical. There are rules."

"There are rules to poetry too."

"I know. Like making it rhyme."

"For me it's harder to make poems that don't rhyme. Rhyme is easy."

"I suppose anything is easy if you know how to do it. We're getting mighty philosophical, aren't we? But really, writing doesn't come easily to me."

"It's the hard things that make us what we are," Derek said. "Raking leaves is easy, but all you get is leaves. Digging is hard, but you might find diamonds."

Mallory laughed. "You want me to think you're wise, don't you?"

He grinned. "Why don't you tell me a poem? You know lots of poetry."

"All right. How about this one:

"Peanuts!
Two bags for five!
They brush your teeth,
They curl your hair;
They make you feel
Like a millionaire!"

His shoulders shook as he laughed. "Did you write that yourself?"

"No. At soccer games in Kenya, the boys that sold peanuts used to call that out."

They talked for a while, and finally she said, "What's the most poignant poem you know, Derek?"

He thought for a minute and then said, "Probably Byron's 'So We'll Go No More a Roving.'" He quoted all three verses and then said, "But that poem's not altogether sad to me. I love one line in particular: 'The night is made for loving.'"

She did not answer, though his tone invited her to respond. "We must be crazy to be spouting poetry when our lives are in danger."

"I think we live more during times like this. The little time I had in combat was like that. It seemed like every moment lasted a year. The good times go so quickly." He straightened up. "Look, there's an opening there. I believe we can get the truck off the road. I think we'd better do it and wait until dark to go the rest of the way."

He maneuvered the truck through a screen of scrubby trees and onto a flat spot. "I'd better get out and see if I can disguise where we came in. Do you think we could cook something?"

"Better not. I'll tell you what. I'll dig out some of those cans—beans, soup, whatever I can find. If you'll put them on the engine block that'll heat them up."

By the time he had disguised their exit marks, the four cans on the engine block were starting to get warm.

"Watch out. Those cans are hot," he warned when he removed them with his heavy gloves. "What is it?"

"I don't know. I didn't even look. It's edible, though, and I'm starved."

They took their cans of food into the truck and balanced them on the dash. She had rummaged through their groceries and found some bread and two apples as well.

"A feast," he said. "Do you ask blessings over food?"

"Yes, I do."

"Why don't you, then."

There in the cold they bowed their heads and Mallory prayed a simple prayer of thanksgiving for the food, then added, "And keep us safe, O God. We know you can, and we're trusting in you. So we ask you in the name of Jesus to get us safe home—safely across the border."

"Amen," Derek said. He dipped a spoon into the can he held. "Some kind of soup, I think. Not real sure—maybe beet." He chewed thoughtfully for a moment. "I like the way you asked God to get us 'safe home.' Those words have a good sound. If I ever have a house and grounds, I think I'll call it that. Safehome. What did you get in your can?"

"It's some kind of beans. Black beans, I think."

"Ooh, I like those! I'll trade you some of my beet soup for black beans."

"Here. Let's just eat out of all four cans. It'll go better that way. Swap the juices all around."

The two ate heartily, laughing at times as the soup spilled down over their chins. When they were finished, he stashed the cans in a bag so as not to leave any evidence that anyone had been there.

Her stomach full, Mallory sighed contentedly. "I guess I should be sleepy, but I'm not."

"I think we'll probably get sleepy eventually, and cold too."

Mallory looked out the window but could see nothing but the scrub trees. "What will you do when we get out of all this, Derek?"

"It'll be difficult, won't it? I can't go back to what I was, and I don't know where I'm headed. I guess I'll be an orphan of sorts. Too young to die and too old to play."

She laughed. "There's your poetry cropping out of you again."

"Was it? Well, at least it didn't rhyme." He leaned back in the seat and took off his officer's cap. "I think I'd better put on Lars's civilian clothes before we go on. This uniform wouldn't help us much out here."

Mallory nodded but was still preoccupied with her question. "You won't go back to Germany, will you?"

"No, I wouldn't be very welcome there. I'll probably wind up in a POW camp in England."

"No, they wouldn't do that to you!"

"I'm afraid they would. I don't think most people can understand what's happened to me."

He leaned his head back on the seat, staring up at the ceiling. He began to tell her about his youth, speaking slowly as he reviewed his life. "I believed in my father mostly," he told her. "He was all I had left after my mother died. He was a stern taskmaster, and his only thought was the military. I grew up with children of military men, so we were all exposed to the same line of reasoning. All my friends were in the Hitler Youth Movement, so I joined too. There was never any question about it. They were all excited about Hitler's promises."

"Did you believe them, Derek?"

"I did at the time, I suppose, but my father was responsible for that. You wouldn't believe how bad it was in Germany after the last war ended. Everybody was hungry. Money wasn't worth carrying home. When Hitler came along, he promised prosperity, which of course was what the people wanted to hear."

"Didn't you get suspicious when you heard some of the stories about the—"

"About the bad things? Yes. And when I saw some of it in Spain and in other places, I knew that something was terribly wrong, but I was caught up in the machinery."

He talked for a long time, and Mallory sensed that he needed someone to listen. He could not have said these things to anyone at his home, and finally he surprised her by saying, "I'd like to see your home."

"You mean in Africa?"

"Yes. I've read a lot about Africa. Tell me about it." He turned in his seat and smiled. "Did you ever play 'Let's Pretend' when you were a little girl?"

Mallory laughed, making a very attractive picture.

"When I was a little girl! I still do it."

"Good! So do I. Let's pretend we've got our tickets, and we're going to Africa together, and you tell me all about your home."

Mallory began to tell him about the Africa she loved, of the vast stretches of veldt and the unbelievable herds that roamed the continent. She spoke about the time, just before she left, when she and Ubo had seen the lion, and this fascinated him.

"What would have happened if the lion had charged?"

"Ubo would have tried to kill him with his spear. I didn't have any weapon at all."

"That's unbelievable that a man with only a spear would tackle a full-grown lion!"

"You do if you're a Masai warrior, and then you make a headdress out of the lion's mane. This one would have made a beautiful one. It had a black mane."

"I've never seen a black-maned lion. All I've seen are tawny ones in the circus."

"I don't think those circus lions are anything like when they roam free."

She amused him by telling him about the Masai's chief diet staple: milk flavored with the blood from the very animal they milked.

"It sounds bloody awful!" he said with a laugh.

"I suppose it's an acquired taste."

"You mean you've tried it?"

"Oh yes. It would have been impolite to refuse."

"I think I'll stick to beet soup. But when we get to Africa, you'll have to teach me how to hunt."

"I never liked to hunt really. None of my family did. We enjoyed watching the animals but not killing them. Nothing is more impressive than an elephant."

"Could you get close to them?"

"I did once without meaning to."

"How could that be?"

"You wouldn't believe how *silent* those monstrous things are. I had gone out by myself from camp. We knew there were elephants in the area, and I wanted to see them. Dad had forbidden me, of course, but I disobeyed."

"You were a wicked, wicked child."

"I was indeed, and I nearly paid for it. I was creeping along in the thick vegetation just seeing what I could find when I heard the elephants. They were in the river. They love to bathe, you know."

"Do they really?"

"Yes, and the babies play just like puppies—and sometimes the adults do too. It's something to see those huge beasts spraying water at each other and shoving each other."

"Well, what happened?"

"I was watching the elephants through the foliage when suddenly I had a creepy feeling—like something was watching me behind my back. I turned slowly, and I tell you, Derek, I nearly died!"

"What was it?"

"It was a huge bull elephant, and it couldn't have been more than fifteen meters away from me. It had enormous curving tusks, and those little eyes were fastened right on me. It had just sneaked up on me with all of its bulk, and I hadn't heard a sound. I guess I was too busy listening to the others in the river."

"Did you run?"

"No, it would have been useless. They're very fast. I just stood there and prayed, but not out loud. I was too scared for that. And it watched me. I didn't move, and the elephant put its ears out like they do when they're going to charge—huge ears like big fans. It was swaying from side to side, and I thought it was all over for me."

"It obviously wasn't. How did you get away?"

"I think it heard some kind of a distress call from one of the elephants in the river—maybe from its mate or one of the young ones. It tore away and went crashing through the jungle. As for me—" she laughed—"well, I just hate to tell you, but I was so scared I threw up."

"No wonder! I don't think I'd like to go through a thing like that."

"After that, as you can imagine, I paid a little more attention to my surroundings when I was out alone in the wild."

"You certainly had a more interesting childhood than most people."

"I know. I'm grateful that I was raised in Africa rather than in America." She opened her mouth in a huge yawn.

"You'd better try to sleep. We need to drive all night tonight, and it'll be slow going in the dark."

"All right. Here, let's fish some of these blankets out."

The two of them got out the blankets and wrapped themselves up like cocoons. Mallory bunched up another blanket and put it between her head and the window, thinking as she drifted off, *I should be scared to death, but I'm not. . . .*

★ ★ ★

Colonel Ritter looked up from his desk, startled as Stahl burst into his office, his face pale. "What in the world is it, Stahl?"

"It's Grüber!"

"Grüber? What about him?"

"He's gone, Colonel, and so is the woman!"

Ritter jumped to his feet. "What do you mean *gone*? He can't be gone!"

"He is, and a truck is missing. He must have taken the woman and they're making a run for it."

Colonel Ludwig Ritter felt a surge of anger flood his whole body. "I knew that man was no good! You should have found him out before this, Stahl!"

"But, sir—"

"Never mind your excuses! I want them captured. You understand?"

"Yes, sir."

"Double the guards along the border. Be sure you give an exact description."

"Do you want them captured or dead?"

"I want them alive. We'll have a little entertainment for them when we catch them—both of them."

He marched over to the map stiffly, trying to get control of himself. He studied at the map and began to indicate the points at which there were guards stationed. "Double all the guards along the border."

"Yes, sir, and I'll build a fire under those in charge. If you don't watch them, they'll be sitting inside by a stove."

"Get them out searching—and arrest those people in the house where she was staying."

"They're already gone, sir."

"Well, put their names and descriptions out too!" Ritter continued to study the map. "They may try to escape by boat."

"That will be much easier to check, sir. I'll see to it."

Ritter turned around and slammed his fist into his palm. "The trouble is that Grüber knows all about our security. He'll be hard to catch, but he must be caught!"

"Yes, sir."

"And that woman—we'll interrogate her first until she gives up her friends. I think we can arrange that." He smiled, his lips thin and an unholy light in his eyes. "Then we'll hang her in the square at high noon."

CHAPTER TWENTY-ONE

CAPTURED!

★ ★ ★

"I never did care much for high places," Derek muttered. "It's a good thing it's so dark. If I could see the bottom of this mountain, I think I'd get out and walk."

Mallory felt much the same way. She glanced out to her right and saw the sheer wall of the mountain that bordered the mountain road, rising upward. This did not bother her much, but peering out through the darkness, she could see the edge of the road on the other side that fell off with breathtaking abruptness. The road had been hewn out of the mountain roughly so that there was barely room for the truck. She leaned over to her left and tried to see down, but the darkness was too great. "That looks like an awful fall. Can you see the bottom?"

"No, and I don't want to." He laughed. "Here we're in terrible danger from the SS, and we're worried about a little thing like driving off the side of a mountain."

"I had an uncle that always made light of things. He would have said, 'Well, if we fall off the mountain and get killed, we won't have to worry about getting caught.'"

Derek nodded, but his attention was on the road ahead

of him. They had been climbing steadily up the mountain, winding around on the hairpin curves that followed the outline of the huge mass of rock that thrust upright toward the sky. He was tired, and he moved his shoulders to relieve the tension. "It'll be daylight soon," he said.

"How much farther is it to the top?"

"I can't remember. I was over this road only once. It seemed a long way, but it can't be too far."

The cold was hardly affected by the small truck heater, and Mallory could barely feel her feet. That made her think of her Lapp friends. "You know, the Lapps don't wear any socks."

"No socks! In this kind of weather?"

"No, they make their boots out of reindeer skins. The women take the sinews of the reindeer and chew them and weave them together into a very tough, waterproof thread. They make the boots oversized, and then they stuff them with hay."

"Hay! That doesn't sound very warm."

"It is, though. I tried a pair while I was with them. My feet stayed warmer than in my store-bought boots."

As Derek guided the truck carefully up the incline, he listened as Mallory told him stories of the Lapps. Some of them were amusing and some were rather tragic. "You really love these people, don't you?"

"They're like children in a way. They're so very *small*. The men are hardly over five feet tall. I felt like a giant among them. And remember how they looked up at you? It was as though you were a different species."

"They must be hardy, though."

"Oh, they are. They're tough as boot leather, and they're very hospitable, as you found out. They'll invite anybody in to share their tent."

"I'd like to have a longer visit with them sometime."

"I wish you could. You'd love them, I know."

Her simple use of the word *love* brought Derek's head around. She used it so easily. "I think I might love them. I haven't had enough love in my life, Mallory."

"That's a shame. You loved your mother, though."

"Oh yes, I did. She was a very gentle woman. Too gentle, my father thought. He always said I was too much like her and not enough like him."

"Well, I'm glad you're like you are."

Derek turned. Murky light was beginning to illuminate the landscape, and he could see her face. "I'm glad you feel that way," he said quietly. He would have said more, but suddenly the engine coughed and began to miss.

"That's it," he said.

"What is it?"

"Out of fuel."

"There's no more in the cans?"

"No, we used it all. These vehicles are hard on petrol."

The truck shuddered to a stop, and Derek shrugged philosophically. "We'll have to go on foot from here. When we get to the top of this mountain, it'll be easy going on skis."

"How far is it to the Swedish border?"

"Quite a ways, and when we get there, it's going to be tricky missing the guards. I'm sure they've been alerted by this time."

The two got out of the truck and very carefully arranged their packs. They knew there would be no stores along the way, for they would not dare stop in a village. Derek divided the load so that he had by far the larger part, and then he said, "I think it'll be easier to carry our skis while we walk up the grade."

"All right."

Derek thought for a moment, then said, "Let me get rid of this vehicle."

"Get rid of it?"

"Yes. We'll shove it over the side. They'll be looking for it, and they won't be likely to find it there."

Derek had put the emergency brake on, and now he got in and released it, still holding the brake. He let the truck roll slowly back toward the edge, carefully cutting the wheel until the rear wheels were headed straight toward the abyss. It would be tricky jumping out in time. If the door caught him as he went out, he would be carried down with the vehicle. Now that daylight was coming, he could see that far below was a small river, but it was a terrific sheer drop of hundreds of feet. Holding his breath, he got ready, then took his foot off the brake. As the vehicle began to roll, he jumped out and slammed the door. The vehicle rolled by and eased off the edge, the front end nosing up, and then it slipped over. The two watched as it rolled and cartwheeled end over end through the air. It finally struck the side, bounded outward, and landed with a loud crash as it hit the rocky bottom. There was no gas to explode, and Derek nodded with satisfaction. "I don't think anyone will spot it there. You ready?"

The two donned their packs and started up the grade, which became somewhat less steep as they approached the summit. Mallory was out of breath and began puffing. "I've gotten soft. I could have done this easily last year when I was living with the Lapps."

"The crest is right up there. Then it'll be downhill. We'll have to leave this road and skirt the village where the guardhouse is located."

The two forged on, and finally the land leveled out and the road became even. The scrub timber had grown rather thick on the crest, and they had made a sharp turn when suddenly a harsh voice cried out, "Halt!"

Instantly Derek reached for his Luger, but he had changed to Lars's clothing and it was underneath his heavy coat.

"Don't move or I'll shoot you dead, Major!"

When he heard the word *Major*, Derek knew that all was lost. He turned and saw two soldiers come out from the copse where they had been concealed. Both of them had their rifles up, and their eyes glittered as they approached. "Major Grüber, I assume." The speaker wore the insignia of a sergeant. He was a small man wearing a heavy overcoat, and he was smiling broadly.

"Kurt, let me introduce you to Major Derek Grüber, the

famous traitor. Major, this is Private Rimmer, and I am Sergeant Jergen. Kurt, relieve the major of his weapon." Jergen raised the rifle and pointed it directly at Derek's head while the private, grinning broadly, laid his rifle down. He came forward, jerked open Derek's coat, and removed the Luger.

"And see if the lady has a weapon."

"It will be a pleasure, Sergeant." The private jerked open Mallory's coat. He managed to brush against her figure as he removed the pistol she carried and laughed as she tried to pull away. "Don't be shy, Fraülein."

Jergen waited until the private had come back, and then he said, "Well, this is a pleasant surprise. What did you do with the truck you stole?"

"It ran out of petrol. We shoved it over the edge."

"Destroying government property? That could get you into serious trouble, Major."

Mallory's heart was like a stone. "We almost made it," she said. "Just a little farther and we would have been in Sweden." She knew nothing good could happen now, and a coldness came over her as she thought of the icy eyes of Colonel Ludwig Ritter and the obvious cruelty of Colonel Uldrich Stahl.

"Well, now, we'll have time to visit when we get to our headquarters. You are valuable people. Did you know that? Colonel Ritter's promised a reward and a promotion for any soldier who captures you. I might even become a lieutenant, and you could have my stripes, Rimmer."

Rimmer grinned and picked up his rifle.

"All right. Head down the road. If you try to run, I'll shoot you in the legs. That will not be pleasant."

They walked down the road for a hundred yards, where they saw a motorcycle with a sidecar parked. "Private, you take the cycle and drive on in. We can't all ride in that pitiful thing. Go in and tell the lieutenant we've captured the famous Derek Grüber and his woman. I'm sure he'll want to come out in a car for such a famous visitor."

"Yes, Sergeant." The private hesitated. "You don't need help to guard them?"

"Not at all. Here, take the rifle. I think this will serve better." Sergeant Jergen pulled Derek's Luger from his pocket and checked the clip. "I could scarcely miss at this range. Hurry. I'm looking forward to our promotions."

Private Rimmer started the engine, then turned and roared off down the road.

"We might as well keep moving," Sergeant Jergen said, gesturing with the Luger. "Start down the road, and if you try anything, you'll be the worse for it."

Derek glumly turned, and with Mallory at his side, they moved away. "I'm sorry about this, Mallory," he said quietly.

"It's not over yet. Don't give up hope."

"That's right. Don't give up hope." The sergeant laughed. "The radio said you were a preacher, that they call you the Jesus woman. Is that true?"

"Some people have called me that."

"Well, I'll be very interested. I know you'll be praying for Jesus to get you out of this, but somehow I don't think He will. Don't worry. The SS will take care of you—both of you. I imagine they'll have some interesting things for you during your interrogation, Major. You, woman, will be hanged—but maybe they will interrogate you also. Oh, I'd like to be in on that!"

Mallory's mind was working rapidly. The sky was light now, and the weak sun illuminated the road ahead of them. The precipice was not so steep here. She glanced over and saw the small river far below. It glittered in the morning light, and she was praying that God would deliver them.

Afterward, she was never able to remember how the plan came into her mind, but it seemed to come from nowhere. She was walking next to the rock wall, and suddenly, she knew exactly what to do.

She looked over her shoulder at the sergeant, who

watched her cautiously. "I don't want to fall into the hands of the SS, Sergeant."

"Nobody does, but that's what's going to happen."

"It doesn't have to."

"What are you talking about? And you keep your head around, Grüber!" He said sharply.

"The one they really want is Major Grüber."

"I expect that's true, but it's always good to catch a spy, especially an American one."

"Look, when I left, I brought everything valuable with me." She pulled off her glove and held up her hand. On her last birthday, Rolf had bought her a huge imitation diamond ring as a joke. When she wore it, friends teased her about being the diamond queen of Norway. Now the imitation stone caught the sunlight, and she said, "This ring is five carats. It's worth six thousand marks. And look here. I've got the rest of my jewels in here." She pulled her bulging leather makeup pouch out of her pocket. "I was going to sell all these and start a new life. They're worth at least half a million marks."

Sergeant Jergen was staring at the ring and at the pouch. "What are you talking about, woman?"

"Take them all and just let me go."

"You know I can't do that."

"Yes you can. For half a million marks, you can do a lot."

Mallory saw the soldier's face grow still. She could almost read the workings of his mind. *I'll take the jewels. I can take some of them out. They'll never know how many she had.*

Mallory saw greed win out over any noble thoughts Jergen might have had.

"Give me the pouch." He changed the Luger to his left hand and held out his right, warning Derek to keep moving. He was walking less than two meters from the edge of the road. When she got close to him, she handed him the pouch and walked alongside as he struggled to open the zipper with his gloved hands, his Luger still in his left hand. Cursing under his breath, he pulled off one glove and stuck it under his left armpit to hold it, along with the pistol. He was so fascinated by the pouch he had taken his eyes off of Mallory.

This was the moment she had waited for. With a sudden burst of strength, Mallory threw herself violently against him.

"Hey, what—!"

Her sudden lunge caused the sergeant to stagger. He tried to both hold on to the pouch and swing the Luger around, but the suddenness of it all caught him unprepared. He was driven to the edge, where he threw an agonized glance downward. He tripped over his own feet, then went over with a scream. He managed to pull the trigger of the Luger, and the sound echoed sharply against the mountain walls.

Mallory almost went over herself. She sprawled full-length and heard the unbelievably shrill scream of the sergeant as he fell. She couldn't look but turned away, shaking. She put her hands over her ears and sat on the icy road, helpless to stop the agony she felt.

Derek had turned at the sergeant's first cry when Mallory struck him. He'd had no time to do anything, for it was all so sudden. One moment the sergeant was walking along the road and the next he was over the edge. Derek ran quickly and knelt down beside Mallory.

"Derek!" Mallory was weeping as he pulled her to her feet. She turned to him weakly, almost collapsing, and he put his arms around her.

"It's all right, Mallory," he whispered.

"I didn't think I could . . ."

Derek knew something of the gentle side of this woman, and he knew that killing a human being was probably the worst thing she could imagine herself doing. He knew that the enormity of what she had done was doing terrible things to her spirit. He held her as she wept, putting his hand behind her head and holding it to his chest. Finally she seemed to get a grip on herself and straightened up. He released her but still kept his hand on her shoulder. "I know you feel terrible about this, but it was the only way. You know what terrible things they would have done to both of us. You did what you had to do."

Mallory brushed her eyes with the back of her gloves and could only say, "I don't think I'll ever forget this."

"We must go quickly." He knew that action was the best thing for her. "We don't know when that car will get back, but it won't be long. Come on. Let's get our packs and our skis."

They donned their skis, and Derek took a quick look around. "We need to leave the road as soon as we find a break."

They picked up speed as they went downhill, and within a mile the countryside had leveled out considerably. Derek waved to his left. "There's a place." He pulled to a stop, and she pulled up beside him. "I wish we could make for the Swedish border."

"Can't we do that?" she asked.

"It's exactly what they expect us to do. They'll call in planes and troops and throw a solid line of men all the way across the border. We've made it easy for them now that they know where we are." He shook his head and bit his lip. "We can't go back, and I don't see how we can get through the line they'll throw up."

"I know what to do," Mallory suddenly said. "We'll go to the Lapps. They'll hide us."

Derek thought for a moment, then nodded eagerly. "Yes, we can go north. They won't be expecting that. We'll cover our tracks where we leave the road. They'll think we've gone on to try to break through their line."

They moved to the open spot where they could leave the road, and he removed his skis. He broke a branch off a tree and went back, carefully sweeping away all traces of their ski tracks. Then he put on his skis and came to stand beside her. "We've got a chance."

"Do you think we can do it, Derek?"

"I believe God is with us. It's the only way we could

have escaped. We were doomed, but now we have a chance. He won't abandon us."

Mallory looked up and saw the light in his eyes. It was the light of hope, and his hope gave her the same feeling. "God is always with us," she said. "Come on. Let's go find the Lapps."

CHAPTER TWENTY-TWO

GOD ALWAYS HAS A PLAN

★   ★   ★

The weather was bitter cold, but there had been no more snowfall, even though Derek had wished it would snow to cover their trail. As they made their way north, Mallory looked up from time to time, but the sky remained clear.

Suddenly Mallory heard a faint sound. "Do you hear that?"

"No. What is it?"

"I think it's a plane."

"Quick, get under these trees!" Derek shoved off with his poles and made his way under the shelter of some of the scrub trees that grew on the tundra at this latitude. Mallory skied in to stand beside him, and both of them looked up into the air. They both spotted the plane at about the same time. It was flying at an altitude of no more than 150 meters. "They're probably looking for us," Derek said. "I'm surprised we haven't seen one before."

"Would they look for us in this direction?"

"They've probably spread out all along the Swedish border and moved inward. Now that they've covered that ground, it may have occurred to whoever's in charge that we took a different path." His eyes were still on the plane, and finally it became a black dot and disappeared. "I'm not sure we can get through without being spotted, but we have to try."

They continued traveling as fast as they could. Now that they were traveling without a vehicle, they assumed it was fairly safe to travel during the two hours or so of daylight they still had. The snow gave them a good surface, but cross-country skiing was one of the most tiring things Mallory had ever tried. They stopped once to have a cold meal and then forged on ahead.

Mallory's arms and legs ached from all the physical exertion. It took every ounce of her determination to keep going. She trudged along, looking up just enough to keep from running into anything.

"Look," she said, pointing at the ground.

"What is it?" Derek asked, stopping and looking back to where she was pointing.

"That's reindeer droppings. A big herd must have gone through here. And see how the snow has been nosed up? They push it back with their noses to get at the tiny plants underneath."

"Do you think it could belong to your people?"

"Even if it's not them, they'll probably know something. We ought to catch up with them soon."

"There's not much daylight left, and you're tired. Come on, let's try to get another few miles."

They forged ahead, and a half hour later, Mallory said, "Look. Reindeer!"

"Do you think it's the Lapps?"

"Sometimes the reindeer aren't owned. They just wander. If we get close enough, we can see if they belong to Jagg's family."

"How could you tell that?"

"They mark all their reindeer when they're tiny calves with a cut in the ear. I've seen Jagg identify one of his at an incredible distance. They have good eyes for things like that."

"We'd better pull up over there and make camp." It was getting dark fast.

They stopped near some scrub trees, where they found plenty of firewood. "I think we can risk a fire," Derek said. They gathered dry sticks and soon had a blaze going. Derek looked up from poking at the fire and said, "Look, those reindeer are curious."

"Their ears are marked. I don't know the markings well enough to know whose they are." An idea came to her, and she said, "You see that female reindeer?"

"I can't tell the difference. They all have antlers."

"You can tell by the udder. Derek, why don't we milk her?"

"Milk her! How would we catch her?"

"Well, she seems pretty tame and she's used to people. You can tell that."

"I've never milked anything in my life," he protested.

"Well, I have, but you have to hold her."

"Hold her! How?"

"By the antlers. Wait, let me get an empty can."

Derek looked askance at her, then shook his head. "I'm not sure this is a good idea," he protested. He looked at the reindeer, which was peering at them from only about three meters away.

"Give her something to eat."

"We don't have much. Here's one of the last slices of bread."

"I'll trade that any day for a cup of reindeer milk. It's filled with fat and is very nourishing. They don't have much milk, but it's much richer than goat's milk. Come on. You go first and get her by the antlers. Feed her and then grab her."

Derek moved forward with some trepidation. He did not like large animals, and although reindeer were small compared to elk or moose, this one was still big enough to have a healthy set of antlers. He advanced slowly and held a piece of the bread out in his hand. The reindeer held its ground and then stretched its neck out and nibbled at the bread. When he put another morsel on his palm, it came closer. "Get ready," he said. "I don't know how hard she'll be to hold."

"I'm ready."

Derek fed the last of the bread to the reindeer, then grabbed her antlers. He was slightly off balance, and when she jerked violently, he slipped to the ground and the reindeer panicked and ran right over him.

"Hey!" Derek yelled. "She's getting away!"

"She'll come back," Mallory said, laughing. "I'm surprised you can't even handle one small female reindeer!"

Derek got to his feet and brushed the snow off the seat of his pants. "All right," he said grimly. "Let's try this again." He found another piece of bread and lured the reindeer back, drawing out the rope he had stowed in his pocket. When the animal took the bread, he let her have it and then grabbed the antlers. This time he was prepared, and he struggled with it for a moment but was finally able to secure the animal to a scrub tree. "Now, you get the lunch," he said, grinning.

Mallory milked the reindeer efficiently, then said, "All right. Turn her loose."

Derek did so, and Mallory handed him the can of milk. "It's good," she insisted at his uncertain expression.

He sipped the milk, and a look of surprise washed across his face. "Never tasted anything quite like it."

After sharing the milk, they managed to lure in two more female reindeer so that by the time they had milked both of them, their hunger was somewhat abated. It was already dark, even though it was still early in the afternoon, and they were exhausted from skiing.

"I don't know about you, but I need a nap," Derek said. "We'll just have to trust that nobody's looking for us out in the middle of nowhere." They pulled their blankets out, and he said, "You get close to the fire, Mallory."

She lay down and stared into the fire. He lay down

behind her and pulled the blankets up but left his arm over her. She felt odd about this, but safe. The day had been hard, and she grew sleepy. The fire made an orange dot in the blackness, and overhead the constellations were bright.

Derek was tired himself, but not too tired to enjoy holding Mallory close as she lay with her back against him. "It's strange how little it takes to make a man happy, isn't it? Here we're in terrible danger, but we've got enough to eat and we've got a fire. We're all right for the moment."

"I remember someone asked Emerson once what he wanted most. He said, 'If I can think of it, it isn't what I want.'"

"I know what he means. What we want most can never be put into words. Are you warm enough?"

"Yes, it's heavenly."

"Aren't you ever afraid of me?"

Mallory was very aware of his strong body pressing against her. "No."

"That's strange."

"You wouldn't hurt me."

"You're right about that."

They lay there silently soaking up the heat from the flickering flames, and finally Mallory said, "Life changes so quickly. Sometimes a person will bend over to pick up something that fell out of his hand, and when he straightens up the whole world has changed."

"That sounds like something from a poem."

"Not really." She smiled in the darkness. "You can put it in one of yours."

"I'll put a footnote on it. 'See the works of Mallory Anne Winslow.'"

"I don't want to be a footnote. You can have it. It's yours."

They lay there enjoying the stillness, and finally both of them dropped off to sleep. From out of the darkness came the cry of a wolf, but they were so deep in sleep they never heard it.

★ ★ ★

The nap lasted longer than either of them had intended, so they decided to stay at their cozy little campsite overnight rather than moving on immediately. They felt rather safe out in the northern wilderness and were a little reluctant to get back on their skis.

The next morning they arose long before daylight, ate the final can of beans, and made a small pot of coffee, leaving enough grounds for one more day. The smell of woodsmoke and coffee laced the thin air and a breeze stirred the snow, sweeping it across the tundra and bringing a musty odor with it.

They set themselves to the journey and skied hard all morning. At noon they were ready to stop for a break when Derek said suddenly, "Look, there are some people and a big herd of reindeer!"

"That must be some of the Lapps. Maybe they'll know where Jagg is."

They advanced and found a family on the move. Mallory did not know them, but an old woman who stood beside her son-in-law said, "The Jesus woman."

Mallory was relieved. "Yes."

"You are hunting for Jagg?" her son said. "He's over there. He's ahead of us no more than half a day."

"Thank you," Mallory said. She turned to Derek and said, "We should be able to catch them. They move very slowly."

"Let's do it. It's going to be a cold camp and a hungry one if we don't."

★ ★ ★

They caught up with Jagg and his family late in the afternoon, long after the sun had set. They were greeted at the rear of the herd by Mayda, who was holding a baby.

"You're back!" she cried, hugging Mallory.

"Yes, and I brought a friend with me. You remember Derek."

Mayda looked up at the tall man. "Yes, I remember. He is so big!"

"Yes, and you are very pretty," Derek said with a smile.

"Who is this beautiful baby?" Mallory asked.

"This is a friend's baby. I'm just watching her for today so her mother can get some rest. Come," she told both of them, "you must be tired and hungry."

They soon came upon the family's small *kata*, their black conical tent. Blue smoke was curling invitingly from the wide smoke hole.

"They look like pictures I've seen of the American Indian tepees," Derek said.

"They're very much like them," Mallory said. "They can take them down and put them up in almost no time."

"Won't we be an imposition?"

"No, you don't even have to knock. The dogs will announce you. In fact, I don't think anyone knocks at a door in Lapland."

Indeed, the dogs did come running out, several of them—two of them black and three of them a strange cream color. They were large dogs but not unfriendly. They swarmed around the pair, and both Derek and Mallory leaned over to pet them.

"The Lapps couldn't do without their dogs," Mallory said. "They are great pets, but they're also used for herding."

When they reached the tent, Jagg and Orva came with Remu, the mother, and Lorge to greet them. They were all saying, *"Pourist! pourist!"*

"That's Lapp for 'I greet you.' Try to say it to them."

Derek managed to imitate the sound and the family glowed at his effort. At six-two, he towered over all of them.

"Come inside. We eat," Jagg said.

As Derek stooped to go inside, Mallory whispered, "Be careful not to walk behind the fire, I mean on the side of the fire opposite the door."

"Why not?"

"Because they keep their food in that place, and they consider that part of a kata sacred."

It took a moment for his eyes to become accustomed to the darkness. The fire was burning in the center, and he noted that the smoke hole was very large—about five feet in diameter. "Doesn't it ever rain through that?"

"They cover it up when it does," Mallory said.

The whole family came into the tent, including the dogs, and they all settled in around the fire in the center. Derek touched the tent cloth behind him, noting that it was made of a lightweight wool. The floor was covered with layers upon layers of fresh twigs, which made a soft, springy carpet that was a little slippery to walk on. There were several reindeer-skin bags on the floor to serve as chairs and birch-bark cases looking somewhat like suitcases. A few pots and pans completed the equipment. He noted that men and women alike wore long coats trimmed with bands of bright cloth. Orva drew out an old-fashioned coffee mill from one of the birch-bark cases, and Derek watched with interest as she sat on one of the rolled-up reindeer skins and held the mill on her lap.

"I used to watch my grandmother do that," he remarked.

Remu, the mother, was busy roasting coffee in an iron kettle.

"Coffee will be good, Mother," Mallory said. She turned to Derek, saying, "They love coffee. They buy the beans and grind them up themselves, and they always serve them."

"It smells good."

Finally the coffee was ready, and Remu opened a reindeer-skin bag and pulled out a piece of dried fish. She pulled off a piece of fish skin, which she put into the pot, scales and all.

"Why is she doing that?" Derek asked softly.

"To settle the coffee, I think. She'll add a little salt to it too."

When the coffee was ready, Derek held the cup, which was fashioned of northern white birch in the shape of a small dipper and beautifully hand-decorated with primitive designs.

"Sugar," Jagg said, reaching into another bag and bringing out a conical loaf of sugar almost as large as a loaf of bread. He broke off a piece with a specially devised pair of pinchers and extended it toward Derek.

He put the piece of sugar in his coffee as the others laughed.

"You people never know how to use sugar," Jagg said. He broke off another piece, put it in his mouth, and then sipped the coffee.

"That's one way of doing it," Derek said.

"We have goat's milk too," Lorge said. He produced a small jar, and when Derek put a small amount into his cup, he found it gave the coffee a delightful flavor.

"We don't use reindeer milk so much as we used to," Jagg said.

"Why's that?" Derek asked.

"Reindeer give less milk. Besides, it's more convenient to keep two or three goats that are willing to stay near the kata. Before, when my wife wanted milk, she had to go run a reindeer down and I'd have to hold the animal. The goats just come when she calls."

The dogs had been keeping a close watch on all the activity, paying special attention to the guest. When Derek leaned over to look at the baby Mayda was holding and stroke the baby's fine hair, he suddenly found his wrist grasped by one of the dogs. The large dog had strong teeth, but he did not break the skin.

"Jog!" Mayda said quickly and tapped the dog on the nose. "It's all right."

Reluctantly the dog released Derek, and Derek rubbed his wrist. "Why did he do that?"

"He didn't mean to hurt you," Jagg said. "Only to protect the baby. That's what his job is. You can see he did not draw blood."

"That's the way it is with the Lapps," Mallory informed him. "They take an old, dependable dog and train it to take care of the baby. The mother has so much work to do inside and out that it's a good way to keep the baby safe."

Both Derek and Mallory were tired, but Mallory knew she had to explain their position.

"Jagg, I must tell you we are being hunted by some evil men. German soldiers. We're trying to get to the border over to the east."

"What men are these?" he asked. He listened as Mallory explained, and then he said, "They never come among us. You will be safe."

"Not if they see me," Derek said. "I'm so tall they'd notice me at once, and they'd spot a fair-skinned woman like Mallory."

"We are moving that way a little every day. It is slow, but you will stay with us."

"It might be dangerous for you if you were caught hiding us."

"The good Lord will take care of us," Lorge said. "We are His sheep, and He is our shepherd."

"That's good, son," Jagg said. He smiled, his weathered face crinkling.

"Mallory, you'll be happy to hear the congregation has grown. We have over thirty now. Thirty-five if you count some who have backslidden a bit."

"Tell me about them," Mallory said. "I'll see them tomorrow, but I want to hear all that's going on."

Derek listened as Lorge eagerly talked about the little congregation. His eyes ran around the circle, studying the faces illuminated by the flickering fire. Mostly, however, he kept his gaze on Mallory. There was an eager light in her eyes that held a loving expression. Her lips stirred pleasantly as she listened to Lorge, and her coat fell away from her neck, revealing the smooth, ivory shading of her skin. Her black hair made her skin seem fairer. He admired the smooth roundness of her shoulders and the delicate lines of her body.

Remu served up some supper, and the family had a lively conversation as they enjoyed the reindeer meat. Before long it was time to settle down for the night.

"I always say a prayer for my family now," Lorge said, "and when I'm done, I would like it very much if you would pray for me, Jesus woman."

Derek was touched by the family's prayer time. With all the many complications in his life, their simple faith moved him deeply, and he longed for the same kind of simplicity in his own life. As he fell asleep, he thought, *It doesn't seem likely that my life will ever be as simple as this. . . .*

★　★　★

For three days Derek and Mallory immersed themselves in the lives of the Lapps. They got up each morning and helped to take the tent down. Derek discovered that everyone carried a part of the tent. He was amazed at how quickly it could be dismantled, and soon their possessions were packed on sleds that were pulled by the reindeer. The animals were driven with a single line attached to the base of the antlers. The adult Lapps never rode on the reindeer, for they were only strong enough to carry the children.

The Lapp dogs were also very important in the life of these people. Derek was amazed the first time he saw the dogs eat, for they were trained from the time they were puppies to take turns at feeding and always in the same order. Jagg strictly supervised his dogs, ensuring that every dog would get his share. Their main food, he learned, was hot soup consisting largely of reindeer blood preserved from the slaughtering time.

As Derek and Mallory moved east with the Lapps

toward the border, the days passed imperceptibly. There was no sign of pursuit from the Nazis, and Derek said one morning, "You know, I think we could leave and make a dash for the border."

"Jagg says the weather's going to get worse. We might get caught," Mallory said.

"I suppose we'd better not chance it, then."

Before Derek went to bed that night, he hung up the hay outside the tent that he had used in the boots Jagg had given him. He had found that the Lapp boots stuffed with hay did indeed keep his feet warmer than his other boots.

The next morning he got up and went out to get the hay. When he realized it wasn't there, he went back in the tent and exclaimed, "My hay—it's gone!"

Orva laughed at him. "The goats ate it. You have to take better care of your things, Derek."

"Why didn't you tell me, Orva?" he asked as he sat down by the fire.

"People have to learn from their mistakes," she said. She came over and sat down beside him and began touching his hair. "You're a pretty man."

Derek saw that Mallory was watching this with amusement.

"I am not!" he exclaimed. "Men aren't pretty."

"You are," Orva insisted. "Why don't you take me for your woman? I could make life very easy."

Derek heard Mallory burst into laughter.

"That's your best offer, Derek."

He suddenly grinned. "Well, that *is* a good offer, Orva, but I'll be leaving here. The Germans are going to keep looking for me, and they'll hang me or shoot me if they find me."

She laughed. "You don't want me anyhow. You like that one."

Now it was Mallory's turn to feel uneasy. Her cheeks flushed, and she left the tent.

Derek laughed. "You're right."

"She is tall enough for you," Orva went on. "I am not, so you may have her."

"Thank you, Orva." Derek got up and left to follow Mallory. When they were outside, he said, "Well, there's one chance I had for a wife."

"I don't think you'd be too happy with Orva. I feel bad about her."

"Well, as she says, I can have you."

Mallory glanced at him quickly, her cheeks still burning. "That's foolishness!" she said. "I've got to go. We're going to have a service tonight, and I need to prepare a sermon."

★ ★ ★

Derek was very quiet during the service that night. As he listened, he noted that no matter what the subject of the sermon, Mallory always spoke of Jesus.

Afterward he rose and said, "Let's take a walk, and you can explain your sermon to me."

"All right. It's too early to go to bed."

They walked through the reindeer herd, and he commented, "They're domesticated, aren't they?"

"I suppose that's all they've known all their life."

"It's amazing how the men can lasso them. They're better than wild west cowboys in America."

As they reached the outer edge of the herd, the sky suddenly lit up with brilliant waves of colors—blues, greens, and reds. "What is that?" Derek asked as he stared in wide-eyed amazement.

"It's the northern lights. I never saw them in Africa, of course, but I've seen them several times when I've been staying with the Lapps." A curtain of yellow blazed across the sky. "Isn't it the most beautiful thing you've ever seen?"

"It certainly is! I guess I've heard of northern lights before but never imagined it would look like this."

They watched for several minutes, until the display faded.

"I wanted you to know your sermon touched me tonight, Mallory." He hesitated, then said, "I want to serve Jesus Christ . . . but I don't see how I can."

"God knows all about you, Derek. He knew about you before you were born. He's brought you out of a terrible way of life, and He has a plan for you."

"I hope so, for I don't have one for myself."

"You're not out of trouble yet. Did you ever hear the story of Joseph?"

"Yes, of course. In the book of Genesis."

"You remember, then, how everything seemed to go wrong for him? His brothers sold him for a slave, and when he made a good place for himself in Potiphar's house, that went wrong too."

"I remember that woman who tried to seduce him. I've always admired Joseph. It takes a strong man to run away from a beautiful woman like that."

Mallory stared at him. "Have you done that?"

"Why . . ." He could not answer. "I haven't always led a pure life, Mallory. I wish I had."

"Did you love those women?"

"I loved Rachel," he said simply. As always, when he spoke her name, a sadness crossed his face and touched his eyes.

"I didn't mean to make you feel bad," she said, "but Joseph came out of it all right. God used him to save His people. God's going to use you too, Derek."

"I don't know how, but I hope so."

"God will help you, and I will help you."

He turned and reached out his hands. When she put her hands in his, he said, "We've become good friends, haven't we?"

"Very good friends indeed."

An impish light touched his eyes, and Mallory knew he was up to mischief. "Don't you think that good friends should express their relationship . . . in some sort of *physical* way?"

She could not help smiling at his foolishness. She had seen this side of him before and loved it. "I think that might be good." She lifted her head, and he bent over and kissed her. A warmth lay between them, strong and unsettling, but at the same time with a goodness and a sweetness in it. His mouth was firm, and he held her gently. When he lifted his lips, he said simply, "I love you, Mallory."

To her own surprise, Mallory knew the truth and spoke it. "I love you too, Derek," she whispered.

"I don't know what our future holds, but whatever happens, I'll carry this love I have for you always."

They stood there in the silence enjoying it, and finally he said, "There are only a few passes into Sweden, even this far north, and they may be closely guarded."

"I'm going to try the radio."

"It's such a small one. Do you think it'll pick anything up?"

"It's the best one I've made. We'll put up an antenna. Maybe it'll pick up something."

They went back to the tent, and she got the radio. It was indeed small, but the batteries were large. She had hated having to add it to her load, but she knew they would need it.

Moving outside, she attached a wire, and he spread it out, looping it over the branches of some trees.

Mallory worked with the radio for some time. The batteries were very weak, but finally a voice crackled. "This is Ajax. I read you, Byron."

"We need to be taken out," Mallory said quickly.

"What is your location?"

Mallory gave their location and voiced the plans they had made earlier. "We will be at Angel Fjord just off North Cape."

The voice came back faintly, "The submarine will be offshore in four days, the first of December at exactly oh two hundred. You must be quick. When you get a signal, answer it. We've made arrangements for a local fisherman to leave a small boat there that you can row out to the sub."

The two were straining to hear, and they barely heard the last instruction before the signal faded completely.

"The battery's dead," she said.

"That's okay. We got all the information we need," Derek said with a glad voice. "We'd better write it down. Angel Fjord off North Cape."

"I'm sure we aren't too far from there. Lorge will guide us. We're going to be all right."

He reached out and put his hand on her cheek. "Yes," he whispered, "we're going to be all right."

★ ★ ★

Adolf Moltmann quickly scribbled the radio message. Jumping up, he found his lieutenant and shared the call he had just picked up.

"I must take this to Colonel Ritter!" he exclaimed.

Leaving the radio room, he went at once to Ritter's office. "Colonel, we just picked this up on the radio. It was very faint, but I think I got it all."

Ritter read the message the radio man had written. "Excellent," he said. "Very good indeed! We have them now!"

Ten minutes later Lieutenant Uldrich Stahl was listening to Ritter, who was walking around the room waving his arms, his eyes glittering with excitement. Berlin had been furious over Grüber's defection and had given Ritter a hard time for letting him escape. Now Ritter said, "We have all we need. We must have a force there to capture them."

"My colonel, let me lead the expedition. It would give me great satisfaction."

"Very well, Stahl. You will be in charge of the team.

Make no mistakes. We must capture them. We'll make an example of Grüber. As for the American woman, she'll have a public trial." He laughed aloud. "She'll be found guilty, of course. It will make the Americans look bad." Then his eyes narrowed, "I will enjoy her execution!"

CHAPTER TWENTY-THREE

DANGEROUS RENDEZVOUS

★ ★ ★

Captain Franz Ubel, captain of the destroyer *Eagle*, fixed his gaze on the visitor to his ship. Ubel was a successful naval commander, having received commendations from no less than the führer himself for his successful action against the British navy. He looked very much like the ideal Aryan warrior—tall and broad-shouldered with gray eyes and a hard-bitten aspect.

As the *Eagle* nudged through the cold gray waters off the coast of Norway, he wished he could pick up Lieutenant Uldrich Stahl and throw him overboard! *The man is an idiot! Command must have lost its mind sending a clown like this on an important mission!*

Lieutenant Stahl had similar feelings about Captain Ubel—and had not attempted to conceal them. He was proud of his assignment and felt that Ubel and the crew of the *Eagle* were nothing but a means of transportation—and a difficult bunch to deal with!

The two men were standing in the wheelhouse of the destroyer. The only light was a pale green glow coming from the instruments and gauges. A helmsman faced straight ahead, trained to ignore the conversation of his betters. From time to time he moved the wheel, keeping to the course his captain had given him and listening to the conversation while appearing to be deaf. He was already composing a letter in his head that he would write to his mother as soon as his shift was over, and he knew he would claim more for himself in the action than was true.

"You cannot seem to understand, Captain Ubel," Stahl said, speaking slowly as if to a slow-witted child. "I want to do two things. First, we must capture the woman and Grüber alive." He waited for the captain to answer, but Ubel simply stared at him without changing expression. "It is important that we do this, for the high command intends to make a public example of them both. Imagine a German officer, a highly decorated one such as Grüber, defecting to the enemy. Oh, we will make an example of him!"

"What part does the woman play in all of this?"

"That's not for you to know, Captain, but I will tell you off the record that she will be tried as a spy and publicly executed. The story will appear in newspapers all over the world."

Stahl had planned the mission down to the last detail. He had argued long with Colonel Ritter about the size of the team he would take. Ritter was in favor of a very large number, but Stahl had finally won out, emphasizing that there were only two of them. "Give me six expert commandos, and I will take them with no trouble." He had argued that it was simpler to move with a small group and had not spoken aloud his real reason for taking such a small crew—he didn't want any more people than necessary to receive the accolades for their success. Stahl had already mentally prepared the speech for the newspapers, telling how he had captured the hated defector and the depraved woman and brought them to justice.

"The second thing we must do is destroy the submarine." This also had been Stahl's idea. The submarine would be a sitting duck when it surfaced, and he could see no reason why a competent German naval officer could not sneak in and accomplish that mission.

"It will be difficult to do both." Franz Ubel's voice was hard and spare. He had dealt with army officers in the past, and their heads seemed to be packed with cement. They simply could not understand that war at sea was different from battle on land. And this fellow Stahl—he was even more stupid than most soldiers! Captain Ubel had checked his record and discovered that Stahl had no combat experience at all, and he felt nothing but contempt for him. "If I understand you correctly, you want me to be absolutely sure that the two are captured before I attack the sub?"

"That is correct, Captain."

"You don't seem to grasp how quickly these submarines can move. They can dive while my ship is making a single turn. These British have become quite adept at that."

"I fail to see the problem," Stahl said stiffly.

"Have you looked outside?"

"Outside? Why, of course."

"Have you noticed that it's a moonless night and even the stars are blotted out by those clouds? In other words, it's as dark as pitch out there. Look for yourself."

Stahl peered outside, and sure enough he could see absolutely nothing, but he would not have his plan interfered with, and he said stiffly, "You have the position of the submarine. You know the exact time, two o'clock, that they will be there. Surely you can find something as big as a submarine."

"As big as a submarine! Have you noticed how large the sea is? On a summer day with the bright sun, it would be simple, but trying to sneak up on a submarine in the dark, we'll have all hands out watching for an enemy it will be almost impossible to see."

Stahl waved his hand impatiently. "That is a technical problem. I was assured you were a capable naval officer, and you have your orders to do exactly as I said in this matter."

"Yes, I have them, Lieutenant." Captain Ubel gritted his

teeth. To put his ship under the command of a mere army lieutenant was galling to say the least, but the orders were clear, and he had little choice. "All right. We won't argue about that, but we can't guarantee our success. Too many factors are unstable."

"What's unstable about it?" Stahl barked. "We want this pair alive. The propaganda will be priceless, and surely you want to add a sunken sub to your record, Captain Ubel."

This was true enough. Ubel was proud of his record, and like all other officers, he sought a promotion. There would surely be great credit in sinking a sub while attempting to take these two off.

"Let me go through the plan one more time, Captain," Stahl said, speaking again as if to someone with a feeble mind. "You will put me and my team ashore in a small boat. We know that they will be in the cape, and they will have to signal the sub. As soon as we see the light, we will go ashore and capture the pair."

"That may not be so easy. These are rough waters, and the coast is jagged. There are very few landing harbors in the fjords."

"I will take care of that. Now, as soon as we capture the pair, we will send you a signal by light, and you can sink the submarine." Captain Ubel saw that further argument was useless. He looked at his watch, holding it up to the green light and said, "It's fifty-four minutes until two. We're very close to Angel Fjord."

"Do you know these waters at all, Captain?"

"Of course. There's actually only one location in the fjord accessible by small boats. The fishermen often land there. They'll have to leave from there. The rest of the fjord has steep walls. A picturesque place, but only one spot for a landing."

"There. You see? We understand each other. You can assume the British submarine will be right off of that harbor in Angel Fjord."

Captain Ubel thought hard, then said, "You have a small force, only six men."

"Yes, but they're all experts. We want to take these two alive, and they will have no guards, we assume. It's not a military force. These operations are always as secret as possible."

Ubel shook his head. "If you make a signal to us with a light, the captain of that submarine will see it. You don't know their code and neither do I."

"I hadn't thought of that." Stahl reconsidered and then said, "Look, Captain, we will see the signal from Grüber and go ashore at once. It will be a simple matter, since they won't be expecting a land force. We'll take them prisoner. From the time we leave until the time we capture them should be no more than thirty minutes. Give us that much time and then move in and sink the sub."

Captain Ubel could think of half a dozen things that could easily go wrong. He had been involved with complicated missions before, but apparently Stahl had not. "I hope all goes well, Lieutenant," he said, shaking his head. "But we have no emergency plan."

"We will not need one, Captain," Stahl said firmly. "Now, I will go give my men their final orders."

Stahl left the wheelhouse, and Ubel stared out at the darkness. "It's a bad plan," he said under his breath.

"I beg your pardon, sir?"

"Never mind, Schultz. Just keep on your course."

★ ★ ★

"I can't see a bloody thing." Captain David Bishop was scanning the shoreline through the periscope. "Take a look," he told his second-in-command.

Lieutenant Charles Moore peered at the shore. "No moon and no stars. I'm not even sure we're in the right spot."

The captain and the first lieutenant of the British submarine *Tiger* were both apprehensive. They had brought the *Tiger* into the North Cape, and both of them knew its waters well. They had come early enough to make sure they were in the proper location, but now that the time of the rendezvous was approaching, both officers were unhappy about the situation. "I wonder what genius thought this up," Captain Bishop murmured.

"I'm sure they have plenty of those at Naval Command." Moore was a young man, short and compact and always cheerful. "Don't worry, Captain. It'll be a piece of cake."

"You said that when we had to go in to pick up that Dane, and we nearly lost the boat." Captain David Bishop was too tall for the submarine service, but he loved it. He towered over every other member of the crew and was continually banging his head on the low compartments. Still, now that he had his own boat, life felt good to him. He looked around at the other members of the crew, who were busy about their work. "Charlie, this thing has to be timed exactly right. We can't stay on the surface any longer than necessary."

"You're right about that, Captain. There have been reports of a pair of heavy German cruisers in these waters. If they catch us, we're finished."

The two men talked quietly, both of them keeping their eyes on the water. Finally Moore said, "This should be pretty simple, Captain."

"Things are never simple." This summed up Captain Bishop's philosophy. He ascribed to the theory that if something can go wrong, it will. He had stayed alive by virtue of the fact that he was a smart, cautious man who knew every boat and his submarine. He also had a healthy fear, which did not keep him from doing his duty but often had warned him in time to take evasive action. As he stooped over in the sub, he had an uneasy feeling. "I think something's wrong with this operation."

"What could be wrong? It's simple enough."

"You keep saying that, but you don't know what's out there. There could be a battleship, for all we know."

Moore laughed. "You worry too much, Captain. Who are these people anyway? They must be important."

"I have no idea. You know how Command is. They like to keep us in the dark."

"You're right about that. Sometimes I think the Krauts know more about our plans than we do."

The two men fell silent, and from time to time, one of them took a look through the periscope.

Captain Bishop checked the time. "We'll surface in eight minutes. We give the signal, and if we don't get an instant response, Lieutenant, we don't wait."

"I'm sure they'll signal. They're bound to be waiting. Any other orders?"

"Yes. Send everybody you can topside. It's black as pitch out there, but they've got ears. If anything's creeping up on us, they'll hear it. Be ready to dive quicker than you have in your life, Charlie!"

★ ★ ★

"There's Angel Fjord."

Lorge had guided Derek and Mallory from the Lapp camp to the sea. He knew the area well, and although he was young, he was serious-minded and understood the dangers.

"I can't see much of anything," Derek complained. Actually a few stars had come out, and his eyes had gotten slightly more accustomed to the darkness. He had discovered that Mallory had better night vision than he had, and now he turned to her, whispering, "Can you see anything?"

"Yes. The sea's right down there, and you can see the steep cliffs of the fjord."

Mallory felt rather calm, which surprised her. She was more worried about what would happen to Derek when they got to England than she was of the actual mission itself.

"I wish we were on board that sub," Derek said as they groped their way down the steep incline.

"We'll be all right," Mallory said. "We wait until the sub signals, and we give them a light. We take the small boat and row out. That's all there is to it."

"I suppose you're right. I'm just jumpy."

The three made their way down to a level spot, and Lorge said, "Here's the boat. It's not very big."

"We don't have to go far with it, Lorge. There are oars, aren't there?"

"Yes. Maybe I should row out with you and bring the boat back."

"We couldn't chance that, Lorge," Mallory said. She came closer and looked down at the small young man. "You've done enough already. Now you go back home."

"When will you come back to us, sister?"

"As soon as I can. But you are the shepherd of the sheep now. When we get to England I'll write to you in care of the Narvik General Store. Then you can write to me and tell me what's happening with the church and with yourself." She hesitated, then said, "We don't know how long the war will be. You may be married with a family by the time I get back."

"Pray God it won't be that long." He put his hands out, and Mallory took them with both of hers. "God go with you," Lorge said. Then he turned and shook hands with Derek. "Take care of the Jesus woman, please."

"I'll do the best I can, Lorge, and thank you. I don't know what we would have done without you."

As soon as Lorge left, the two turned their eyes toward the sea. "What time is it, Derek?"

"Four minutes to go. We got here just in time." He stared out at the sea and shook his head. Doubts filled him, but he did not want to speak of them to Mallory. They simply stood there with the cold wind biting them as it came off the sea.

"Look, a light," Derek said suddenly. "It's got to be the sub. Here, give me the flashlight."

Derek took the flashlight and gave the signal. He received a confirmation and said, "Are you ready to go?"

"Yes, but—" Mallory didn't finish her sentence, for they heard the sound of running footsteps. Frightened, they both whirled, but it was Lorge crying loudly, "There's a boat filled with soldiers! They're coming down the coast-line!"

"What kind of a boat?"

"One with a motor!"

"We can't outrun them," Derek said. "Not if they have a motor."

"We've got to try," Mallory said. "Quick—maybe they'll miss us in the darkness."

Derek knew they had no choice, so the two scrambled into the boat and Lorge shoved them off. The sea was not rough, but still the waves tossed the small boat around as they rowed with all their strength. They had rowed for five minutes, one of them on each oar, when suddenly they received another light from the submarine. "There's the second signal. We've only got a few minutes."

Mallory pulled as hard as she could, rowing until her arms felt like lead.

Suddenly Derek said, "Listen." But Mallory had already heard it. "They're coming," Derek said. "I don't think we can make it, Mallory."

"We've got to try."

They could now make out the small German craft as it cleaved the water, headed toward them.

"They've seen us!" Mallory gasped.

"It's too far to the sub—we'll never make it!"

The small boat shot toward them, the roar of the engine getting louder. Derek pulled out his pistol and began to fire, but they kept coming. Throwing the pistol down, he pulled with all his might on his oar. "Pull, Mallory, pull," he yelled.

Three soldiers in the other boat were standing up, their

automatic weapons trained on Mallory and Derek. Mallory's heart went dead within her. When the boat came closer, a German officer in the front ordered, "Stop your rowing!"

Both Derek and Mallory put down their oars. When the officer and a private leaped into their small craft, she immediately recognized Lieutenant Uldrich Stahl.

"Well, Miss Winslow and Major Grüber. You've given us quite a run, but it's over now." He waved his Luger. "We have some entertainment planned for the two of you, but I'm sure you knew that."

Desperately Mallory tried to think of some way to escape, but the soldiers in the German boat were alert.

"You can just row us back to land. That submarine is due for a surprise in a few minutes. It's quite a feat capturing an American female spy and a turncoat German officer *and* destroying a submarine. I think I will be a major before this is over, and I'll be there for your hangings—both of you."

Mallory turned away from the leering face of Stahl, and her eyes met Derek's.

"Well, what is this? A love affair? That will make even a better story. All right. We'll just wait here until your submarine is sunk. Then the destroyer will pick us up."

★ ★ ★

Captain Bishop had excellent night vision, and he had been watching the pair row the small boat as it approached. They were no more than a hundred yards away when the rumble of the engine from the German boat reached them. "Something's wrong," he said to Moore.

"What is it, Captain?"

"I can't be sure, but I'm afraid our people may have been captured by a German squad." He watched as an officer leaped into the boat waving a pistol.

"What should we do, Captain?"

Captain David Bishop was a man noted for quick thinking and quick action. He saw his mission going down the drain and considered the fact that if the Germans knew about the escapees, they could also have a moored ship in the area. Still, he wasn't afraid to take chances when he felt it might be worthwhile.

"You gunners, get ready to fire!" He looked up and yelled, "Put a light on those boats, Ensign."

Instantly a bright searchlight stabbed out into the darkness, and all the men on deck saw the two boats. "That's a German boat to the right. Blast it out of the water, Hartness!"

Almost before he had stopped speaking, a fifty-caliber machine gun broke the silence of the night with its raucous noise. Captain Bishop could see the slugs tearing into the side of the German boat, splintering it. Two of the men fell at once. The others opened fire with their automatic weapons, and Moore yelled, "Give it to them! Sink the dirty Krauts!"

The private standing over Derek lifted his weapon and began firing toward the searchlight. Derek, seeing his chance, sprang up and knocked the soldier into the water. He turned to pounce on Stahl, who was lifting his pistol, but before he had a chance, Mallory struck the man's head with her oar and he fell limply to the bottom of the boat.

"Quick, we've got to get out of here!" Mallory exclaimed. "They might hit us by mistake."

Derek returned to his seat and the two rowed as hard as they could. As they watched, the German attack boat, which was sinking fast, was riddled with bullets, leaving the rest of the crew dead. They heard the sergeant whom Derek had pushed into the water calling out for help, but in the frigid water he could not stay afloat long, and his cries dwindled, then were gone.

They reached the sub, and hands reached down and pulled them aboard.

"What about this German, sir?" one of the sailors asked. "Is he dead?"

"No, it looks like he's coming around."

"Bring him on board."

At that instant a voice cried, "Captain, enemy vessel approaching off port bow!"

Bishop turned and saw the destroyer coming directly at them. "There's no time to dive," he yelled. "We'll fire all forward torpedoes and hope for a hit. And get that deck gun firing, Swanson!"

The deck crew was ready, and they began firing the gun at once. The fifty-caliber weapon rattled loudly, sending a stream of bullets toward the fast-approaching destroyer.

Captain Bishop had relayed his orders to the third lieutenant. The submarine rotated around by Bishop's orders until it was squarely facing the oncoming destroyer. "Fire all forward torpedoes!" Bishop yelled.

A voice below echoed the order, and the submarine shuddered beneath Mallory's feet as the tracks of the four torpedoes spread out. Derek put his arm around her, and they watched the destroyer, which obviously intended to ram them. The deck gun was firing rapidly, but there was no sign of any damage.

"Not much chance, Captain, firing blind like this head-on."

"There's always a chance, Charlie," Bishop said tersely.

He had no sooner spoken than a torpedo hit the destroyer directly in the bow. The big ship swerved, and then suddenly an explosion ripped through the sky.

"We must have hit their munitions store!" Bishop yelled.

"Quick, let's get out of here! Everyone below!"

Derek and Mallory knew nothing about submarines, but they were shepherded down below and waited until the hatch was closed.

"Dive—dive!" the captain ordered.

The submarine at once began to dive, and Derek and Mallory held on to the closest thing available to maintain their footing. It gave Mallory an eerie feeling to think they were going under the sea.

Captain Bishop commanded, "Periscope depth!" And then a few minutes later he was peering through the periscope. "She's going down!" he said happily. "Here, take a look, Charlie."

The second officer had his look, and then the other officers took their turns.

"You two were a lot of trouble," the captain said to Derek and Mallory before he introduced himself.

"My name is Derek Grüber, and this is Miss Mallory Winslow."

"And who is this?" Bishop asked as Lieutenant Stahl got to his feet. Blood was running down over his face, which was as pale as paper.

"Let me introduce you to Lieutenant Uldrich Stahl of the SS," Mallory said.

"Well, I'm happy to know you under these circumstances, Lieutenant. I'm sure our people in London will want to talk with you."

"How long will it take us to get to England?" Mallory asked.

"We'll make a very quick trip. We'll get out of here as soon as that ship is completely down."

"Mason, guard the lieutenant well," he said to his third lieutenant. "I think he might be of some use to our people." Then turning to Mallory and Derek, he said, "It was close there for a while. I thought we were going to lose you."

Mallory suddenly felt all the pressure that had built up inside of her leave. She took Derek's arm and said, "Thank you for coming to get us, Captain. You look like an angel."

"I've been called lots of things, but never an angel. Come along. We'll have tea, and you can tell me your story."

CHAPTER TWENTY-FOUR

"WE'LL BE TOGETHER"

★ ★ ★

The door to Colonel Ludwig Ritter's office burst open, and Ritter looked up, a curse on his lips for whoever dared to interrupt him so rudely. The words died when a burly man wearing the uniform of a general seemed to fill the room. Ritter leaped to his feet and saluted, for he knew this man well.

"General Dengler! I-I wasn't expecting you, sir."

General Otto Dengler was a massive man with a broad, brutal face. He was feared and dreaded in the SS and known for his cruelty, not only to his enemies, but even to his own men on occasion.

"I'm sure you weren't expecting me, but you should have been, Ritter!" Dengler's voice was harsh, and he glared at the smaller man with disgust. A major dressed in the black uniform of the SS had entered with Dengler, and he shut the door firmly. He had a face like a shark, and there was a cruel smile on his thin lips as he studied Colonel Ritter.

"General, if I had known you were coming, I would have—"

"You would probably have tried to leave the country! What a dismal mess you have made of this business!"

"What business, sir?" Ritter squeaked, his voice almost leaving him. He hardly had the breath to speak, and the faces of the two officers told him all he needed to know. Ever since Lieutenant Stahl's failure to capture the two fugitives, he had been dreading just such a moment. "I'm sure I can explain. It was all Lieutenant Stahl's fault!"

"You were in command, I believe," Dengler snarled. He advanced closer, and Ritter seemed to shrink before the bulk of the brutal form. "What idiocy possessed you to send a force of only six men on a mission like this? We had troops stationed on shore. You could have had a company surround the area!"

"Lieutenant Stahl felt it would be better—"

"Shut your mouth, Colonel Ritter! And, by the way, it's not Colonel Ritter anymore. It is now *Lieutenant* Ritter, and you're lucky we don't plan to have you shot!"

"But, General Dengler, you can't do that to me!"

"We'll see whether I can or not! You're incapable of running a desk, so we'll see how you do in a combat outfit. We're making you a first lieutenant in a crack company of the Fifth Army. I think he'll like that, don't you, Major?"

The major smiled and looked more than ever like a shark. "I believe the combat life of a lieutenant in that company is something just under three minutes, General."

The former colonel had turned as pale as paste. His lips trembled, and he could not say a word.

"Get out of here! You'll get your orders at once. Be ready for some action. I expect you'll win the Iron Cross, a brave man like you. Now get out!"

As soon as Ritter had left, General Dengler said, "Watch him, Major! He may try to kill himself. On the other hand, if that's what he wants, let him do it."

The major smiled smoothly. "It will be his choice either to kill himself here or get himself killed for the glory of the Fatherland."

★ ★ ★

Captain Bishop was saying his good-byes to Derek and Mallory. Their time had been short, for the journey to England had been quick. A flotilla of heavy ships had escorted them in, allowing them to travel on the surface. Now they had docked, and standing on the deck of the *Tiger*, the major said, "I wish you the best of luck, Major."

"Not a major any longer, Captain."

"I suppose that's true." Turning to Mallory, he said, "And you, Miss Winslow. Will you be going back to Africa now?"

"I think that will be up to the authorities. I would like very much to help with the work in Norway."

"I expect you would get rather a warm welcome," Bishop said wryly. "But I doubt very much if that will be possible."

"Perhaps not." Mallory lifted her chin defiantly. "But one day I'm going back. My heart is still with the Lapps."

Captain Bishop was aware of the problems that faced the two, especially the German. He studied Derek's face and shook his head. "Well, Grüber, I wish you the best of luck."

"Thank you, Captain."

"And now this is good-bye, Miss Winslow." Bishop watched as they walked off the sub onto the dock. They were met by two uniformed guards and a civilian. "Strange pair," he said. "A war produces some funny stories."

As Derek and Mallory stepped onto the dock, a small man stepped forward and put out his hand. "My name is Hadley, James Hadley. You are Major Grüber, I take it."

"Not major any longer. Just mister, I suppose."

"Ah yes. Well, that's true, I take it. And this is Miss Winslow?"

"How are you, Mr. Hadley?"

"Very well, thank you." Hadley looked rather frail, as a

matter of fact, but there was a quickness about him that neither of the pair missed. "We will be seeing quite a bit of one another. I will be taking your stories."

"Are you with the Secret Service, sir?" Derek asked directly.

"Something like that. You may consider yourselves guests of the British government."

Derek glanced at the two heavily armed guards wearing large pistols in their belts and holding rifles in their hands. He smiled and nodded. "Of course."

Hadley did not miss the sudden bit of humor and smiled also. "A necessary precaution. You are a very valuable man, sir. And, Miss Winslow, you will be wanting to speak with your parents—to contact your family, I'm sure."

"Yes, I would, Mr. Hadley."

"For the time being you will be housed at an estate just outside of London."

"Mr. Hadley, what's going to happen to Derek?"

"Why, my dear Miss Winslow, it's far too early to say." He knew more about this young woman than she supposed, having checked into her background thoroughly. He said nothing of this, however. "If you'll follow me, we have a car waiting. I'm sure you'll welcome a bath and a good meal after your adventures."

★　★　★

"This is a beautiful place, isn't it, Derek?"

"Yes, it is. And we've been treated most royally."

The two were seated in a large room with high ceilings and beautiful paintings on the wall. The carpet was expensive, and a fire crackled in the huge fireplace built of native stone. They were drinking tea, and from time to time, one of them would glance at the man who sat a short distance away. He appeared to be ignoring them, but they were sure he was actually a guard keeping a close eye on them. He wore no uniform, but they had no doubt he had a concealed gun.

"It's been an odd time. I feel like I'm in limbo," Derek murmured.

"Do you suppose we'll be interrogated again today?"

"I expect so, although I don't know what else I can tell them."

"Mr. Hadley knows more about us than he lets on. Why, he even knew about things that happened to me when I was young."

"I don't think you have any problem, Mallory, but they can't make up their mind what to do about me, can they?"

"I think you're right, Derek."

James Hadley, they had quickly discovered, was a very important man in British intelligence. He was never rough or abusive, but he had a way of picking a man apart that impressed Derek. He had grown to like the man, even though he was a bit weary of spending time with him going over his past.

"I'm afraid this story's not going to have a happy ending," Derek said to Mallory.

"Yes it will."

"You think life is like a movie or a magazine love story." He smiled and reached over to take her hand. "I wish it were."

"I'm confident it's going to be all right, Derek."

He shook his head. "You really believe that, don't you—that everything's going to be fine?"

"Yes, I do."

Derek squeezed her hand and smiled at her affectionately. "I'm glad you believe that. I hope you can make me believe the same thing."

"God has delivered us from the hands of our enemies. Back when Stahl caught us in that open boat, all I could do was cry out to God."

"Ah yes, Lieutenant Stahl. I don't think Mr. Hadley has been quite as gentle with him."

"I don't know how Hadley knows all these things. How

did he know about Major Ritter being relieved and sent to a combat unit?"

"He has his ways, I guess. He's like a fox. I'd hate to try to lie to him."

"What does he ask you at all these sessions you have, Derek?" Mallory picked up her tea and sipped it. "I can't imagine."

"No detail is too small for Mr. Hadley." He smiled ruefully. "I've told him my life story. Everything I can think of. It's like I said. I don't think he knows what to do with me."

She leaned forward, and her eyes were bright with hope. "It will be a good ending, just like in the love stories. We'll get married and live happily ever after."

He laughed. "You make me believe that when I look into your face and see your eyes and all the goodness and hope that's there."

After a time, they were interrupted by Hadley, who strolled into the room. "Ah, here you are," he said. "May I join you?"

"Of course, Mr. Hadley."

"Why don't you call me James. I've asked you to do that before."

Derek gave him a mischievous glance. "I'm trying to be on my best behavior. I want to impress you."

Hadley took a seat. "Well, I have a bit of news for you. I know you've been nervous about your future, especially you, Derek."

"What is it?" Mallory asked. "Is it good news, James?"

"Well, I think it is, but you'll have to decide. You, of course, Miss Winslow, are free to go. Do you think you'll go back to Africa?"

"I can't make any decisions until I find out about Derek."

"Well, then. You have two options, Derek. We can't just turn you loose to roam around. I believe you've told the truth, and I've managed to convince my superiors of that. So here is what I'm authorized to give you. One option is you can go to a prisoner-of-war camp. It's not too bad, I assure you. That would be for the duration of the war."

"What's the other choice?"

"I suppose you know what I do."

"You're in intelligence," Derek said, studying the man carefully.

"That's correct, and I've been given a new assignment. And I must confess I'm not sure how to handle it."

"What sort of assignment?" he asked.

"I'm not at liberty to discuss the details. Suffice it to say," Hadley said slowly but with a strange light in his eyes, "I will need someone to help me. Someone who knows the ways of the German mind. Better still, someone who knows the ways of the German *military* mind. It is a secret assignment, and I must tell you at once that it involves considerable risk."

Derek glanced at Mallory, then looked back toward Hadley. "Are you telling me you want me to become an agent in British intelligence?"

"That is what I would like to see you do, Derek. I've become convinced that you could be a great help to us in this matter and in other matters to follow. You speak several languages. You've been around the German military organization all of your life. I would like very much for you to work with me on this."

Derek regarded the smaller man for a moment, then turned to face Mallory. "What do you think, Mallory?"

"You must do it, Derek. All of Europe needs people like you to help stop Hitler before he does any more damage." She turned to Hadley and said, "And if he has to go, I have the feeling he will be going underground."

"That's exactly right, and in dangerous territory."

"Then he will have to have a contact, won't he?"

"Yes, he will." James Hadley cocked an eyebrow. "May I take it that you're volunteering?"

"Yes. That's what I want to do."

"That would be excellent from our point of view. Well, I'll leave you two to talk it over."

"You already have our answer," Derek said.

"Good." Hadley got up and shook hands with Derek. "I'll go prepare the way. My superiors will be very happy to hear this. But you are going to be two very, very busy people."

Hadley got to the door, then turned. "Oh, by the way, you won't need this gentleman anymore. Dickens, you are relieved."

The guard got up, smiled broadly at Derek and Mallory, and left the room.

"You were right, Mallory," Derek said. "We're going to have a happy ending." He took her hand in his own and kissed it. "Now you will have to marry me so we can live happily ever after."

"Oh, Derek, it's going to be wonderful!"

"The war won't be so wonderful. It's going to be very difficult."

"But after the war, it will be. We could settle in America. Or maybe we should go back to Norway. Maybe—"

Mallory did not finish, for Derek had risen and pulled her into an embrace. He looked down at her as she fit closely within his arms. "We won't talk about all the *maybe*s. For now we're together."

"Yes. We'll be together no matter what happens." She pulled his head down and kissed him. "I'm starving. Let's go eat some of this terrible English food."

The two left the room holding hands, then Derek put his arm around her and held her tight. "You were right. God is good, and we'll always be together."

Stories of
Courage, Faith and Love
on the Kansas Plains

Lured by the promise of true freedom, a thriving community, and land to call their own, sharecroppers Ezekiel Harban and his three daughters set off for Nicodemus, Kansas. When their wagon train arrives, they are shocked at what they find, and many give up and head back home. But Ezekiel's family is determined to build a new life in spite of the disappointments.

Dr. Samuel Boyle and his family also are drawn by the wonderful potential of the Kansas frontier. When the Boyles settle in nearby Hill City, the struggling people of Nicodemus get word of a doctor in the neighboring community and seek his help. As the lives of the Harban and Boyle families intersect, neither community will ever be the same.

First Dawn by Judith Miller
FREEDOM'S PATH #1

◈ BETHANYHOUSE

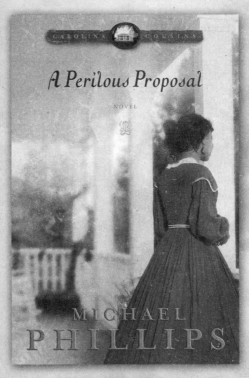